**JAEL WHISPERED A SILENT PRAYER.
THERE COULD BE NO DOUBT
TEETEE'S MURDER AND THE OTHERS
WERE SERIAL KILLINGS.**

She was suddenly reminded of the fear that overwhelmed her at the first crime scene. Now it seemed to make sense. It had been a forewarning.

She walked to the end of the block to find Brenda. Gently as possible, she whispered her friend's name. Brenda fell into her outstretched arms.

"I knew you'd be here. The police are asking a thousand questions about my brother, but I can't seem to talk right now."

"I know," Jael said, embracing her tightly.

"I'll call you later. We'll get together with the Prayer Warriors and pray, okay?"

"Sure, when you're up to it. In the meantime, I'll be wearing out the Lord with my own prayers and petitions for guidance."

At least that got a weak smile. "He'll never let us down, Jael. We'll understand all when He is ready to reveal the why's."

Jael kissed Brenda on the cheek. "I plan to give Him all the help He needs." To herself she added, *The battle lines are drawn, Satan. It's on!*

ALL THINGS HIDDEN

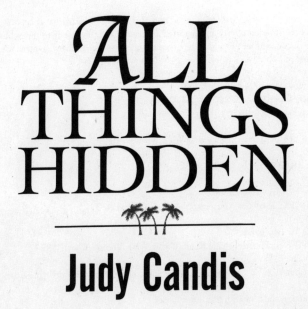

Judy Candis

Walk Worthy Press

West Bloomfield, Michigan

WARNER BOOKS

NEW YORK   BOSTON

Published by Warner Books with Walk Worthy Press™

Warner Books

Time Warner Book Group
1271 Avenue of the Americas, New York, NY 10020

Walk Worthy Press
33290 West Fourteen Mile Road, #482, West Bloomfield, MI 48322

Visit our Web sites at www.twbookmark.com and www.walkworthypress.net.

Printed in the United States of America

First Printing: September 2004
10 9 8 7 6 5 4 3 2 1

Library of Congress Cataloging-in-Publication Data

Candis, Judy.
    All things hidden / Judy Candis.
        p. cm.
    ISBN 0-446-69315-4
    I. Christian women—Fiction. 2. Police—Florida—Fiction. 3. Divorced women—Fiction. 4. Single mothers—Fiction. 5. Policewomen—Fiction. 6. Florida—Fiction.
I. Title.
    PS3603.A536A75 2004
    813'.6—dc22   2004003033

Book design and text composition by L&G McRee

To My Mother
Emma Lillian Henry
November 2, 1922–July 27, 2001

We miss your presence every day,
but your spirit remains and gives us solace.

Acknowledgments

To my heavenly Father, may I acknowledge you in all my ways. You are first and last in every endeavor.

To my daughters, Amelia (Mia) Howard and Tiffany Trenier Candis:

Mia, there are no human words to express the blessing you have been to me since the day the Lord put you in my arms. Your wisdom and genius have been my lifeline. Thanks for happily reading every word I have ever written and staying up late into the nights to brainstorm with me to make my scenes come alive.

Tiffy, you believed in me when I was ready to give up. You've encouraged me and been my best source of advertisement. Thanks for being so protective of my writing time and interceding to tell people, "Mom is working on her novel. If you want to chitchat, please call back when she's not busy." I love you, sweetheart.

To my sister, Alicia Henry. Girl, what would I do without you? Your pride in each of my efforts in life has made me the woman God knew I could be. Your support is over-whelming.

To my brothers, Virgil, Daryl and Keith. You guys never wavered in your faith that I could do it. You're the best.

To Denise Stinson. Thanks for holding on to the line and never letting me plunge over the edge of unrealized dreams. A special thanks for walking with me through those crazy moments when the adversary tried to knock me down. God certainly put you in the right place at the right time as a spiritual warrior in my journey of life.

To Monica Harris, the best editor in the country. Girl, you make me look good. You're tough, and you know what you're doing, but does everyone know how really sweet you are too?

To Colleen Tripp, for reading the first draft from cover to cover and having the nerve to say, "Wow, this is a really good book." I love you, and thanks for all the great ideas and your perspective from the other side of the coin.

To Officer Susan Bowers of the Tampa Police Department, for all your technical support and giving me all your phone numbers so I could call you at any time, anywhere, with any question.

To Betty Bradford Byers and Vee W. Garcia, for taking time out of your busy writing schedules to reread my final edits. You're my "golden girls."

To the members of the Nathari Writers Guild: Doris Johnson, Chris Wallace, Dr. Idelia Phillips, Bill Liggins, Frances Keenan and Judy Smith. Thanks for being there from the start.

To the many friends who have encouraged and supported me along the way. I could not have done this without you: Felicia Wintons, Darlene Harris, Pastor Ricc Rollins, Lorenzo Robinson, LaQuanda Gamble, Mary Cochran, Anthony and Nell Kemp, Pastor Willie Dixon and family, Lieutenant Jason Mims, Kay Wells and Iris Holton and the entire *Florida Sentinel* family, and the gang at BAR-B-Que King.

To my dear pastor, Superintendent Jesse Smalley; First Lady Sharon Smalley; and all my family at Emmanuel Cathedral Church of God in Christ.

To the Nubian Queens of the National Organization of SISTUHS Incorporated. I can't wait to have my own membership *ankh*.

And last but most assuredly not least, to my father, Virgil J. Henry. YOU'RE THE KING!

ALL
THINGS
HIDDEN

Therefore judge nothing before the time, until the Lord come, who both will bring to light the hidden things of darkness, and will make manifest the counsels of the hearts: and then shall every man have praise of God.

—I Corinthians 4:5

Chapter 1

God had not given her the spirit of fear. Jael knew this like she knew there were sixty-six books in the Bible. She knew this like she knew the exact hour and second that she accepted Christ as her Lord and Savior. More important, she knew this like she knew God's Word was eternal and true. Yet the pounding of her heart was so rapid, so profound, it threatened to burst through her rib cage.

From the moment her foot touched the bottom step of the vacant, notorious crack house, waves of unexplainable panic washed over her. Why she suddenly felt so nervous made no sense, especially since she'd been on calls at this very address a number of times. She had not experienced this kind of gut-quaking since the time she had first laid eyes on Phyllis Wilcox, early in her Christian walk. She'd realized later that the "quaking" was actually her first real experience with one of the gifts of the spirit: the "spirit of discernment," a small nudging in the innermost being of one's soul.

In that case, it had been the alarm of envy and vile hatred

to come. But that was not what was going on here. There was no suggestion of a personal attack on her or on those she loved. Just another Code 223, a reported shooting, something Jael had handled many times before.

Or was it?

She shook her head with denial. *Satan, you have no power over me. I rebuke the spirit of fear in the name of Jesus.*

The grip of anxiety lessened but did not completely release its hold. Tiny knots of nausea tugged at her midsection, causing her a moment of confusion.

Lord, I need you. I need your supernatural strength and control right now.

Jael's pulse, racing seconds ago with Olympic furor, slowly began to quell. Still, she had to dig her nails into her unnaturally sweaty palms to keep a firm grip around her .38, a *silver* .38 special, standard issue. She prayed that no one—especially the officer now pressed in a similar pose against the outer doorway across from her—noticed her trembling gun. Her anxiety was clearly out of the norm, but she couldn't allow herself to focus on it now. She was the commanding officer, and needed to act like it.

Above, the starless sky was black, ominous, layered in sinister premonition. Around her, red and blue rotating squad lights swept the darkness with flashes of waning colors, illuminating the desolate neighborhood and the unlit porch where she stood pressed against the wall. Through the doorway, hazy yellow light spilled outward from somewhere deep within the house.

She glanced back at the other officers crouched around their blue and white cruisers a few feet away, waiting for her nod to advance. At the same second, her mind diverted, attaching itself to the feel of the peeling paint of the frame house scraping against her jacket; to the tickle of sweat on her brow even as the cool night air brushed across her flesh. Even to the odd thought that her stockings would be a lost cause no matter what happened tonight, since she'd paid her dues—years in a drab officer's uniform—to wear a skirt on duty.

These rampant thoughts seemed to minimize the shawl of doom, but instantly, Ramon, her nine-year-old son, flashed inside her mind. In moments such as this, Jael often wondered, if something were ever to happen to her, if she could count on her ex-husband to continue to raise Ramon in the knowledge of God. Would he see that their son went to church on a regular basis, said his prayers each night and read his Bible daily? She quickly answered her own question. Naw, no way was her ex suddenly going to admit there was a greater power than himself.

A police walkie-talkie crackled, forcing her to refocus on her immediate surroundings. She had entered dangerous ground like this a hundred times, yet there was always a certain measure of fear for any active-duty officer; on any given day, your life was on the line.

The 911 call of fired gunshots from this known crack house could mean anything. Any one of them could end up toast if there was a fool or whacked-out madman waving a weapon somewhere inside. Yet, as commanding officer of this operation, she knew her men were waiting intently for her signal. *The Lord is my protector,* she prayed silently.

Rearing back her shoulders, Jael sucked in a deep breath, as if she were about to plunge into a sea of icy water. It was time.

Jael lifted her right index finger, counted ten seconds, then jerked her head in a silent *"Now!"* As she propelled her body into the doorway, every fiber of her being was alert to the possibility of imminent danger. With her stomach muscles tightening, she braced herself for anything.

A fat white candle on a tin jar top flickered weakly from the room beyond. Intermittent light from the street only scratched the darkness through the broken and boarded windows. Expelled puffs of air from fellow officers vibrated around her as she dropped just within the door into a crouching position and swung her gun back and forth before her. Other than the heavy breathing of her men, she heard nothing.

Stealthily, the team moved in behind her, spreading themselves in strategic positions to cover one another. Her nerves prickled like live wires as she moved forward.

The team quietly spread out toward different areas of the house. Two officers stayed with her as she passed through the foyer and into the main room, her gun poised to fire. Her second in command was right behind her, his high-beam flashlight giving her an even circle of light to scope out what lay ahead.

"There!" he hissed, almost in her ear.

Jael followed the direction of his light and saw a slumped form on the floor of the archway leading to a back room. Cautiously, in case the assumed victim was playing possum, she trained her gun on the body and moved slowly toward it.

Within a few feet, any doubt the victim was dead fled like scattering pigeons. The glare of the flashlight glinted off his eyes as they stared lifelessly at the peeling ceiling above. His fear was over.

Before stooping beside the body, Jael took another look around to ensure no one was using the corpse as a decoy. Finding nothing, she pocketed her weapon, then kneeled beside the man and pressed her fingers against his throat. He was still warm. This bit of knowledge flooded her with caution.

"He's been down only a few minutes," she softly warned the nearby officer. "Alert the team to be extra careful. His assailant may still be on the premises."

The officer behind her whispered the command into his walkie-talkie. Jael rose, retrieved her firearm, carefully stepped over the body and moved into the other room. From the flashlight of the officer with her, she could make out a tattered mattress lying not far from a window covered with cardboard. Trash and filth were everywhere, typical of transient dwellings and drug houses. The scent of stale cigarettes, urine and even dead rodents permeated the area.

Moving to the open closet to her left, Jael peered inside. Nothing. She checked both windows as possible escape routes. Again nothing. Then she nodded at her officer and they returned to the main room of the building.

Two other officers entered from the back rooms, shaking their heads to indicate they had also found nothing.

Now it was time for a closer inspection of the dead man. He was a young brother, possibly in his early twenties, dressed in jeans and a silk shirt open at the collar. Thick gold chains draped his charcoal-colored throat. She sighed. It always seemed to be the young black guys involved in these kinds of crimes. As the only black woman in her division, she found the disappointment rough sometimes.

Jael pocketed her revolver in the shoulder holster just

beneath her suit jacket and kneeled again by his side. Her fear was ebbing, but not her caution. One didn't become a lead homicide detective through foolish bravery, but with intelligent caution.

"Think it was a rival dealer, Detective?" one of her men asked. Though the question was directed at her, she didn't get to answer first.

"Who else could it be?" Jael recognized the voice as belonging to Detective Ernest Billups. "These guys fight all the time over a drop of that poison. This one just didn't come out the winner."

In response to his statement, Jael flashed him a warning scowl. As usual he missed it, or pretended to. Though she resented these kinds of prejudgment remarks, she'd been in law enforcement long enough to understand how certain things were often accepted as patterns.

"Search for any clues that might give us a better idea about what happened here," she ordered. It wasn't a good idea to reprimand Billups in front of his fellow officers, but she was darn tired of his prejudiced answers for anything dealing with black men.

"Why bother," he argued. "We know what the hell went on here."

Obviously he *had* missed her earlier scowl. "Watch your language, Billups," she said between gritted teeth, still stooped beside the victim. "And since you seem to have the up on this situation, why don't you tell us what we don't know."

Billups had a way of getting on her last nerve. It took as much control to keep from barking back at him as it did to stay sane on a seven-day stakeout. For now, she had to keep her mind focused on the job.

"Another drug deal gone bad," he answered, waving his gun toward the victim. "That's all it is."

The other officers took this as a cue of some kind and scurried toward the front door.

"Can't we get some better light in here?" she growled. There would be time for a down-dressing for Billups later.

"No juice," someone said. Again, typical of drug hang-outs.

"Bring in the floodlights and tell everyone to be careful where they step." She raised her voice slightly. She could see by the departing looks on some of the officers' faces, it was obvious they thought this was an open-and-shut case. The men might get sloppy if they assumed this was a simple drug theft. As lead detective, she'd learned to never assume.

Rising from her crouched position, she sent up a silent prayer for the victim's family, as was her custom for the last ten years of police service. She had witnessed more than any normal person should of death and violence, but never once regretted the profession she had chosen. In many ways it had been her destiny since that infamous day, October 17, nineteen years ago. A day forever etched in her brain. A frown crept to her face. Jael quickly banished the uncomfortable thought from her mind.

Instead, she admitted it was certainly days like this, while working with an irritating imbecile like Billups, that she thought twice about her career choice.

Now, after close inspection of the remains, she determined the victim had died from at least three gunshot wounds to the chest. His torn flesh lay open in three places like small anthills saturated with blood. The autopsy would tell her later which bullet penetrated what and the ultimate cause of death.

As she backed away from the body, the heel of her boot connected with the victim's outstretched right arm where it lay on the tattered linoleum. Watching her step, Jael eased around, took a penlight from the inside pocket of her jacket and aimed it at the floor. Two thick plastic bags of rock cocaine lay beside the body, and near his open hand, a large stash of bills. She stood there for a second absorbing the scene, grateful she had discovered this before the other officers. It was not unheard of for an officer to pocket money at a scene such as this one. She decided to stay put until the forensics team arrived and all the money was accounted for.

More important, she wondered why the money was even there. This was not a drug deal gone bad. If it were that simple, this much money, along with a commodity of street drugs she estimated to be well over $4,000, would not have been left behind. Of course, there was the possibility that they had arrived on the scene before the assailant could grab the money, but the body had sprawled backward from the impact of the bullets. It was as if he'd been shot by surprise, while the money and drugs were still gripped in his hands, almost as if in offering. Was he about to pass them over when he was shot? Was he boasting and the shot came after? But why leave it all behind? It couldn't have taken long for the assailant to grab the goods and rush for the back door.

This scenario was a new one for her and naturally raised questions. And, with these thoughts, her earlier fear kicked in with a wallop.

She was no psychic and trusted completely in her heavenly Father for anything she needed to know about the future. At the same time, she felt an undeniable check in her spirit. Had she stumbled onto something that would personally affect her in some way? Was there something here she was missing? The tingling in the base of her stomach felt like an inner warning of bad news ahead, and the sensation was making her edgy.

"Have the techs arrived yet?" she barked, attempting to wrap her mind around what this scene was trying to tell her.

"They're pulling up now," someone answered.

"Get them in here, pronto!" she ordered. "I want photographs of this on my desk before the night is out."

Officer Rick Sills, three inches taller than her five-foot-eight frame, with thick reddish-blond hair that forever stayed in his eyes, leaned over her shoulder. Though she was no longer a street cop and just happened to be with Sills when they heard the code over her police radio, she had agreed with his suggestion she be the first on the scene. Kudo points, he'd said, toward her promotion. He tended to carry their office camaraderie with them everywhere, which humored Jael to no end. It was kind of comforting now.

"Man, it looks like all hundred-dollar bills, Lieutenant!" he whispered.

Jael smiled. "Not lieutenant yet, Sills, but I love the way your mind works."

"Only a matter of time." He turned and looked at her with respect. "Only a matter of time. No one deserves this promotion more than you, and soon we'll all be calling you *Lieutenant* Jael Reynolds. First name, by the way, pronounced *Jay-el*,"—he let the "el" roll across his tongue for effect—

"for the benefit of those who might try to use your name in unsavory jail jokes."

"I've heard them all before anyway," she said with a grin. "But could I stand to leave you at your desk alone and move into my own office?" This light banter was just what she needed now, as she kept her gaze on the dead man.

"Yeah, that may put a major crease in my day-to-day work duties. Who would I have to tease?"

"I have a few names in mind, but for now I'll run my ship as if I'll still be here for a while. So, can I get the techs in here, Rick, please? We need photos of this."

"Yes, ma'am," he answered, teasing back. Then, almost in her ear, he yelled, "Hey! We need the photographer, STAT!"

Jael sighed and tried not to roll her eyes playfully. Instead, she began counting to ten. She had just made it to seven when shouts from the backyard stopped them all. Her adrenaline kicked in again. She pulled out her gun, and she and Sills took off running toward the back door. The night was far from over.

Chapter 2

Her body screamed in protest against the sudden, and long-forgotten, physical workout. Tonight she was exercising more muscles than she had in the last twelve months. Since it meant she no longer had to do street patrol, advancement in the department had softened her physically. Sweat was dripping down body parts she'd forgotten sweat glands existed in. As she slammed her way past two awaiting officers guarding the back door, she absently wondered about the freaky change in the weather. The temperature was constantly reverting from jacket-chilly to T-shirt-hot, mirroring the rapid change in her emotions.

Dashing toward the backyard, only inches behind Sills, she acknowledged the weird thoughts that went through one's mind when the adrenaline was pumping. Things could get pretty bizarre when it was dark and death and danger were in the air. As an officer of the law, she could attest to that. Police officers tended to deal with stress and fearful situations in unusual ways. She, maybe more than most.

As they raced down the back steps, a distant train whistle

broke through the steady hum of freeway traffic a few blocks away. The sound added a touch of normality to the otherwise tense atmosphere. With her gun drawn, Jael tried to keep from stumbling over all the scattered junk as she rushed across the ground. Thankfully, she was wearing her favorite, all-purpose, low-heel pumps.

In the dimly lit yard, she could see two other officers, with their guns trained on something moving against the metal fence at the far end of the yard. They huddled around a mound of debris. Had they captured the perpetrator so quickly?

The whining man balled into a fetal position against the dilapidated fence was by no means a killer but more likely a frightened witness to the crime. The smallness of his body and the sour smell of urine that enveloped him was a sure sign he was a crack-head who had possibly landed in the wrong place at the wrong time.

Rick Sills moved around to the side and aimed his flashlight on the man. Jael elbowed her way between the deputies and went up to the vagrant.

"Okay, talk to me. Who are you and what are you doing back here?"

"I didn't do nuthin'," he whined, never looking up as he folded his body even tighter into a ball. "I was just passin' through. I swear. I didn't do nuthin'!"

The weed-covered, dilapidated chain-link fence behind him screeched in protest, threatening to fall inward as the man pressed his bony frame farther into it. The movement made the man's hair part at the nape, exposing the pale skin of his neck. He was definitely a white guy, just filthy.

With a sigh, Jael glanced around the small neglected yard.

Unrecognizable structures stood in varying shapes in the heavy darkness beyond the beam of the alley light. Other than the frantic scuffling of the man on the ground, the night was still. Overhead the orange moon hid behind a gauze of clouds, creating eerie shadows around them. A shiver caught her off guard. From his position a few feet away, Sills swept his beam of light several times across the yard before aiming it back on their captive. He, too, was taking no chances.

Looking down at the bedraggled vagrant, who had evidently heard the shots, Jael knew he might have also seen the killer escaping. Getting the frightened man to say anything would be a waste of breath. She asked anyway.

"Who did you see run back here?"

"I didn't see nuthin'!" he screamed, fear choking his words. "Nuthin'!"

"What did you hear?" Her voice was even and patient, betraying none of the anxiety she'd felt a few seconds ago.

"Leave me alone! I ain't done nuthin'. I didn't know those two guys, I swear! Let me go!"

This was getting her nowhere. Jael snapped an order at her men. "Send someone to find out who made the call, then continue searching the surrounding area." Pointing to the vagrant, she added, "Bring this one down to the station."

"Hey, no . . . leave me alone. I didn't do nuthin'!" The man kicked his legs to fend off the officers as they tried to pull him to his feet. His shouts grew louder. "I don't know nuthin' about those killings, I swear. It wasn't me. . . ." He gripped the fence with both hands, forcing the officers to peel his fingers away.

Jael closed her eyes and rubbed her temple to ease the

headache creeping in just above her right brow. The rush of excitement was wearing off and her pounding heart had slowed to a reasonable thumping in her chest.

Releasing a pent-up breath, Jael snapped her jacket lapel straight and headed back to her squad car at the front of the house.

The wind had picked up again, and she knew that with Florida's crazy February weather, the temperature could drop like a brick in a matter of seconds. The newly applied yellow crime tape across the front of the house flapped its vote of confirmation as she passed.

A few neighbors had congregated across the street, and for a moment Jael thought she recognized one of the oglers from her previous years on the narcotics beat. Before she could confirm this, he eased back into the crowd. Though she knew most of the more enterprising dealers and users, it struck her at that moment that she did not know what the guy in the backyard looked like, since he'd never let go of the fence and kept his face buried in the mounds of trash.

As she settled in her car, she saw her men bring the struggling derelict around front in handcuffs. He was squawking his head off. His loose-fitting jeans and worn floral shirt made it look as if he hadn't changed his clothes in weeks. From this distance, she still didn't recognize him. He appeared to be somewhere in his late twenties and there had been no weapons found on or near him. She knew from experience they wouldn't get much out of him and he'd be back on the streets in a few hours, hunting down his next hit. A user like him would soon forget the horrors he'd just witnessed, in favor of satisfying the need of his body. For an instant, she wondered how much horror she had stored in *her* memory over the years. Horrors she was determined to erase with prayer every waking moment of her life.

Still, this man's terrifying fear seemed far deeper than what one expected from a simple arrest. He must have seen the killer. Had the killer threatened him? She wondered why the man said "killings"—plural. What did he know?

Jael turned her body away from the scene and started the engine. The passenger door opened as Rick Sills climbed in beside her.

"He's not our man, you know," he said, closing the door.

With a sigh, Jael glanced out the window, taking in the row of cheap frame houses, many with sagging front porches decorated with kitchen chairs and plastic plants. The weeds embedding the flat tires of the late-model cars testified to the vehicles' lengthy stay in the yards. The side-walks were nothing more than simple dirt paths, and the few palm trees that lined the streets seemed to droop with despondency.

She knew that folks in this immediate area survived by keeping their mouths shut, many struggling to maintain a blind eye to everything around them, even the filth. The neighborhood, one of three such areas surrounding Dadesville, had been at death's door for many years now. Soon it would give up the battle, if urban renewal didn't come along to save the day.

Finally turning from the view, Jael answered Sills's statement. "Yeah, I know, but you also know he knows something."

Sills tilted his head. "He'll never snitch."

"He might, if we threaten him with the right thing."

"We're up against a cold-blooded murderer. This bum

will know his life, however pathetic it is, won't be his for long if he rats."

"We have to do what we have to do."

With that, Jael shifted the gear into drive and pulled off, heading toward the east side of town and Dadesville's Eighth Precinct. She had appointed herself designated driver after only three experiences riding shotgun with Officer Rick Sills. She was in more danger of losing her life with Rick behind the wheel than she had ever been on the streets.

Jael glanced at her partner, remembering the first time they had met. He had been assigned to her during roll call that day, and Jael had been sure it would never work the minute he'd lit up a cigarette within the confines of their Homicide Department–issued vehicle.

She'd been a little rough around the edges then, expecting everyone to challenge her, and was maybe more forceful than she'd meant to be when she told him she'd prefer if he didn't smoke around her.

Sills had surprised her by flicking the still lit cigarette out the open window and, with a lopsided grin, saying, "Hey, I need to quit these things anyway."

Sills was a big bear of a fellow, but his weight was more muscle than fat, which certainly worked in his favor as a police officer. His huge, open face, which sometimes broke out with little red blotches, boasted thick brows over cobalt eyes that could turn into chilling blue if provoked. A thin mustache outlined a thinner upper lip. The bottom lip was full, with a hint of natural red coloring, and those who knew him knew that his face was always ready to break into laughter. It was a simple and honest face.

Over the two years they spent together, she'd shared with him her newfound commitment to Christ, and though Sills had yet to actually step foot inside any holy sanctuary, there'd been a gradual change in him everyone could see. His wife of thirteen years called her often to thank her for softening the "bear" and making living with him a whole lot easier.

Jael had not given up on her partner about attending church yet, knowing that God was working on her buddy every day. Each time he questioned her about how God would expect him to handle a given situation, or why the Bible said this or that, she gave the Lord praise for using her to plant the seed.

It was now 6:28 P.M., according to the clock on the dashboard, and another hour before she was off duty. She had a feeling it might go hours beyond that with the added paperwork. She decided to make a quick call and ask Terrell if he could stay late . . . again.

Pulling her cell phone from her jacket pocket, she punched in her home number, using her right hand and steering with her left. Maybe she could get the boys to throw some hot dogs in the microwave, she thought as she waited for someone to pick up. She knew neither boy would mind the delay on her part. As for Terrell, any excuse to keep from going home was a treat for him.

"Hello, Reynolds residence."

"Terrell, hi, sweetheart. I'm going to be running late again. Can you handle dinner until I get there? Maybe hot dogs in the microwave?"

"No prob, Ms. Jael. I need to beat Ramon at Madden 2003 again anyway."

"Is he near the phone?"

"Naw, he's taking a leak. I'll have him call you when he comes out."

Jael cringed at the terminology. "That's okay. Just tell him to leave some hot dogs for me. I'll call again from the office." Before she could say good-bye, Terrell added, "Pastor Smalley called from church."

"Yeah? Did he leave a message?"

"Said to remind you that next Tuesday night a Reverend Mathews was guest speaker and you promised to pick him up from the airport."

"Got it. Don't forget, you and Ramon are doing the welcome sketch. You know your part?"

"Like Halle Berry knows she's beautiful."

"You'd better," Jael said, laughing.

She clicked off and laid the phone beside her.

Rick Sills was peering at her with that sickening hero-worship look again. "It's like you have two sons instead of one. That's a nice thing you're doing, Jael, letting Terrell hang around you guys all the time like that."

"It's a two-way deal, Rick. Ramon is crazy about Terrell, and Terrell seems to shake off a lot of that mess he picks up at home when he's around us. Plus, I have someone to help look after Ramon when I work late."

Jael had met Terrell while coaching baseball at the Police Youth Athletic League about two years earlier. A scrawny fourteen-year-old at the time, with no evident parental guidance, he had attached himself to her and never let go. She had only met his mother a few times, and during each episode she'd felt sorry for the boy. The woman was a foul-mouthed alcoholic and drug addict with four other unfortunate offspring. Terrell fell somewhere in the middle of the crowd and was rarely missed. He had come into their lives at the right time, a time when things were personally falling apart for Jael. He also held a tender spot in her heart because he reminded her of her brother, Edward, who was the real reason behind her joining law enforcement.

Rick interrupted her thoughts with more immediate matters.

"That addict from the alley kept yelling about 'two guys.' Says he wasn't one of them."

Jael turned to Rick with a quizzical look on her face. "Two guys?"

"He wasn't making much sense. You know how they all are. He's probably brain-fried."

"Yeah, brain-fried." Jael drove the rest of the way to the police station thinking about what was on *her* brain lately. She had no idea her life was about to turn inside out, and picking up a visiting minister would be the last thing on her mind.

The familiar smell of burned coffee, computer ink and old metal file cabinets enveloped Jael as she stepped inside the inner office of the Eighth Precinct. Accompanying sounds of fax machines, gurgling water coolers and phone conversations were right in sync. The atmosphere was as much a part of Jael as breathing.

With a wave of his hand, Rick headed off in the opposite direction, taking the belligerent witness to an isolated room for questioning. She offered him a thumbs-up sign as they parted ways.

"Detective Reynolds, your messages," the slightly overweight, platinum-blond clerk said from behind the reception counter as she waved a couple of pink WHILE YOU WERE OUT slips at Jael.

"Thanks, Tammy," Jael replied, accepting the slips before stepping through the inner doors and to where her desk sat amid a triangle of six other marred wooden desks in the cramped police station. Only two other officers were at their desks.

Kicking off her shoes as soon as she flopped in her seat, Jael pushed aside piles of folders and briefly glanced at her messages. *First things first,* she decided. She'd check for any calls that needed her immediate attention *after* filing her report.

Jael clicked on her computer and pulled up the report file format and began typing in the initial name, date, time of arrest, etc., etc., before pulling out her bottom left drawer and reaching for the WORLD'S GREATEST MOM coffee cup. Only hers had a slight alteration. Right above the word MOM, Ramon had scrawled in POLICE with a permanent black marker. It was her most treasured possession.

It was also a symbol of her rites of passage. Her unofficial initiation into the predominantly male department was considerably mild compared with what it could have been. Just a few tricks on the part of other officers, such as placing masking tape over the word MOM and changing it to LEGS, then stuffing the cup with someone's used panty hose. Jael debated preaching to the men right then about God and His saving grace, but understood that would all come in time. It would take smarts on her part to make the men comfortable around her, then let the Lord use her as He saw fit in *His* own time.

Thus, Jael successfully passed her test with time and plenty of police cases to earn the trust of her colleagues, finally becoming "one of the boys" the day she joined the prank and taped her own words, THE LORD SMILES EVEN ON THE MENTALLY CHALLENGED, in a borrowed cup on the coffee counter along with six blowup cigars. The joke got a good laugh and a few pats on the back. Since then she'd kept her own cup in her bottom drawer—after bleaching it to death—whenever she was away from the office.

Over the past two years, though never preachy, she presented her faith in many ways. Though several coworkers edged away from her, others would come to her for counsel about certain decisions or with questions in a debate about whether the Bible really stated certain things.

Those new avenues eventually led to a budding Bible study group that met each Wednesday at the station after normal work hours. Though members changed on a regular basis, several remained faithful, and Jael thanked the Lord for the chance to witness and bring another to Christ. She smiled now, as she glanced up at the handwritten plaque one of her former coworkers had taped over the top of her computer. THE SUPER CHRISTIAN CRIMEFIGHTER. It was a gift she cherished, and she found it could lighten her day at the worst of times.

Feeling around for her shoes under the desk, Jael was about to head to the break room for some stale coffee with lots of cream when a shadow crossed her shoulder.

"Don't you think you should be down there as part of the questioning team?"

Jael looked up into the ruddy face of Officer Ernest Billups. A familiar wave of annoyance coursed through her veins. She frowned. Billups had continually declined her numerous offers to participate in their Bible study, a reminder that she could only plant the seed, not convert the sinner. He was a walking testament to the fact she was not *the* Super Christian, knocking down every stronghold; in Billups's case, she knew, only prayer and God's divine will would prevail.

Looking at him from the corner of her eyes, she answered, "I thought drug dealers were low on your priority list, Billups. But since I happen to be the lead detective on this assignment and can do what the heck I want, I've assigned Officer Sills to handle that. He's as capable as I am."

"I know that's the method you used to make detective in the first place, but you don't get to work your way to lieutenant by shifting your responsibilities onto others. Affirmative action doesn't cut it in this arena."

"Excuse me, but I don't remember asking for your advice about how to handle this case."

"You don't have to cop an attitude. Just trying to help a fellow officer keep things in perspective. It won't hurt your image to ask for advice from a seasoned officer every now and then." He reached up to push a few strands of hair back on his balding head, exposing a sweaty half moon beneath his armpit.

Jael's lips thinned into a straight line. She felt the tension tighten her jaw, and clenched her teeth. "I'll keep that in mind."

"We're a team here, Reynolds. We succeed by working together. Everyone carries their own weight."

Jael rolled her eyes as Billups walked away, her coffee forgotten. *Yeah, right. Like you have the slightest idea what the word "team" means,* she thought.

She turned back to her computer and began typing with sharp, precise strokes. It was times like these that made it difficult to remember she was a Christian. Billups's remarks were nothing more than an opportunity for him to take another unwarranted jab at her. One step beneath her in rank, he obviously resented her presence on what would otherwise have been his crime scene at the crack house, and

rarely masked his anger at her possible promotion to lieutenant over him.

Peace, be still, she whispered to her mounting anger as she
jabbed at the keys.

An office loner, Billups had declined every offer by
coworkers to participate in various activities; some had even
suggested joining them at the nearest watering hole after
work, hoping that would loosen the man up. So far, no one
had ever piqued his interest. The only pleasure the man
seemed to get out of his job was jabbing at her.

She couldn't let Billups get under her skin. She knew what
she was doing and knew how best to handle her watch. She
also knew her men would not chance her displeasure and
would meticulously document and label every piece of evidence carefully; they would be at the scene with the crime
technicians for hours.

As for her, she would review the crime scene videotape
before leaving, if she was lucky enough to have it on her
desk before finishing her report. She wanted to have as
much done as she could by the time she sent her report to
the homicide sergeant. Since the dead man was black, she
had to be extra careful to see that everything was done correctly. Because he was a dealer, few would care enough to
push for justice on his behalf. As always, it would be on her
shoulders to see that someone did care.

Confiscating so much money off the dead man's body
could help. Jael wrote herself a note to have all prints found
near the alley matched with those of the vagrant. Of course,
there would be numerous prints found at a drug site such as
this one. It would be like hunting for a clean needle among
a stack of addicts.

Jael picked up her phone. "Forensics, please." She drummed her slender fingers on top of her unchecked messages.

"Forensics."

"This is Detective Reynolds, Homicide. May I speak to Larry?" She waited several minutes. "Hi, Larry. Jael."

"Don't start, Jael; I haven't even had a chance to review the body. I have other corpses here too, you know. And your boy's body bag just came in."

"I just need to know one thing: Which bullet was responsible for the actual cause of death?"

"That's going to take a while. The report says he was hit three times in the same area."

"Yeah, but what is that to an expert like you? You know you're rarely off base, Larry. Just one look, please, and I'm in your debt forever."

"You're already up to your neck in 'debt forever' to me. What's another eternity?" Jael heard her friend sigh. "Hold on a second."

After a few lengthy minutes, filled with the sound of zippers and plastic fumbling, she heard the phone being picked up again.

"Of course, this is off the record. You'll get my full report like everyone else. But my preliminary assumption is that it was the bullet that penetrated the myocardium."

"I thought so. You're a pal, Larry. You know you're my boy."

"Yeah, yeah, but just because *you're* determined to work your butt off all the time doesn't mean the rest of us are willing to devote twenty-four/seven to our jobs."

Without his offering a good-bye, the phone clicked in her

ear. Jael smiled. Her buddy wasn't fooling her. Larry was just as much a work fiend as she was.

It took almost an hour and a half to complete her supplementary report. She needed to insert her personal impressions while they were still fresh in her mind. She would then add the coroner's report and collected evidence as the information was released to her, and all of it would be added to the Homicide Division's preliminary. For a moment, she thought about heading down to the interrogation room to see how things were going, but immediately realized that would give Billups the pleasure of thinking once again that he knew it all. He was wrong in all his assumptions

She was a darn good officer, and knew it. She had solved nearly 98 percent of all her assigned cases. And as far as she was concerned, the 2 percent of cases she hadn't solved were still open. She did everything strictly by the book and with little or no unnecessary harassment. She was pushy only when she had to be, and when she had to be, even the assisting officer knew to stay back.

She'd proven herself more times than not, sacrificed more than she cared to admit. The men in her unit knew it too, even Billups. So, for now, she put him out of her mind. She had to get home, and it would still be at least another fifteen minutes to break down the initial call and log in the times and first condition of the body. At home over the weekend, she would add the coroner's complete report, evidence found by the last officer on the scene and the witness's statement. In most cases like this, it could take weeks if not months before they even had a solid lead.

She reached for the phone again. "Yeah . . . this is Reynolds. Get me Sills."

"One moment."

She waited.

"Sills here."

"How's it going?"

"As expected. He denies having seen or heard anything. He's been searched and questioned about who his dealer was and who else came through there. You know the routine."

"Think I should come down?"

"Naw, we were just about to let him go anyway. I'll hit the streets tomorrow to make sure we didn't miss anyone who might have seen anything. The initial call came from a little old lady two doors down. I'll visit her again. Otherwise, we've got everything covered, so stop bothering me. It's Friday—go home and play with your kid. Forget this place for a while. Don't you have the weekend off?"

"Yeah, that's something that hasn't happened in a while."

"So stop hanging around here and go home. If anything comes up, I'll call you."

"Okay, Rick, see you Monday morning."

"Have a great weekend."

Which for Jael would not be the case by any stretch of the imagination.

Chapter 4

Ah, shoot!! Shoot, shoot, *shooooot*." Jael slammed the brakes just before pulling her '96 Bronco into her driveway behind her ex-husband's Mercedes C280. How could she have forgotten he was to pick up Ramon for the weekend? Screwing up her nose, she hissed through her teeth as she backed her car up and parked in front of her small colonial-style home at the mouth of a cul-de-sac.

This was the last thing she needed—another confrontation with her ex. Before she was out of the car, Virgil was storming from the house, ready for the attack. Jael braced herself with a prayer for calm and patience.

"It's about time," he yelled, hands on his hips, Samurai warrior–style. "I've waited over an hour and a half. Unlike *yours*, my time is accountable."

Turning off her engine, it occurred to her how Virgil loved any opportunity to engage in this familiar dispute in front of his old home for all their neighbors to witness. And, of course, he never thought her time was as valuable as his. If she sat in her car, he would just come toward her yelling at the top of his lungs; better to let him vent inside.

Jael stepped out of the car as Virgil marched down the pathway toward her. He wore his usual style of loose dark pants, white shirt with tie and suit jacket. His hair was still cut in the same close crop, and his deep-set brown eyes, once so adorable, were now pinched at the center of his brow, flaming in anger. Stoking his anger just a notch higher, Jael moved past him without a word.

"I don't even want to ask why you're late again," he barked. "Is it possible that for just once you could have my son ready on time?"

"I forgot you were coming."

"Forgot! I've told you twice I would be here by seven P.M. It's almost eight-thirty and you've left Ramon here alone again with that . . . that . . ."

"His name is Terrell. You know that." Jael continued toward the house and moved as fast as she could to the door.

Sometimes it was hard to believe that she had actually prayed to win this man's heart. Well, not prayed in the sense that one requests a specific blessing from the Lord, since at the time she had little to do with spiritual things. But she had wished, and her wish had been granted. *Be careful what you wish for,* Rhonda, her cousin, had told her at the time. Cuz had seen through him even then.

She had met Virgil at a card party, on the south side of town, right after graduating from the police academy. His wide, sensual smile, along with his tall, muscle-rippling body, had called to her as if she were a slobbering pup. She'd always admired a man who knew where he was going, and Virgil had his life completely mapped out. Even down to the

number of children he wanted and where he intended to be
financially when he retired at fifty-five.

They had dated off and on for a while, not really making
a serious commitment, until the day Jimmy, a former
boyfriend of hers, stepped on the scene. She and Virgil had
joined Rhonda and Rhonda's current beau at Cuz's house to
watch the NFL playoffs. Jimmy dropped by unexpectedly,
having just arrived back in town.

Jael had been too naïve at the time to realize that when
Virgil's arm slipped tightly around her shoulders, it was
more a sign of his true possessive nature than an act of
undying love.

She'd thought it romantic at the time, when Virgil proclaimed before the entire group that she was *his* woman and
they were soon to be married. She'd beamed from ear to ear
and thought how lucky she was.

As time passed, she'd had to push him for a wedding date,
and only got him to the altar on time when she threatened
to pick up where she'd left off with Jimmy. But Virgil had
been a lot of fun then, back when they both thought fun
was the same thing. He was ambitious and proud to intro-
duce her as the first African-American female to join the
Criminal Investigation Division in the Dadesville Police
Department. They worked together to have the best of
everything. Because, boy, did Virgil love to boast.

So, it really irked him that she had continued on without
him, reaching every goal they had set for her career. He had
expected her to fail, to be nothing without him there to
direct her. He had no idea that the God she served had even
greater plans for her life than the two of them could have
ever imagined.

During the divorce proceedings, Virgil reluctantly relinquished his half of the house they'd bought together, back in a time when life and love still had a promising new appeal. It was a modest three-bedroom home, among other well-manicured homes, with a nice-size yard for Ramon to romp around in. If not for Virgil's timely child-support payments, Jael would have had to move out long ago. Naturally, she never had to worry whether she thanked him or not—he did enough of that for himself.

"Is nothing more important than what you want to do? Ramon isn't even packed! I had to get his things together myself, among what I could find *clean.*"

Behind his back, Jael made an ugly face. She'd just bet he had a great time probing through her things, looking for signs to accuse her of mishandling the court-ordered custody of their son. *Who, by the way,* Jael wanted to add out loud, *had also conveniently forgotten this was his weekend to spend with his dad.* For Ramon's sake, she wouldn't include him in their argument.

As she stepped through the door, she saw the two boys leaning against the wall that divided the living-dining room from the kitchen-den. Ramon shrugged his shoulders at her as if to say, "Sorry." Terrell moved back into the den, knowing this was a private family moment.

Virgil was right behind her, still spewing his usual belittling harsh words. For her, they had lost their sting long ago; she'd done her time, in more ways than one. Thankfully, when Ramon was around, Virgil held back from saying the hurtful things he didn't think twice about saying in private. So she made sure she was rarely alone with him. Now, Jael ignored him as she bent before her son to give him a farewell kiss.

"Do I have to go?" Ramon whispered.

"Ramon, we go through this every time. You know you love these trips with your father. You just hate leaving Terrell behind, but he'll be here when you get back."

"But we were into a great game, and Terrell just ordered a double cheese pizza with sausage," he pouted.

Jael rose and ran her palm across her son's smooth cornrows. Though she'd fought Virgil and won about not letting her son play video games filled with violence, she had lost the battle to deny him video games altogether. Her pastor had suggested she play with Ramon and Terrell herself and use the time to teach them about violence and why such behavior was not acceptable for a Christian. She'd even enjoyed playing, once everything was in perspective.

She'd also lost a smaller battle when Virgil went against her wishes and allowed Ramon to wear his silky, thick, black hair in cornrows, a style that reminded her of prisoners. At first she'd been livid, but couldn't find anyone to back her up. Even her mother had said, "Let the boy be a boy. God's not going to be upset with him because he braids his hair. Just don't let him start wearing earrings, though." The incident had made her wonder if maybe she was going a bit overboard, as Virgil claimed.

After asking the Lord to show her how He felt about the matter, she finally gave in when Ramon showed her photos of several young gospel singers sporting similar styles, and told her that he'd copied his style from a member of the third-generation Winans Phase II.

When the ladies of her Prayer Warriors group commented about how handsome Ramon looked with his new hairstyle and that he was growing into a fine young man, she'd exhaled a sigh of relief. Now she could snub her nose at Virgil, showing him one didn't have to be a geek to be a Christian.

She took a long look at her son now, who was small for his age. Ramon was nothing more than a pint-size sack of bones in baggy jeans and a Spiderman T-shirt. With a square chin and full nose and lips, he favored his father. But he had her huge rust-colored, oval-shaped eyes and screwed his mouth up like hers when he was forced to do something he didn't want to do. An overwhelming and unexpected need to protect him surged through her. Yet, she knew better than to express it. Like most boys his age, he hated for her to mother him in front of witnesses.

Virgil was still taking verbal shots behind her back. "I just can't understand how you continue to place Ramon last on your list of priorities. I've asked you time and time again . . ."

Turning toward him, Jael expelled a tired sigh. "I don't feel like one of your lectures, Virgil. All you had to do was call and remind me."

"I did call! Twice! But I can never get that sorry excuse for a receptionist at that station to realize the importance of my calls."

And of course Virgil assumed everything he did was important and the world should stop and take notice whenever he opened his mouth. But this time she wished Tammy would have mentioned that one of the pink slips was from her husband. Tammy knew a little of her past with Virgil, and often assumed more than she should, sticking her nose a little too much into Jael's personal life. She'd noticed a change in Tammy's attitude recently, that she'd become a bit more nosy than before. She would have to speak to the woman, and soon. Jael turned back to her son.

"Ramon, do you have your homework with you?"

"Oh man, Mom, I can finish my homework when I get back." He rarely called her "Momma" when Terrell was within earshot. Jael smiled.

"Okay, this time only. But your father needs to see what you're doing in school. A good way would be for him to help you with your homework."

Virgil was irate. "I know what he's doing in school! Maybe more than you do!"

Jael blew exasperated air through her lips. *Patience, patience.* She kissed Ramon again, then led him to the door. Virgil grabbed Ramon's overnight case from the chair by the door and followed. It was a shame, she thought. She was rushing her only son out just to hurry and get rid of his dad. Virgil was on to her, and added a parting shot just above a whisper.

"Remember, I'm watching you. One screwup and my son comes to live with me."

"And you keep forgetting I was adjudicated!"

She could have slapped herself. What a lame answer. Virgil always did that to her, making her guilt override her common sense. Once she'd closed the door behind them, she leaned heavily against it. The exhaustion was finally catching up with her. Suddenly she felt drained, tired *and* hungry. The smell of cheesy pizza pulled her into the kitchen-den, where Terrell sat on the carpet before the television. His eyes brimmed with a hopeful plea.

"Well, I guess I'd better be going," he said lamely.

"Hey, aren't you going to at least help me eat all this

pizza? A lady in my position has got to keep her weight in check if I'm to fight all those criminals out there."

It was almost heart-wrenching to see the grateful gleam that came into his eyes. Then he gave her one of his challenging grins. "Only if you let me whip you at Smackdown." He was a handsome boy, well over six feet tall at sixteen and only slightly heavier than Ramon. He wore the same baggy jeans, and the Christmas gift from her and Ramon: a black T-shirt with WWJD across the front in gold tones.

"Whip me? Boy, I know you done lost your mind. I'm the WWF champ around here." Jael moved into the kitchen and lifted the top of the Pizza Hut box and inhaled. *Calories for days.* Dropping the top again, she carried the box into the den and sat it on the cocktail table before the TV. "I'll give you two chances. Who do you want to be?"

"The Rock."

"You were The Rock last time," Jael said, returning to the kitchen to get a couple of Pepsis from the fridge.

"And I almost beat you last time."

Flopping on the floor beside him, Jael kicked off her shoes and lifted a sticky slice of pizza with both hands. She bit into the steamy clump of dough and let the cheese stretch into a long string as she pulled it from her lips. Virgil would have frowned on her choice of dinner, but this was as much her favorite as the boys'. She left money for times like this, and Terrell and Ramon often used the stashed cash to order out, rather than taking her hint to pop dogs in the microwave. This time she was glad. After her encounter with Virgil, anything hot, rich and fattening was just what the doctor ordered.

Popping her Pepsi lid, Jael took a deep swallow as she

looked around the room, which was filled with pictures of Ramon at various ages. Right over the TV was a photo of him taken two years ago in his karate outfit. She'd had it enlarged because the pose had been so cute. He looked adorable—although she was never to say that out loud—with his foot kicked high in the air.

She would miss Ramon over the weekend. Since she often had to work with only occasional weekends off, they rarely had a chance to do things together. Virgil rubbed that in her face too whenever he got the chance, reminding her that he took more time out with their son. But Jael didn't want to reminisce about her relationship with her ex. That delicate and hopeful dream had turned into a suffocating nightmare for both of them. Remembering only reminded Jael of the terrible role she'd played in bringing about their separation.

Taking another bite of her pizza, she picked up the control, pressed the AGGRESSION button and slugged The Rock in his jaw.

Chapter 5

Tires screeching as she raced into the First Temple Church of God in Christ parking lot, Jael leaped from the Bronco, barely making the 10 A.M. Saturday morning prayer session. Offering the ladies of her Prayer Warriors group a sheepish grin, she slipped into the second row of purple-cushioned pews beside Sister Jamerson, and was instantly enshrouded by an ambiance of White Shoulders perfume. She was just grateful to make it on time. Without Ramon around the house making his 8 A.M. noises, she'd slept like Lazarus before Jesus called him from the tomb, dead to the world.

Jael glanced at the pews to her left and spotted her friend and personal prayer-partner, Brenda, giving her "bud" a thumbs-up. Brenda's lips indicated she was compressing a giggle. She knew Jael was always rushing somewhere.

"As I was saying," Sister Otis continued, her smile indicating she was not put out by Jael's tardiness either, just glad everyone was present and accounted for. "We want to add Mother Cooper to our weekly prayers. As you know, her husband was admitted into St. Joseph's Hospital three days ago after another stroke. Right now, the doctors are not very hopeful."

"But our Lord is Jehovah Rafa, our healer," Sister Phillips shouted in her thick, raspy voice.

"Yes, He is, and this will be just another testimony in the days to come. Any other special prayers we need to add this week?"

Jael raised her right index finger. "Yes. We had a homicide victim yesterday. I'd like to add a special prayer for his family."

"Yes, of course, and you're a good soul, Sister Reynolds," Sister Otis replied. "The Lord has put you in His perfect place."

The women all nodded in agreement, and within minutes, hands were clasped, heads bowed, as the group began its weekly assault on the devil with powerful prayer for friends, relatives, church members, public officials and the town in general. It was a time Jael looked forward to and cherished. She received a spiritual surge each time she joined with others to combat the assaults of the adversary. She'd not missed a meeting since joining First Temple COGIC four years ago. She left each meeting with a new awareness of the power of God and the mind to do His calling with every fiber of her being.

A little past noon, Jael revved up her Bronco and headed for her cousin Rhonda's house. She'd missed last night's birthday party—as she intended—but knew her cuz would never forgive her if she didn't acknowledge this momentous occasion in some manner.

Rhonda had spent weeks planning her celebration, and

though Jael had stopped attending affairs long ago where lots of drinking and light drugs were the standard, Rhonda always extended her an invitation, just in case.

Passing along Durant Avenue, Jael considered the town she had resided in since high school. A smaller version of its neighboring city of Tampa, it had the usual divisions of any major city: well-to-do neighborhoods and middle-class neighborhoods, separated to some extent according to color; poor areas, definitely determined by color; and a sizable downtown area. Still, for her the pieces all fit comfortably, not as spread out as in a bigger city.

Jael pulled in front of the single-family home that was no more than a clapboard box with no discernible architectural style. With gift in hand, a beautifully wrapped Victoria's Secret "Tropical Nectar" gift basket, she stepped from the Bronco and heard a tiny, sweet voice calling her name.

"Hi, Auntie Jael."

The singsong words rejuvenated Jael's spirit like crystal droplets of rain on a scorching summer day. She moved across the bare lawn with a spring in her step toward the walkway and two little girls.

"Hi, sweetheart." She stooped to plant a kiss on her niece's brow. "I see you're busy getting Barbie all dolled up today."

With the fickle Florida weather flaunting its variations of temperament, LaTesha was dressed in skinny jeans, a pink short-sleeved top that tied at the waist and a pair of those little thongs from Payless.

"Is Ramon with you?"

"He's with his father for the weekend. Who's your friend?" Jael asked.

"This is Shenica," her niece said proudly of the little girl dressed much the same as she and playing beside her.

"Well hi, Shenica."

"Hi." Shenica gave Jael only the briefest of glances, quickly returning her attention to fashioning the latest hairstyle for Barbie.

Jael shifted the package to her left arm. "Your mom inside, sweetie?"

"Uh-huh. Is that a birthday present for Momma, Auntie Jael?"

"You bet, but here's a little something for you, too," Jael said, passing a package to her niece. "Don't tell anyone."

Her niece giggled with a conspiratorial inflection as she ripped open the small box of Barbie hair accessories. "Thanks, Auntie!"

"You're welcome, honey. See you in a few."

Jael walked up to the front step and knocked on the door. Her cousin's throaty voice called out from inside. "It's open!"

"Hey, girl," Jael replied, stepping into the room.

"Hey, yourself," Rhonda answered as she looked up through the partition dividing the kitchen from the front room. In a voice that always seemed just on the edge of laughter, she added, "Missed you last night."

"I had to work late. A homicide."

As Jael stepped into the living-dining area, the air was spicy with the lingering aroma of last night's delectables. Somewhere in the mix was a nose-wrinkling hint of stale cigarettes.

Other signs of the birthday get-together were still visible. Paper cups and stained napkins were scattered on the coffee table in front of the couch. On a table to Jael's left was a worn pack of playing cards, several drink rings and two empty Salem cigarette packages.

Moving toward the kitchen, Jael smiled at her cousin, who was busy washing a sinkful of dishes. Rhonda was and always had been a beauty. She had rich butter-colored skin and voluptuous curves that would have made the biblical Salome seem like a boy. From head to toe, sister-girl dripped with sensuality, even dressed as she was in a faded pink terry cloth robe. Her huge brown eyes held a sassiness that captivated many a young man's heart, and they were set above full lips that were always ready to smile. Add to this feminine drape her beautiful thick hair, which this morning was slightly pressed to one side from sleep, wrapped bouffant style with a multicolored strip hanging along the side of her face.

"You ain't fooling me, Cuz." Rhonda grinned. "You weren't coming anyway."

"Okay, I'm busted, but you know your fortieth birthday is special to me."

"I shouldn't, but 'cause I love ya, you're forgiven." Rhonda pulled her hands out of the suds and shook them over the sink. "What you got me, girl?" she added, wiping the excess dampness across her robe.

Jael raised the basket. "Your favorite."

Rhonda squealed, hugging Jael and taking the gift at the same time. "Now this is a birthday gift. I'm so tired of those cheap 'our version of.' They all smell like rubbing alcohol. You're a sweetheart, even if you are the police."

"From your lips to God's ears." Jael watched her cousin set the basket on the kitchen table and slowly turn it around, peeking at the items behind the see-through wrapping. "So how does it feel being forty?"

"Ask me that when I'm not fighting a hangover," Rhonda answered over her shoulder. "Or better yet, wait six more years and tell me yourself." Turning around, Rhonda gave her cousin a full once-over. Though Jael was taller, standing barefoot at least five foot eight, unlike Rhonda, she'd never had a problem with weight because of what their mothers called "thin bones."

When they were teenagers, everyone would tease Jael about her height, which instead of making her timid and withdrawn had only made her more aggressive. She had played some serious sports during academy training, but over the years had transformed into a beauty of her own. With skin the color of silky cappuccino and eyes a blend of hazelnut and gold, Jael had given Rhonda a real run for her money with the boys back in their heydays, even forcing Rhonda to use a few underhanded techniques, such as wearing skimpy, tight-fitting dresses and low-cut tops, to keep the boys' eyes where they belonged—on her.

She never needed to worry, though—Jael was one of those sistas with natural-born beauty that could be taken for granted. Having no concept of style, she often grabbed any old worn-out thing to put on as long as it was comfortable.

Rhonda twisted her mouth, lowering her eyes to give Jael a smoldering gaze. "And when you gonna stop wearing that ugly ponytail? What happened to that great style I gave you a while back?"

Jael's hand instantly went to her hair, loosely pulled back with a simple beige scrungy. "It's just easier to handle this way. I never seem to have the time to maintain all those fancy dos."

Rhonda put her hands on her hips, shaking her head. "Girl, I don't know what to say 'bout you. I told you before, if I were blessed with all that rich auburn hair, I'd have it hanging down my back all the time, calling the brothas with each swish of my head."

"You don't need that to call them. They come like flies to a picnic each time you pop on the scene. Besides, Toad would have a hissy fit if someone looked at you the wrong way."

That was the kind of stuff Rhonda liked to hear, and they both knew it. Rhonda tilted her head in a "you got that right" gesture and laughed. "Girl, you ain't never lied."

The drone of a TV wafted toward them from the back of the house. "Toad still sleeping it off?" Jael asked.

"Naw, he left about an hour ago to catch up with Derrick. LaTesha left the TV on again." Rhonda finally lifted the basket and placed it on the kitchen divider. "I'm not going to open this now. The package is so pretty, I just want to look at it for a while."

"Girl, you crazy. You get a lot of gifts?"

"You know how these folks are around here. Party means free food and liquor. You're lucky to get a 'Happy Birthday' wish. Toad did give me forty dollars in a card, and a few friends brought cards and extra bottles of E&J and Seagram's, but I wasn't expecting nothing. It was just having the fun that made it for me."

Rhonda loved to party, and judging from the decorations stuffed in the trash can and the few deflated OVER THE HILL balloons lying around, she had gone all out.

"There's still lots of food left. The crab shalah was gone as soon as I took it off the stove, but you can fix a plate for you and Ramon from all the other stuff."

"Maybe I'll take a piece of cake home," Jael said, pointing to the huge Kash n' Karry pastry box on the counter beside the stove.

"You got it."

Jael settled herself at the table, which was squeezed between the refrigerator and the broom closet.

"How's Auntie Nadda doing?" she asked her cousin.

"Frisky as always. She sent me some money in a card, along with one I got from your momma, who sent me a fifty-dollar gift certificate to Dillards."

"Go 'head, Cuz, money to burn."

"Yeah, gonna get myself that Coach purse that I've been dying for. Give your cuz some class."

Rhonda's mother, Nadine, was the older sister of Jael's mom, Esther. About four years ago, Esther had moved back to Miami after Nadine's husband died, to live with her older sister and sort of look out for her. Both women had deep religious ties and pretty much ran the church they belonged to. Being two bossy sisters, their antics never ceased.

Jael had received a lot of support and encouragement from her mother after the divorce, especially in regards to her returning to the church.

"Auntie Nadda wasn't home last week when I called Momma," Jael said.

"I think she met somebody. Aunt Esther told me a certain male member at their church had an eye for Momma and that lately she's been spending a lot of time away from the house. When I asked her about it, she avoided the subject by going on as she does about you and how I should model myself after you. Says they won't stop praying for my soul until I come around."

"And of course, adding *my* prayers, you don't have much of a chance of not making it into heaven."

"Yeah, well . . ." Rhonda left the sentence unfinished, busying herself with opening the cake box and reaching for the foil before changing the subject. "That homicide you were working on last night didn't happen to be the one they were talking about on the news this morning, was it?"

"What did the news say?"

"That a suspected drug dealer was murdered over on 29th Street. Shot five times, I think," Rhonda said as she sliced two huge chunks of the frosted cake and placed them on a plastic plate.

"Three."

"Oooh, sh . . . I mean shoot. So you were there? Is it related to that other drug killing over by 10th Street?"

Jael's police antenna went up. This was the first she'd heard of another drug murder. "What other killing?"

"You know, Zap Man was shot to death too, supposedly in the middle of a drug transaction. It makes me wonder what's going on with these dealers. They trying to keep up with New York and L.A. or something?"

"Or something." Jael would have to check the files, but the only way she could have missed this was if the murder had been in another jurisdiction. "Did you know Zap Man?"

"Not personally, but you don't live on this side of the track without hearing the names of the more notorious ones." Rhonda moved to the refrigerator. "Want something to drink?"

"Depends on what you're offering."

Rhonda laughed. "You know I'm real proud of you, Jael. Once you made up your mind to leave the fast life behind, you stuck to it. Maybe someday I *will* follow your lead. But right now it would be like giving up sex. Even though I feel like sh . . . well, even though I don't feel so hot this morning, it was worth it. Girl, we put one on last night! It was the bomb! There was so many folks in this house you couldn't move. Even you would have enjoyed yourself."

"I don't doubt it. But my success is based on avoiding certain situations, and lots and lots of prayer. I've told you time and time again, I couldn't have done it alone. I—"

"Okay, okay," Rhonda interrupted. "No preaching this morning, all right? My head can't take it. Your invitation to convert my lifestyle is branded on my brain. When I decide to give up the good life and start going to church with you, you'll be the first to know."

Jael couldn't help but laugh as she shook her head. "You'll be surprised about what is really the 'good life.' Anyway, whenever you're ready, the doors are open."

Rhonda shut the refrigerator and passed Jael a can of 7UP. "Well, at least we always have lots of chaser around."

"Is anyone talking about the killing?" Jael popped the tab and took a long swallow.

"They will be after the news gets around. Two dealers in three weeks means somebody's mad at somebody."

"Yeah, you're right about that." Jael had to wonder how this tied in with the dealer they found last night. She'd check the files on her computer when she returned home, then give Sills a call and have him see what he could find out.

Rhonda was now stacking another plate with potato salad and chicken wings. If she heard Jael groan, she ignored her as she covered both plates with foil and turned the conversation in another direction. "Toad invited this guy over, even though I told him you weren't coming. But you know Toad, always bragging about you. You know, being a police detective and all and looking so fine to boot. But after this man he brought had a few drinks in him, girl, I wouldn't have wanted him myself if I were single. Although he didn't look too bad at first. But dang, can liquor make some people stupid. Brotha lost all his fine looks with each slurred word that came out his mouth. He was fuc . . . I mean drunk as a skunk. They had to carry the fool out of here."

Jael smiled, appreciating Rhonda's attempts to curb her cursing around her. A few years back she'd had a long talk with Rhonda about cursing in front of LaTesha. Since then, Rhonda always watched her mouth when anyone four feet or under was present, though look out if she was drinking or in a foul mood. Still, Jael admired her efforts. "When will your husband stop trying to hook me up with men?"

"Whenever you stop working so hard and realize Ramon needs a real father figure, not a police mom. And believe me, Jael, it's not the same, sweetheart. And I don't mean to get all up in your business but shh . . . shoot, girl, ain't the physical needs there no more or what?"

"Hey, I ain't dead yet. But with my kind of job, you're too busy to think about men."

"So I guess those things walking around in pants at the station don't count as men? Ain't no job out there could make me forget about a little hum-hum. Damn, Jael, all you work around is men. Do you ever stop and notice the difference?"

Well, so much for curbing the foul language. In her need to express her thoughts on Jael's incomprehensible celibacy, Rhonda hadn't noticed the slip. "God's got his time, Rhonda."

"Well, if for no other reason than to get you hooked up, I guess I'll start doing some praying of my own."

Jael roared with laughter. "Whatever it takes. I guess God's going to pull some unique strings to get you on your knees in prayer."

"Yeah, ain't that the truth."

"Well, I'd better be going," Jael said, rising from her seat and heading to the front of the house. "Don't see many of these free weekends, you know."

Rhonda pushed the two plates at her cousin. "You'd better slow down and take it easy. You're the only high-ranking black police officer we've got, you know, and female besides."

"You don't stay on top taking it easy." Jael had not mentioned the possible promotion to anyone outside the station; she'd wait until she had a definite reason to celebrate. Opening the door, Jael looked back at her cousin. "And if you hear anything about those murdered dealers, call me, will ya?"

"Hey, you know I'm your eyes and ears on the street. But if there's something I need to know for my own safety, make sure you tell *me!*"

During the drive home, Jael couldn't get what Rhonda said about the other dealer out of her head. Was it possible the two murders were related? What were the dealers saying? After all, they would certainly have a better spin on this than outside spectators.

With that thought, Jael made a sharp turn and headed in the opposite direction toward Main Street, a notorious hangout for drug dealers. Thankfully, she was in her Bronco instead of her unmarked car, though she knew that a few of the dealers recognized it anyway. Still, she hoped to talk to someone who could get this nagging itch out of her head— that there wasn't a drug war going on in Dadesville.

She didn't need to be an officer of the law to know that this poison was a multibillion-dollar industry, seeping into every crevice of society. It spread like a virus. Not even small towns were immune—to that she could attest. Prior to her promotion to detective, she had thrown herself into being a street cop to prove she could handle the job, and the temptations. She had done almost two years of undercover narcotics work and learned to be a credible witness, known as an officer devoted to doing her job. Only solid evidence could convict, and Jael avoided the entrapment law by handling all her assignments strictly by the books.

In less than five minutes, Jael was cruising down the South-side district of Dadesville, black folks' downtown. Black-owned businesses were on either side of the street and people were already out in numbers. It was Saturday—a little breezy now, since the earlier humidity had given way to crisp gusts of chilled air, but Saturday, nonetheless. In another six hours, this street would be crawling with the partying crowd.

Jael looked for a familiar face and just as she suspected, one was at the corner leaning against a trash barrel, overflowing with last night's remnants. Jael pulled up slowly beside the curb.

"Hey, Deke," she said, leaning out the window.

"Whoa, now, Detective Reynolds. I ain't doing nothing but taking in the sun." Deke did a little two-step as he backed away, his hands slightly raised in defense.

Deke was just a small-time dealer, a corner boy who had yet to reach the status of "the man." Though he wore at least two heavy platinum chains around his neck over an Orlando Magic jersey with shiny gray FUBU pants, he probably didn't own much. Jael knew he lived with his girlfriend, who already had two kids and paid the majority of their bills.

"No problem, just need to ask you a few questions." Jael gave him what she intended as a reassuring smile. She still hoped to add Deke to her list of CIs—confidential informants. So far he wasn't showing any interest.

"Now you know that ain't kosher. Can't be seen talking to

no vice." Though his eyes shone with a hint of amusement, his skinny frame was instantly tense. He was a walking paradox. He wore his hair in short cornrows and his facial features had a baby-fresh look of innocence that threw most people off guard. In court, minus the earring and wearing the right suit and innocuous expression, he'd look like a college student awed by his arrest.

"Would it make it easier if it looked like I was taking you down?"

"For what?" A dumbfounded look crossed his handsome face. "Y'all always messing with folks."

"Just one question, around the side, and then I'm outta here." Jael tilted her head sideways with a "you can't deny me this" smile.

Deke pursed his lips and glanced up and down the street as if looking for oncoming traffic. Jael suspected he was debating whether to make a dash for it. She decided to help him make up his mind.

"I know where you live."

Rolling his eyes, Deke shrugged his shoulders and defeatedly moved toward the backside of the old laundry building. Jael did a hasty U-turn and parked on the other side of the road. She locked her Bronco and casually moved across the street as if she were a part of the afternoon scene. She certainly looked the part in snug stonewashed jeans, K-Swiss sneakers and a red and white Old Navy pullover.

Deke was waiting near the Dumpster with his back turned in case anyone saw them.

To his back, Jael said, "I just need to know if you heard about the dealer killed over on 10th Street a couple of weeks ago."

This was safe ground. Deke turned toward her, his hands playing with the cell he had pulled out of his pocket to camouflage their meeting. His fingers ran nonchalantly across the face of the portable phone, never pressing the SEND button.

"Hey, who hasn't?" His smart-aleck inflection quickly changed to a look of astonishment when Jael continued to silently stare at him. "You don't think I did it?!"

"Did you?"

"Hell, Zap Man was my dog. We often pooled our funds for . . . for certain business deals."

"Any idea who might have?"

Flabbergasted, Deke twisted the side of his mouth. "And you think I'd tell you if I did?"

"If your butt was on the line."

"Hey, don't know nothing, ain't heard nothing. So stopping me was a waste of time." Deke pocketed the cell phone to indicate their little session was over.

"He wasn't the only one, you know."

When he looked at her again, his expression said he did know and that he'd been thinking just that. He quickly regrouped with a nonchalant air. "Hey, what can I say, it's the kind of life they lead."

"But what if he's not the last?"

This also got his attention. It seemed Deke had been doing some serious thinking on this matter and probably had a lot of questions of his own. Of course, Jael had no illusions Deke was about to make her his new confidant.

"All I need to know is if there's some kind of vendetta going on with the drug boys."

"Hell, Detective, you're Homicide. It's dangerous just

looking at you." To reinforce his statement, Deke took a nervous glance around them. Though it was even cooler in the shade of the building, Jael noticed a sheen of sweat across his brow.

"If it's not a vendetta, then we may have a serial killer on our hands." This thought hadn't occurred to her before, but if there was no gang war going down, then what else? A vigilante killer?

Obviously this was one line of thought that hadn't crossed *Deke's* mind, either. It put a whole new twist on things.

"Well, it ain't no vendetta. Both brothas worked for Big Jake, and so I hear he was pissed like a motha." With that, he decided he had said enough and took off swiftly down the opposite end of the alley, without even a good-bye. The interview was over.

Jael's thoughts were racing. Two dealers popped, no rival drug war supposedly going down; plus, she hadn't missed the fact that Deke was suddenly scared to death, and not of the police.

Chapter 7

Less than an hour and a half later, Jael was on her stomach searching under Ramon's bed, hoping to find at least two pairs of matching socks. That boy could lose more socks, so getting him brand names like Spiderman and Nike wasn't working out. She'd have to resort to her old standby, all white.

After leaving Deke, it had crossed her mind to ride around and look up Big Jake, though it could take hours just to locate his latest hideout; to avoid police scrutiny, the dealer moved around a lot. Then again, she'd decided, it probably made more sense to have more info under her belt about the other dead guy before approaching Big Jake. The man could fiddle with your mind if you weren't up to par, and it would be a wasted trip if she didn't have the right information to fire back at him. So instead of driving around in circles, she'd come home, choosing to throw a load in the washer before going on the Web to see what she could learn about the other killing.

"There," she said in triumph as she found another match.

Two dirty Nikes and a pair of Adidas. For just a second, as she eased herself from beneath the bed, she thought of pulling one of her mother's old tricks and make Ramon gather everything from under his bed in one big pile and then let *him* sort through all the junk. But of course, if she didn't stand over him every minute of the process, socks would end up in the trash, never to be seen again.

Rising to her feet, Jael looked around her son's room. His bed was still made, in that haphazard way of his. Lumps poked everywhere under his NFL All-Star comforter. The pillow still had indentations where his head had lain. Jael reached over and fluffed the pillow and pulled the spread a bit tighter.

The action caused her to remember the time he had pulled the pillow to the floor to pad his knees while saying his nightly prayers. He'd bruised them pretty badly at karate practice that day and was still nursing tender and scraped skin. Like a champ, though, he was never whiny.

"Momma, you think they do things like play ball and eat pizza in heaven?"

"Well, if God is a loving Father, what do you think?"

Ramon had been silent for a moment, his head turned slightly as he looked up at her from his position on the floor, his fingers folded together on the bedspread.

"Well, maybe He won't let us eat a lot of pizza because it's not healthy for you all the time, but ball—man, I hope they play sports up there."

"Well, think about this just before you go to sleep," Jael said, sitting on the bed. "If Jesus came to earth to give us life and to give it more abundantly, wouldn't heaven be even more than what we have here on earth?"

"I certainly hope so. I mean sometimes I think heaven might be kind of boring."

Jael had laughed. "I seriously doubt that."

It had been a topic that came up often. Though Ramon was a good student and had never had trouble in school, Jael had eventually transferred him to a Christian school not far from their home, making it easier for him to socialize with other kids who would help reinforce his new attitude toward life.

Looking around his bedroom now, she knew that, though financially it may have been a little tight, it had been a good decision. Certainly Virgil liked and supported the idea of "private school." It was another thing to boast about to his friends.

Just overhead was a built-in bookcase Virgil had put up years ago, cluttered now with robots and spacecraft, a children's Bible, several Early Reader Books, and things Jael couldn't even put a name to. Around the walls were posters of The Rock and other WWF wrestlers, his favorite basketball stars, Phase II, Mary Mary and the empty space where she'd made Ramon take down the picture of a well-known rapper. Though she didn't consider herself fanatically strict, she made sure her son understood some things would not be tolerated in their home. One of those things was a foulmouthed rapper, no matter what his claim to fame.

Ramon's dresser was just as loaded with schoolbooks and sheets of lined paper, showcasing his fourth-grade scrawl and a recent photo of his dad Virgil had framed and delivered himself, looking for all the world like the smug bug he was. Jael sneered at the photo before leaving the room.

Taking the socks and pants she'd gathered earlier, she

headed for the washer and dryer in the little room behind the kitchen. She tossed in the clothing, dumped in some Purex and twisted the knob to WASH. The rhythmic sound of the washer was pleasingly hypnotic. This would be a great time, she thought, to turn on the CD player, kick back and listen to some contemporary gospel as she whiled away the hours indulging in selfish fantasies. She resisted the temptation. Maybe later.

Moving to the refrigerator, she reached in and pulled out a Caffeine Free Pepsi, her latest addiction. Popping the lid, she strolled into the den, where the computer sat on a Wal-Mart self-assemble wooden desk, a postdivorce accomplishment.

Jael took a sip of the caramel fluid, then sat before the computer. Turning on the PC, she clicked the mouse to bring up the DPD file. Entering her password, ROMY, Jael began a search of all recent homicides in neighboring districts.

After about fifteen minutes, she found what she was looking for: the homicide report on Bartholomew Walker, alias Zap Man, a twenty-seven-year-old Dadesville native.

The entry date of the report was less than two and a half weeks earlier, processed by a Sergeant Donald Nichols. Jael jotted the name on a piece of paper. She would contact the officer later and get a personal accounting. Different districts often worked together, sharing information on various cases, and she'd worked with this particular one on several occasions.

Scrolling down the report, she read how the body had been discovered in an alley off 10th Street behind the Walgreens a block away from 32nd Avenue. The victim had been shot three times in the chest, just like her boy. According to the report, Dr. Larry Steinberg recovered three slugs during the postmortem, which were now secured in District Five's property room.

And just as with her boy, listed under confiscated evidence retrieved at the scene was a large amount of cash— $2,150, to be exact—and two kilos of powdered cocaine, plus a spent .38-caliber slug, a pair of metal-framed sunglasses and a dirty white pillowcase. This information brought a frown to Jael's brow. Yeah, maybe during the last incident the assailant feared getting caught, she thought, but what was his excuse in this case? Was the murderer opposed to drugs and drug money? How ironic would that be? None of it added up. There was a pattern here, but what did it mean?

Jael searched the investigation report for any clue that might present a beacon of light into this confused madness, but there was nothing, no leads or probable suspects. Reading between the lines, Jael surmised that both the original investigating officer and the second officer concluded it was a retaliation hit of some kind, not completely unlike the conclusion her men had come to at last night's crime scene. Now she knew better. The similarities in the two cases spelled only one thing: premeditation.

Jael nibbled her bottom lip in concentration. Was she going off the deep end here? Making things up to suit a scenario? Even with all her years in Narcotics before moving into Homicide, she couldn't possibly know every dealer on a first-name basis, and unfortunately, she'd never crossed paths with either of the two dead men. She stared at the keyboard, wondering what the connection was.

She remembered Terrell telling her something about his mom attending a young man's wake, but had no idea the deceased had been murdered. She knew only that his mother, in her usual alcoholic state, had passed out over the coffin. Her thoughts at the time were more directed toward her concern for Terrell and regret over his upbringing than toward the recently departed young man.

In many ways she understood Virgil's concern about Ramon spending so much time with a young boy of Terrell's background. Though Virgil had fought her tooth and nail over what he called her so-called conversion and her "ramming religion down his throat," he was a worldly snob in his own right, with gobs of false pride. Of course, she admitted that Terrell had a very unsavory background and that he would not have been a good choice of friends for Ramon without her close supervision. What Virgil didn't understand was that Ramon was a good influence for Terrell, who had a heart as big as Texas, and a brain to boot.

She'd had plenty of talks with the boys about the dangers of drugs and street life. Her firsthand knowledge ensured that the boys got a full stomach of the real horrors, and not the glamour preached by thoughtless rappers of the "gangsta life" that seduced so many. Even with her busy hours, she watched over Ramon like a hawk.

Jael stared intensely at the computer screen, as if the words would suddenly rearrange themselves and reveal the secret of what was happening in Dadesville. These senseless murders were an aspect of just the kind of life she warned the boys about. Now even more so, because this was all so unusual. In fact, this was downright scary.

Jael jumped when the phone rang.

"Hello."

"Jael, Sills here. Seems we may have another drug-related homicide on our hands. A guy known on the street as Zap Man was murdered much the same way as our boy less than three weeks ago."

"Man, are you psychic! I was just looking at the report. I'm going to call the officer who handled the case and compare notes."

"I just did. No one thought to connect the two shootings until now because the first was considered a random killing, not drug-related. What do you think? Drug deal gone bad?"

Jael could hear the trepidation in Rick's voice as she visualized him leaning back in his chair, twirling a pencil around his knuckles.

"I don't know what to think. I talked to Deke and of course he swears he knows nothing, but I have a feeling whatever is going on, the local dealers are a little shook up, but quiet. So it seems we've got some kind of outside force working here."

"Maybe I should ask around. Stick my nose in certain places where it's not wanted, and drum up a few CIs."

"Good idea. I'm going to—"

"You're going to keep your butt at home and spend time with your son."

"Can't do. He's spending the weekend with his father."

"Well, rest, read a book, clean a closet. We can handle this until you return on Monday."

"Why does that suddenly sound so far away?"

"Because you're a sicko, not like a normal human being who'd leave others alone to do their job on her days off. I just called to keep you abreast of where this investigation is going."

Jael smiled, holding back her standard retort. "Okay, but do me one favor: Check to see if the bullet the men were struck down with came from the same gun."

"Already on it. Anything else?"

"Yes, find out where they usually did business and if that was a known fact. It seems these fellows were sought out, and at a time when no witnesses were around."

"You got it. I'll call again if something comes up."

"You'd better, or you're going to see my chocolate butt before the night is over."

"Such threats, and from a Christian woman at that. Naughty, naughty."

Sills hung up before Jael could reply. If given the chance, she would have told him that the word "naughty" is used once in Proverbs 6:12. Knowing her so well, he probably figured that and hung up before she broke into another sermon.

Jael spent the next half hour attempting to piece together what little she knew about the two cases. No miraculous inspiration transpired. Finally giving up, she threw a Lean Cuisine in the microwave before driving to pick up a few movies from Blockbuster, R-rated movies that Ramon was not allowed to see because of the violence. Halfway into the first movie, a Samuel L. Jackson runaway hit, Jael was fast asleep, dreaming dreams she would mercifully forget the next morning.

Chapter 8

Jael hit another sour note, but thankfully no one in the choir pew cringed openly. She did get a "Lord help me" roll of the eyes from the chorus director, but all in all, no one outside of the choir picked up on her lapse in euphony. If only she wasn't so darn loud, Jael thought. Then again, blaring vocal cords came naturally. It was a family trait. Her grandmother had been loud, and so had her momma, her aunts, her uncles. Even the family tomcat had gotten on more than a few nerves with his vehement meows.

She'd never forget that day, so many years ago in high school, when she'd tried out for the majorette squad. It was the one sport all the girls salivated to be a part of, because the majorettes were considered the campus glamour girls. Besides, all the boys went nuts over the short, sequined outfits. Yet even then, fate had a way of calling Jael to its own selected vocation.

On a day so beautiful Jael would have sworn God had kissed the earth with His approval, to her horror she'd dropped the baton in one of her skyward swirls during tryouts. Quickly retrieving the silver baton, she had yelled across the field, where Mrs. Roberts sat several yards away on the center bleacher.

"Oh, please, Mrs. Roberts, let me try it again," Jael shouted, appalled by her clumsiness after having practiced the maneuver with Rhonda the entire summer. Her voice carried so far across the school football field that even the track coach, standing by the far gate, stopped waving his pencil at a reluctant student and looked up.

Always the comedian, Mrs. Roberts broke out in laughter, apparently glad for the hilarious interruption in the otherwise tedious auditions. "Young lady, I believe you've missed your true calling. With vocal cords as strong as yours, I'm sure the cheering team would *pay* to have you among their ranks."

To hide her humiliation, Jael laughed along with everyone else.

Failing to make majorette, she had reluctantly tried out as a cheerleader for the Pep Squad. At least she was a big hit with *that* coach. Within a year, her outgoing personality and leadership abilities landed her the spot of captain. She still got to wear colorful short skirts, and Jael's popularity soared.

However, an earsplitting voice in the choir stands that overpowered the others, and that was always off-key, was something else altogether. Finally, the song ended and a much quieter Jael watched for the signal to be seated with the rest of the members.

"I did it again, didn't I?" she whispered to her prayer-partner, Brenda, as they sat in unison.

"Girl, you know you can get loud," Brenda teased, pulling her purse and Bible from beneath her seat. "I'm sure you never have to request a bullhorn at work, do you?"

"I know, I'm sorry. Sometimes, I just can't help it. I get so carried away with the words of worship I forget I sound like a frog."

"Just another reason to be grateful. The Lord doesn't care how much you're off-key, or how loud, only the sincerity of the worship."

"Well, I've got plenty of that. I might—"

She was interrupted by a commotion at the far end of the choir pew. All heads turned as Brenda was passed a folded note down the length of the pew from member to member. Since she and Brenda were sitting next to each other, Jael couldn't help but glimpse a part of the note sprawled in big black letters as Brenda unfolded it: COME HOME QUICK

Whatever was in the rest of the note Jael didn't see as Brenda shot from her seat, dropping the note and ignoring Jael's "What? What?" She quickly brushed past the members, not even apologizing as she bumped people trying to get out. Everyone in the choir stand was abuzz with curiosity, attracting attention from the pastor, who narrowed his eyes as he shook his head in a reproving gesture.

The look of horror on Brenda's face before her abrupt departure frightened Jael, so she reached down and picked up the fallen note. She read the second line.

TEETEE SHOT!

Impatiently, Jael had waited the remaining twenty minutes for the end of service, but didn't hang around after Brenda's swift departure. Instead, she quickly disrobed, hanging her gold and purple vestment on the choir rack. The choir room was dizzy with speculation, since the original note-passer had willingly disclosed what was inside.

"Isn't TeeTee Brenda's baby brother?"

"I heard he was messing with drugs."

"Oh, Lord, this will certainly kill Brenda's grandmother."

The members tried pulling Jael into their heated question-and-answer session, but she escaped any direct replies by saying she was headed over to Brenda's in case she was needed. Others quickly followed her example and decided to rush to Brenda's aid. And of course to find out more about what was going on.

Once in her Bronco, Jael pondered this new development, even as she worried for her friend. TeeTee was no stranger to the police department. She'd had a few run-ins with him herself, but because Brenda was a close friend, Jael often called her first whenever TeeTee was in trouble. Brenda had tried unsuccessfully to get her brother to stay away from dealing. But the pull of the streets and the smell of easy money had a power that surpassed clear thinking and a loving family influence.

On her way to Brenda's, Jael prayed that TeeTee wasn't another victim of this madness and would not only survive, but be able to give her a description of the shooter.

Brenda lived on the west side of town, not far from the church, and Jael came to a screeching halt in front of her house in no time. There was already a crowd hanging around outside the white frame home, with its massive porch and burgundy trim. A blue and white patrol car was parked in front, its lights still and dark, a bad sign.

As she pushed herself through the gathering crowd, someone shouted in her direction.

"What y'all gonna do, Ms. Police Officer? Just takes some notes and call it a day?"

Jael quickly looked around, but didn't recognize the voice.

Obviously, whoever had shouted out at her knew she was an officer of the law even though she was dressed in her Sunday best.

When Jael finally made it inside the dimly lit house, cluttered wall to wall with overstuffed furniture and whatnots on every available space, she quickly scanned the room for any sign of Brenda. In the far corner, a lanky officer with short blond hair questioned a middle-aged male member of the household.

Notifying the families of victims was often the hardest part of her job. It was a part she never ventured into without sincere prayer for the wisdom to use just the right words. With a nod of recognition, Jael left him to his task and moved toward a cluster of people near the unused fireplace.

Brenda's grandmother, an eighty-year-old woman with leathery mocha skin and stark white hair tied in two braids across the top of her head, was slumped in a chair with her head lowered. Several people stood around her, dropping soft words of sympathy. Brenda was nowhere in sight. As Jael moved forward, one of the ladies recognized her and moved away to allow Jael a place before the agonized woman. Brenda's grandmother moaned and rocked back and forth, her thick arms wrapped around her midsection. Her words, strangled by tears, weighed heavily on Jael's heart. The worst had happened.

"He's dead, killed like a dog," she said in a low-pitched wail.

Jael placed a hand on the elderly woman's slumped shoulder. "Mrs. Davis, it's me, Jael Reynolds. You have my deepest condolences. I'd like to speak to Brenda. Do you know where she is?"

"All I know is my baby is lying out there on the street like an animal. Shot like a dog! Killed by some no-good trash. And they won't even let me see him!" Her tear-strangled voice was rising, and the lady sitting next to her pulled Mrs. Davis into her arms.

So TeeTee was dead, killed like the other two. Was TeeTee now the third victim of a serial killer? Was the killer getting bolder? Jael moved to a quiet part of the house and pulled out her cell phone. She punched in Sills's number. He answered on the second ring.

"Rick, looks like we might have another one."

"When, where?"

"I'm at the victim's home now. I don't have any details yet, but it seems like the same M-O."

"So, it seems the guys going down are dealers. And since the first guy was in another district, the killer's not working in one given area." Without a pause he added, "Let me pull up what I can, get over there, then get back to you."

"Okay. Call me as soon as you hear something. I'll try to—"

From the doorway came another commotion: the press. The murder had become headline news.

"I gotta go." Jael quickly clicked off, then slipped out as quickly as possible, hoping no one in the press would recognize her. This was not a time for her to make any kind of statement. Heck, she didn't know anything, nothing more than anyone else. Which was scary.

Jael knew it was time to see Big Jake. There wasn't a second to waste. Her ex-husband would be dropping Ramon off about five. Jael glanced at her watch. She had about four hours to run down Jake and be home before she had to listen to Virgil's mouth again.

Chapter 9

She had been searching all Big Jake's local haunts for over an hour and had come up with nothing. She couldn't even find Deke. Probably for the first time in street drug history, not a single dealer could be found at the local hangouts. Even the junkies were rattled beyond their usual state of jumpiness, because they couldn't find their next hit. Crack houses were suddenly ghost houses, something Jael would have loved to see under different circumstances. Whoever was behind this drug evacuation had cleaned the town of Dadesville as if he were the pied piper of illegal street drugs.

Jael reached out to the polished wood-grain dashboard and twisted the knob from her favorite gospel station to the local twenty-four-hour news channel. As she sat there waiting through the stock market update and fast-talking commercials, she racked her brain over the three murders. Within minutes, a broadcaster began the hourly report. The recent murder was the headliner.

"A black male was fatally shot earlier today on Lake Avenue in South Dadesville just outside the Jensen Liquor

Store. The assailant is currently still on the loose. Though family members attest to the high moral character of the victim, Jonathan David Merrill, News Radio 650 has learned that Merrill has a record for dealing illegal drugs. His murder places the Dadesville Police Department on full alert. This is the second such incident within the past week and, according to informants, there have been several others. Details are sketchy, but all indications point to the possibility of a 'drug weeder.' Mayor Alton White has informed the media that the matter will be investigated to the fullest and that the perpetrator or perpetrators will be brought to immediate justice. We will have further updates on the six o'clock report as the situation develops. In other news . . ."

Jael hit the OFF button. How were these guys getting their information so fast? Who was informing the press? And wasn't it just like the media to dub the murderer with a fancy tag—the "Drug Weeder." Also, if the mayor was making statements, it wouldn't be long before a special task force was assigned. A crime that might have gone unnoticed before, because of bias against the criminal element, was now big news, and people wanted answers. Where would she start? Who had the answers?

The answer came as a brainstorm. Where would it be safe and the last place the perpetrator would look for his next victim? Jael headed back to Brenda's house.

The crowd outside the Merrill home was much the same as she had left it, with maybe even a few heads more, creating a greater camouflage for anyone wanting to melt into the sea of bodies while at the same time learn what was going on. Jael parked her Bronco across the street near a magnolia tree.

From inside her car, she watched the crowd. Most of the people were curious neighbors, a large portion about TeeTee's age. They were all strangers to her. But there, near the fence, lurking behind a middle-aged woman with rollers still in her hair, was Booley, a dealer known to use more of his product than he sold. He was wearing a pair of miniature John Lennon sunshades, his hair cropped close to his head. Nothing that could be pawned for cash adorned his slim frame. With his hands buried deep in his pockets, Booley scanned the crowd with obvious trepidation.

Jael got out of the car and headed in the opposite direction with her head lowered, so as not to attract attention to herself. She walked completely to the end of the block before turning around, crossing the street and heading back.

Jael pressed her way through the throng of gatherers, getting a nasty look from the woman in rollers, who stepped back in indignation. She was behind Booley before he realized it. He was much taller than Jael, so she rose on the balls of her feet to whisper in his ear.

"My 9mm is trained at your back. Do not move a muscle or you're joining TeeTee selling only heavenly hash." Jael hoped God would forgive her this little white lie. "I don't want you, I want Big Jake. And if you're smart, you'll tell me where he is so I might just be able to save his sorry life."

No one would have ever accused Booley of spontaneous acts of bravado. Even as his body language tensed, he never turned around as he quickly blurted in a frightened whisper, "He's at his mother's house."

"Where?"

"On Monroe Street."

"What's the address?"

"I don't know, just that the house is the only yellow one at the corner of Monroe and 15th."

Jael jabbed the finger sticking through her suit dress pocket harder against the center of Booley's back. "You see that Bronco across the street?"

Booley turned his head slowly. "Uh-huh."

"Walk casually toward it. Don't shout, don't run, don't even breathe more than you have to."

Cautiously moving away from the pressure at his back, Booley headed for the car; then, before Jael could fall in step behind him, he bolted. Head lowered, Booley dashed across the street in a zigzag pattern to elude any bullet that might ignite from the finger he thought to be a gun, then squeezed between two tall hedges and ran around the back of a bright orange house and out of sight.

"Dang!" Jael threw her arms out in frustration. She should have known better. Now he was sure to call Big Jake before she got there, wherever "there" was. At least thirty pairs of eyes focused on her as she turned back toward Brenda's house. *Might as well go inside and see what developed while I was away,* she thought.

As she moved toward the crowd, some stepped back to let her pass, but others seemed hostile; Jael had to push her way through. She was about to place her foot on the bottom step when someone brushed against her, forcing something into her open palm. Instinctively, Jael closed her fingers around the item while drawing away in a defensive stance to see who had touched her. The look on her face must have conveyed her own mounting hostility, and the rest of the spectators backed away, but not before Jael realized that what she held was a crumpled piece of paper. She hurried up the steps and moved to the corner of the porch, where she scanned the crowd with an angry glare. Several eyes were looking back at her, but now with a little less self-assurance. Teeth gritted, Jael looked down at the note in her hand.

Her blood froze as she read:

THERE WILL BE MORE IF HE'S NOT STOPPED.

Chapter 10

The sun was scorching by the time Jael arrived at the crime scene. The Bronco's air-conditioning was blowing full blast, but it wasn't enough to quell the heat of trepidation plaguing her. The weather forecast had mentioned the possibility of late-afternoon thunderstorms—the cooling rains would be appreciated. It might even wash away some of the confusion, she hoped.

The crumbled note lay open in a clear plastic bag on the seat beside her. Jael glanced at it again. There was no question what the message meant to convey: TeeTee wasn't going to be the last if this maniac was not found. Pulling her eyes away from the threatening note, Jael glanced through the window at an EMI van, a media truck and another growing crowd of spectators.

This time, the murderer had struck on an active drug corner, near a mom-and-pop grocery and liquor store, soon after dawn, when few were around to witness the crime. As she pulled forward, most of the activity now seemed to be centered in front of the liquor store. Parking her Bronco behind the second of two blue and whites, Jael noticed the techs were still busy gathering whatever evidence they could find. Since it was an outdoor crime scene, it would be harder to contain; much of the area was already polluted by curious observers before the 911 call came in. She didn't envy her fellow officers as she watched them trying to ignore the inquisitive onlookers and sidestepping the media. For the press, this was the ultimate story.

Jael remembered that TeeTee was a hardhead and refused to adhere to commonsense advice—but he didn't deserve to die in the street. She knew that by now the body was bagged and headed for the morgue. She had no love for drug dealers, but no one had the right to be judge and jury.

Detachment was one of the tools many officers used to stay out of the psychiatrist's office. For her, detachment was unacceptable. Each case was as personal as if it were her own family member. God alone kept her strong and able to deal with each murder as a personal vendetta—a vendetta forever at her heels, since that day nineteen years ago.

From her seat in the Bronco, she looked for either Sills or Brenda. Among the throng of moving bodies, she saw the back of Sills's reddish-blond head. Leaning over the shoulder of one of the crime technicians, he was nodding in agreement as the tech pointed at something near the ground. Jael finally pulled herself out of her SUV, using her hand remote to lock it behind her.

"'Scuse me, please, let me by," Jael said as she pushed her way through the crowd toward Sills. Hearing her voice, he stood erect and turned in her direction. In two quick strides he was at the roped-off section, lifting the crisscross yellow crime tape for her to slip under.

"I was going to call you," he said in a dejected tone. "You didn't have to come down to this madness. They're still trying to locate one of the stray bullets and check for any more personal items that may have flown out of his hand when he was hit."

"What have they found so far?"

"Money in his pants pocket, a beeper and about ten ounces of rock cocaine in his vest jacket."

For a moment, Jael stood stunned. For her, there could be no further doubt that these were serial killings. What was the killer, or killers, trying to say?

After several hours in the sun, the pungent smell of blood was overwhelming when Jael and Sills stepped toward the chalked-off area. Deep crimson stains spread in haphazard circles, penetrating the cement walk around it. A trail led backward about eight feet, then zigzagged to the front of the liquor store, as if TeeTee had attempted to run for shelter.

Jael thought of the man she once knew and whispered a silent prayer, adding a single question mark at the end. Not sure how to petition her request, she counted on God's supreme knowledge to fill in the right words.

Over her shoulder, Sills volunteered a bit of technical information. "He was struck down sometime this morning, when the area was pretty quiet."

"Yeah, a quiet Sunday morning. A time when life is usually gentle and serene. When a person shouldn't have . . ." Her words choked up before she could complete the statement. The noise around her melted into a heavy hum of sounds, its melancholy undertone threatening to pull Jael into a void of despair. She was suddenly reminded of the

fear that had overwhelmed her a few days ago at the first
crime scene. Now it seemed to make sense. It had been a
forewarning. She shook off the ominous mood seeping into
her veins like ice water. "Where were the wounds?"

"Three direct hits to the upper chest. The predator was
precise, missing only one shot."

Jael shook her head. "What's going on here, Sills? What's
happening in our town?"

"Beats me. But the bold viciousness of this killer scares
the shit out of me."

Normally, Sills watched his language whenever he was
around her. The slip was a clear indication these murders
had gotten under his skin. Sills wiped his hand across the
back of his neck, Jael ran her fingers along the side of her
chin, both dealing with their own troubled thoughts.

Jael was the first to speak. "You seen any relatives? I'm
looking for his older sister, Brenda."

"Yeah, they're round the front, outside the grocery store.
His sister is really shook up. The wind blew up the covering
just as she walked up. She got a stomachful of all the blood
and gore, and man, was there a lot of blood for such a
skinny guy. It's . . . It's . . ."

"Aw, man." Jael reached out and placed her hand on Sills's
shoulder. He seemed to need the touch of consolation as
much as she. For a supposedly tough guy, these senseless
assaults hung around him like a cloak of hopelessness. The
more Jael professed the love of Christ to Sills, the less he
could stomach the killings. It took a lot out of her sometimes too. Even with the heavy heat of the day, a shiver ran
through her. "If the Captain doesn't call an emergency

meeting—which I'd be surprised if he didn't—I want every available man in the main conference room first thing in the morning to organize a task force."

"You got it." Sills seemed thankful for the quick transition back to business. "There may be one bright spot in all this; I think we may finally have a witness." Tilting his head in the direction of the empty building across the street, he added, "He's waiting over there in case we need anything else. A Mr. William Walters."

Jael glanced across the street and saw a middle-aged man wearing a rumpled dark suit, leaning against the trunk of a late-model Oldsmobile, his hands shoved deep in his pockets. She moved toward the opposite yellow tape, lifted it and headed in his direction. The man stood upright, yanking his hands from his pockets as he watched her approach.

Removing the badge clipped to the waistband of her skirt just beneath her jacket, Jael flashed it at the man. "I'm Detective Reynolds. I understand you witnessed the shooting."

"I don't know if you could call it 'witnessing.' It all happened so fast, I didn't see much." Up close, Jael guessed the man to be in his late forties. His weathered, bark-colored skin and strong build told of a life spent outdoors doing strenuous manual labor.

"Where were you when the shooting took place?"

"About fifty yards away on this side of the street. I was checking for any remaining trash that might have been overlooked last night. We have a little church around the corner and do some street ministry on Saturdays. Just before

Sunday service I usually check around to make sure every-thing's cleaned up good, and no loiterers hanging around, you know."

"Did you get a make on the car?"

"Like I told your fellow officers, it was an old Ford sedan, white with rust around the bottom. My back was turned when I heard the shots and when I looked up I saw this car speed away. I never thought to check the license plate. I just ran across the street, and there was this young guy holding his chest. I didn't see who shot from the car. I was more con-cerned about getting the paramedics here. I used my cell phone to call 911."

"Did you see if there was more than one person in the vehicle?"

"Naw, the only reason I mentioned the car in the first place was because it was the only automobile cruising by at the time. And the way it took off after the shots, was . . . well . . . sort of obvious. Another drive-by shooting."

Jael didn't bother to correct him. He'd learn soon enough that this was more than a street gang seeking revenge. Jael looked back at the scene across the street, breaking down the entire area in her mind. Photos would be on her desk later, but for now she wanted to get a feel for it herself.

"Hey, Detective," the man said, breaking into her thoughts. "I'm sorry I didn't have more to tell you."

Jael shook her head in understanding. "No problem. Take my card and call me if anything else comes to mind." She handed Mr. Walters her card, then walked to the end of the block before crossing to the other side of the street, where she hoped she'd find Brenda.

There were now two things they had that they didn't have

before: the note someone had slipped into her hand at Brenda's house, and a witness. She was afraid it wasn't enough.

She noticed Brenda immediately. Her friend had an arm draped over the shoulder of an older man, as if holding him up. As she got closer, Jael recognized the man as Brenda's uncle, whom she'd met once outside the church. Several other people stood around them. Moving closer, Jael got a good glimpse of Brenda's face. The woman seemed like an unflinching rock of strength. Jael suspected that if her friend displayed even one ounce of the emotions surging inside her, the floodgates of pain would explode.

As she approached, Jael prayed that her voice would come across softly, suggesting her sympathy but hiding her desperation. She prayed for the right words, words that might convey that the police had a handle on the situation—though, of course, they didn't.

Gently as possible, she whispered her friend's name. Brenda instantly looked up. Thin lines of dried mascara cascaded down her cheeks. So she *had* let go.

Seeing Jael, Brenda dropped her arms from around her uncle and moved toward her friend, her face suddenly a mask of misery. She fell into Jael's outstretched arms.

"I knew you'd be here. The police are asking a thousand questions, but I just can't seem to talk right now."

"I know," Jael said, embracing her friend.

"I still need to get home and contact the Prayer Warriors and Pastor Smalley, and of course, do what I can for my grandmother. I know you'll do all you can. I'll call you later. We'll get together with the Warriors and pray, okay?"

"Sure, we'll do that as soon as you're up to it. In the meantime, I'll be wearing out the Lord with my own prayers, lots of questions and petitions for guidance."

At least that got a weak smile. "He'll never let us down, Jael. We will understand all when God is ready to reveal the why's."

Though steadfast in her faith, Jael was still amazed by Brenda's countenance. The woman was a walking testimony that "God will see you through."

Her thoughts reverted to the many times Brenda had been there for her, praying, encouraging and simply saying all the right things when Jael believed she would never conquer her demons. Jael was positive that without Brenda there, walking her through each struggle, each nightmare, things might have turned out a lot different.

She kissed Brenda on the cheek. "I plan to give the Lord all the help He needs. I'll be home waiting for your call." To herself she added, *The battle lines are drawn, Satan. It's on!*

Chapter
11

Whether she wanted it to or not, the impact of what it felt like to lose someone dear came rushing into her mind with the force of a Mac truck. While certain things remained vividly etched in her brain, others were mere snatches of sensation, wrapped in swirling blocks of fog—such as the choking rattle of the window box air-conditioner unit that night, as it went off and on; the infuriating buzz of a mosquito at her ear; the weight of the suffocating darkness in the hall outside her bedroom.

The time had been approximately 11:45 that fateful evening, nineteen years ago. She'd just given up the fight to hang late watching TV with her big brother, Eddie, and was about to drift into blessed sleep when she heard the noises. Those awful, life-altering noises.

After the sounds, her memory of that night metamorphosed into distinct frames, frozen in time like photographs. It always began the same, seeing herself creeping down a hall shrouded in thick, unrelenting darkness; the muffled sound of struggle, just before the explosion of light in the room ahead; the rush of panic to come to her brother's aid, only to trip and fall at the mouth of the front room entrance. The impact of the fall, transforming everything into slivers of slow-motion action.

That's how her mind played it out, anyway; quick flashes of bright images, high octaves of sound and then the brightness, followed by quick jerky unforgettable fragments.

Frame 1: Looking up to see him, the unwelcome stranger, standing in the doorway, the porch light reflecting off his cruel ugliness. The greasy black skullcap, the deep-set, hatred-filled eyes under thick bushy brows, the wide nostrils flaring like those of a horse, the evil grimace across crooked yellow-stained teeth. The cheap dirty white ski outfit with red stripes down the side. The tattered, out-of-season winter gloves, over huge hands clutching their twenty-inch front room color TV.

Frame 2: The porch light illuminating the entire front room as the shadow of the stranger flees into the night. Her, pushing up from the floor, only to feel the cause of the fall. Looking down to see . . . Eddie, dear Eddie, covered in blood, oh, so much blood.

Frame 3: Eddie, reaching out to her, his other hand clutching the object embedded in his chest—a simple kitchen knife.

Frame 4: Her reaching out, clasping the object, cutting a deep gash in her hand in the process, her blood blending with Eddie's. The gurgling sounds he makes in his throat.

Frame 5: Eddie motioning for her to get the phone and call 911. His strangled words reaching her from the depths of a tunnel. The paralysis that consumes her. Eddie rising slowly, struggling to push her to the phone. Telling her what police codes to give the 911 operator. His chest heaving in rhythm with her own.

She remembers Eddie's moans of pain reaching her frozen brain and she sees herself reach for the phone cord and pull the phone off the end table to the floor. Her eyes revert to her brother's pain-riddled face as she nods and tries to hear everything he's attempting to tell her. Wiping away the wetness in her eyes with a hand saturated in crimson, making it hard to see the numbers. Dropping the phone when Eddie slumps back to the floor. Eddie whispering to her to remember every detail, how to give the information to the police, what not to touch. Even then, he is meticulous about the crime scene, even though it is his own.

At that point, a haze of darkness punches a big hole in her memory.

Frame 6: The house alive with people, sounds, cries, the pungent smell of lingering blood, whispering blood, whispering to her. She clearly remembers the feel of the cloth her momma presses to her face and hair. The cloth coming away each time with more of Eddie's blood. The bandage wrapped around the wound in her palm.

Frame 7: Eddie, lying only a few feet away from her, in a long cherry wood box, draped with flowers of varying colors. He lies before her, a shell of the brother she loved. The one who never allowed her to miss the presence of a father, because his role was significant enough. The one who taught her everything he knew on those nights when Momma worked late. The one who let her sleep in his bed, when she had bad dreams or was scared of the dark.

Then finally the last frame. The sound this time is that of the preacher's voice, talking about how Eddie was supposed to leave in two weeks for the police academy, to fulfill his single ambition in life. To be an officer of the law. To protect and serve.

It was then that it became her ambition also. Through the rivers of tears that fell from her eyes, she made an oath to her brother and herself. She solemnly promised to learn all she could, to follow in Eddie's footsteps and bring his murderer to justice. She wanted to stop this madness from ever happening to another family again.

Even today, only her mother knew that with every criminal she captured, with every face she looked into on the streets, was carried the hope of finding Eddie's killer. It was like an indirect satisfaction of justice for Eddie whenever she brought in a criminal, taking her one step closer to her ultimate goal. It had driven her for most of the years on the force. While others saw her choice of career as a way to honor her beloved older brother and carry on his legacy, for her it was a personal vendetta.

Jael shook the painful thought from her mind, unconsciously rubbing the scar in the palm of her right hand. A reminder of many things, including the fact that Eddie would want her to stay focused.

BeBe Winans's rich, rhinal alto spilled from the radio with his message of how God "Lifted Up," but right now Jael wasn't hearing a word of her favorite song as she steered the Bronco down Howard Avenue, heading home.

A tangle of conflicting thoughts ravaged her mind, especially about the note. She hadn't mentioned it to Sills at the crime scene—too many people around, too many ears that could leak info to the press. What was the note about? What exactly had she been given? Who knew that more deaths would occur? The person who'd passed the note to her didn't want anyone to know who he or she was.

Deeply buried in her thoughts, Jael didn't notice the silver Maxima passing swiftly alongside her until it swerved to the right within inches of her front bumper. Instinctively, she slammed on her brakes, barely avoiding the other vehicle or hitting her head on the steering wheel.

"What the . . ." she hissed as her heart hammered inside her chest and the adrenaline of surprise raced through her body.

Jael had no time to react further. The passenger door of the other car burst open and a huge, burly man dressed in loose-fitting jeans and a large pullover shirt advanced to her side of the car.

How dare he act as if she were at fault, she thought. Well, she was ready for him. He was in the wrong, and didn't have any idea who she was.

His next words confirmed he knew exactly who she was.

"If you want to talk to Big Jake, pull your Bronco over and get out," he said so close to her passenger window that she could see his chipped front tooth and a mass of acne scars.

Jael had never seen the man before, but he was big and obviously expected to be obeyed. "Who are you?" she demanded.

"Don't ask any questions, Detective Reynolds—Big Jake will be the one asking the questions. Now, if you want to talk with him, you'll do as I say. Leave any weapons behind."

Though it was certainly not one of the smartest things she'd ever done, she followed the stranger's orders. She knew

Big Jake, and if this guy called her by name, Booley had reached Big Jake in record time and he was now turning the tables in pursuit of her. Jael prayed that the Lord had finally put "the fear of God" in the dealer and that Big Jake merely wanted to know what was going on in Dadesville as much as she did.

Jael gave the guy a slight nod, backed her Bronco up and pulled to the side of the curb. She removed her shoulder holster from beneath her suit jacket, not wanting the men to have reason to frisk her and maybe keep her weapon. She placed it in the glove compartment, climbed out and locked the car. She'd trust the Lord to get her out of this one. Besides, she still had her trusty forefinger, she mused.

Though the big guy never displayed his weapon, the way he waved her along with one hand in his pocket indicated he was packing something more deadly than a finger.

The rear left door of the Maxima suddenly swung open before her. Jael hesitated just a beat, then stepped inside and looked straight into the glaring, malicious eyes of Big Jake. The burly fellow with the chipped tooth climbed in the front with another buddy and raced the engine, but didn't drive off.

Big Jake was more menacing and dangerous-looking in appearance than anyone Jael had ever laid eyes on, and wore his name rightly. At six and a half feet tall, he exuded a danger not defined by gangland scars or the ugly remnants of acne, but a deeper, sinister evil—rooted to the bone.

The last time Jael had spoken to Big Jake, he had worn his usual self-assured, snide grin. Today the grin was missing, replaced by a hateful scowl. He still wore the lavish attire of an open silk shirt over a white T-shirt and a huge J held by a platinum chain around his ornery neck. A diamond-studded ring in each ear of his shaved head seemed to make his appearance even more intimidating.

"I just love your method for meeting women," Jael said as she settled back against the rich leather seat before turning to face Big Jake.

"Why you looking for me, and what the hell is going on?" he barked without preamble.

"If you're going to curse, this conversation is over before it starts." The smell of marijuana saturated the car's interior, but it was something she'd have to overlook for the moment. She had more urgent matters to deal with than a drug bust.

The car suddenly pulled off, and Jael glanced at the back of the heads of the two men in the front seat. They sat like twin stone pillars, staring straight ahead.

Jael's attention was drawn back to Big Jake as he sputtered his indignation.

"Are you . . . do you . . . have you really lost your last mind?"

"We go way back, Jake. This is important to both of us, so let's get the ground rules straight. Someone's offing your boys, and you need me like I need you or you wouldn't volunteer to make my search for you easier. Now, let's lay everything out on the table so I can do my job and get out there and find out who's behind it."

Big Jake stared silently at her for an interminable length of time, as if he were trying to make up his mind. Jael waited, never letting her gaze waver; two could play the intimidation game. When next he spoke, it was to say the last thing she'd have expected.

"I think I might know where you should start. You've got one chance to do your cop stuff and only twenty-four hours to do it in. If you can't handle it, my boys will take care of this situation for you. Unofficial deputies, you might say."

The ugly grin was back.

Chapter 12

Jael pulled into her driveway just as Virgil drove his Mercedes to a screeching halt in front of her house. Always appreciative of small favors, she sent a grateful "Thank you" heavenward, that she had beat him to the house this time.

Before Virgil could shut off the engine, Ramon jumped from the passenger seat and ran to meet her as she stepped from the Bronco.

"Momma, you'll never guess what we did this weekend. We spent all day Saturday at Islands of Adventure. Can you believe it? Dad gave in and let me eat as much as I could hold and even rode with me on the Space Blaster. It was the bomb!"

"That's great, honey." Jael wrapped her arms around her son in a welcoming hug as she looked over his head at his father. If Virgil had let his hair down over the weekend, there was no sign of it now. He was dressed, as always, to the nines. And, as always, the first thing to come out of his mouth when he saw her was criticism.

"Do you realize that Ramon needs to see a dentist? Don't you ever bother to look closely at your son?"

Since she hadn't fallen smack on her face after their divorce as he'd expected and had even gone so far as to be considered by many as somewhat of a local hero, Virgil could eat bricks. He resented her success without him. It wasn't supposed to go that way, especially since he felt trapped in a job that kept overlooking him during promotions. For her it only proved how God protected His own.

"What's wrong with his teeth?" Jael asked as she pushed Ramon slightly back and gently spread his lips apart. "You weren't having any problems, were you, honey?"

Ramon assisted her efforts with a wide grin while rolling his eyes, knowing his father, standing behind them, couldn't see. The expression was so comical Jael had to press *her* lips together to keep from laughing out loud. With her knee, she nudged him to behave.

"Dad says I need braces," he whined, ignoring the nudge. "Please, Momma, not braces."

"The boy needs his teeth corrected," Virgil said, moving toward them. "Do you still have dental coverage? Or should I apply through my plan?"

"I have coverage, but we'll let the dentist decide what he needs." With her arm still around Ramon, she turned and headed for the front porch. "Okay . . . Well, see you, Virgil."

"Wait a minute, not so fast. The Omega's Fathers and Sons Banquet is next Thursday, and I need to know if you can have Ramon ready . . . and on time."

"You never told me about a father-and-son banquet," she said over her shoulder.

"Let's not even go there. I tell you these things all the

time, but you always conveniently forget. Anyway, I'm telling you now, again, so I won't have any problems with you later."

Very slowly, Jael turned to face her ex. "Listen, Virgil, I resent the way you always insinuate that I'm attempting to keep Ramon from you or that I'm some kind of monster mother."

"Oh, how soon we forget. But I don't have time to give you a current list. Just remember to have him ready. It's a suit-and-tie affair." With that, her ex marched back to his car.

Ramon had taken off inside the house, leaving his overnight bag on the front steps. Jael picked it up as she passed, mumbling unintelligible words at the departing car, then added a final hiss.

Once inside, she again grabbed Ramon, who was dancing around in a circle, and gave him a big hug. "Boy, did I miss you!"

"Yeah, I bet. Did you have a great time in this house alone? Did you eat right?"

"Hey, without the boss around, I pigged out on so much fat my cholesterol count is probably off the chart."

"Tsk, tsk, good thing I got back here in time. Can't leave you alone for more than a day or two."

"Yeah, yeah." Jael pushed her son ahead of her toward the kitchen. "Had dinner?"

"We went to Red Lobster earlier with Dad's . . . uh . . . I mean, yeah."

Jael shoved him playfully. "You don't have to be elusive about your dad's new girlfriend. I'm sure she's fat and ugly."

Ramon laughed, then tilted his head as if seriously considering the matter. "Well, actually, she looks a lot like Halle

Berry, if you go for that type." Then he exploded with laughter at his mother's astonished expression. "Just kidding, Momma. She can't touch you by a mile. I can't figure out what Dad sees in her; she looks worse than the woman he dated after you guys split."

"Oh, sure, words of comfort out of the mouth of an adoring son."

"Who says I'm adoring?"

"Why, you little turkey," Jael teased, reaching her hands out in a death grip toward her only child. Ramon took off in a peal of laughter toward the den as she bolted behind him. While she was in heavy pursuit, her police cell phone rang. Giggling, Ramon dashed to his bedroom.

"Don't think you're saved by the bell!" Jael shouted after him. "You 'done tried a colored girl' and your little skinny behind is mine as soon as I finish this call."

Jael could hear his chuckled reply, and grinned to herself. Lord, she really did miss that boy when he was away. She moved toward the couch and lifted the cell phone from where it lay beside her purse on the end table. With a note of merriment still in her voice, she said, "Hello."

"Is this Detective Reynolds?"

Instantly, the gaiety in her voice disappeared. The person at the other end sounded as if he'd never laughed in his entire life. She answered in her most official tone, "Yes, this is her."

"This is Harold Watson."

"Well, isn't this weird. I was going to call you." After talking with Big Jake, and learning of his suspicions that MAD DADS, a grassroots antidrug group, was somehow involved in all this, she'd meant to contact Harold first thing

Monday morning. At least this saved her some office time. It also proved Big Jake might have pointed her in a more likely direction.

"You mean you already know about the threat?"

Jael slowly sat on the couch. "Threat?"

"The threat to my life!"

"Wait a minute, Mr. Watson, let's back up here. Someone threatened *you?*"

"Some fool thinks I know something about these recent murders and left a note at my house demanding I confess, or else."

"*Do* you know anything about the murders?"

There was a solid moment of silence.

"Do I . . . ? Listen to me and listen good. I'm the founder and president of MAD DADS. We try to clean up drug-infested neighborhoods and *rescue* those who are addicted, not kill them!" he shouted in a self-assured, self-promoting manner.

"I know all about your organization, Mr. Watson, but you haven't answered my question. Do you have any idea who might be behind all this?"

Again Jael picked up on the slight hesitation in his answer. "Why would anyone think I know anything? Yes, we walk the beats, try to keep our streets clean of the drug scum, but we never hurt anyone, never take advantage of our position in the community."

"If I remember correctly, a young man was knocked around pretty good a year ago, and your organization was held responsible."

"How can you even call that lowlife 'a young man'? He was caught in the act of trying to sell drugs to one of our members' own kids! If the father went off rather physically, who can blame him? At least it showed those dealers we meant business. We've kept our neighborhood clean because we don't take no mess."

"How far would members of your organization go to send out the message, *We don't take no mess*'?"

"Not enough to kill somebody! Look, Detective Reynolds, I called you to alert you to the fact someone's trying to threaten me, *and* to warn you that I will take any precautions necessary to keep myself and my family safe. If the dealers want a war with us, then . . ."

"Hold on a minute, Mr. Watson. That's not the case at all. It seems the dealers are scared to death someone's targeting *them*. I was pointed in your direction because of your actions against them. So, forget retaliations. We all need to work together here."

"I have no desire whatsoever to work with that scum to keep their butts safe. They've brought this on themselves and deserve any mishap that falls their way. I applaud whoever is behind this. Since the police don't seem to be able to do anything, maybe someone figured out a way to eliminate the germs."

"Mr. Watson, are you suggesting that you know who's behind . . . ?"

"Take it however you want, Detective, but you'd better tell them to stay away from me. I have every legal right to defend myself. Threats don't scare me! And I'm not afraid of any drive-by shootings, either, because I'll be waiting for them!"

The line went dead before she could respond.

Chapter 13

A half hour later when she stepped out of the shower, Jael continued to play the phone call with Harold Watson around in her mind while she absently toweled off. She was not surprised by his "devil may care" attitude toward those who pushed illegal drugs on kids. Many in the community would have the same sentiments. No one was going to have any serious qualms that dealers were being offed.

But for her, life was precious, no matter whose it was. Murder was never to be considered a means to eradicate a problem. As a child of God on the police force, she came up against the criminal element on a continual basis. With many, there was simply no supreme power other than what they strived to achieve on their own. Still, every now and then, using the right words, and with just the right measure of kindness, she sensed the curiosity and wonder she left behind, and knew that another seed had been planted.

Moving into the adjoining bedroom, Jael donned a pair of comfortable cutoff jeans and her favorite Tampa Bay

Buccaneers T-shirt. She was a do-or-die Bucs fan and reveled in the fact that Virgil detested the team.

A knowing smile passed her lips for a moment, as the thought flashed through her mind about what her reaction to this recent rash of murders would have been if she was still with her ex. Certainly not a pleasant one, that was for sure. But that was then. Now she was stronger. Now she had an inner force that fought her demons on a daily basis. She whispered a soft *"Thank you, Jesus,"* something she did a lot, but even more so these last couple of days. Had it been only two days ago that she'd discovered the first slain dealer in the crack house? So much had happened since then.

She didn't believe Big Jake and his boys were behind this; they were too scared. And it was far-fetched to think Harold Watson and MAD DADS had gone to this extreme. The men were a great asset to the community, cleaning up drug-infested neighborhoods and then patrolling them to deter any future returns. They worked closely with the Dadesville Police Department, and had even received a recognition award from the department for their service. Yet there was something nagging her about her conversation with Watson. He knew something—she felt it.

With Ramon now snugly in bed, Jael decided to call Watson back. Reaching for her phone, sitting beside her bed in its charger, she pressed *69, but got his answering machine. She left a message for him to call her later or tomorrow at the office. Replacing the phone in its cradle, she jumped when it rang right away. Man, she thought, her nerves must be shot. She'd become a ball of jitters in just a few days.

The person on the other end did not wait for her to speak.

"Hello, Detective Reynolds?"

"Yes?"

"Gwen Hayes, from the *Florida Sentinel*."

Jael exhaled a sigh of relief. She settled on the bed and slid back against the queen-size headboard. Gwen was a reporter for the local black newspaper, an honest journalist with a smart head on her shoulders. Jael had liked the woman ever since they'd met six years ago at a drug-related crime scene. Gwen had even gotten the scoop on Jael's unpublicized leave of absence from the force two years ago, yet had never printed a word of what she'd learned. Though Jael had let Gwen know that she would be forever grateful for that, the young woman never acted as if she was owed a favor.

"Hey, Gwen, what's up?"

"Hoped *you* could tell *me*. About what's going on with the street dealers, I mean."

"Yeah, well, we haven't got much to go on right now, Gwen. You know you'll get the exclusive from me when anything turns up."

"I understand there was a witness to the last murder?"

Boy, did this gal work fast. Jael wouldn't waste breath asking how she'd found out.

"I can't give you his name, but the witness did see a rusty old white Ford sedan speed from the scene of the crime, seconds after the shooting."

"Can I print that?"

"It's all yours, and you can add that the police department is also looking into written threats to certain members of MAD DADS and will enforce the law to the fullest degree."

"Wow, now this is all beginning to make sense."

Jael frowned, not sure she understood Gwen. "How so?"

"Well, I heard through the grapevine that Daniel Foster, a relatively new member of MAD DADS, was sending out feelers for someone who would accept a contract hit."

Jael sat straight up. "What?"

"Of course, I have no proof of this, only stuff I picked up along the way, but from what you're telling me, it seems to add up."

"Why would he do something like that?"

"Payback, from what I hear. His own son is strung out, stole everything out of the house that wasn't nailed down, then jumped Foster's wife when she wouldn't give him money out of her purse. The rumor goes, Foster put a gun in his son's face and dared him to step foot on the property again, but the boy's been back twice. Foster told a friend he was going to have his son put out of his misery."

"My God!" Jael was dumbfounded. None of her CIs had even hinted at this. Could all this madness be occurring because a father had gone loony? Was this what Big Jake was hinting at? Drugs always affected more than just the user, and oftentimes an enabler or other family members suffered to great extremes. But to put a hit out on your own son and those you felt were responsible for his deterioration was too much.

In her line of work, strange things happened every day. For many law enforcement personnel, it was easy to become a skeptic about spiritual intervention. For her, it had been the grounding rod of her life. The confirmation that even amid the hatred, abuse, death and horrors man could inflict on his brother, there were beacons of kindness, and salvation, and moments of bravery and unselfish giving; and awe at the mercy of God when, say, an infant could fall from a sixth-floor building and land safely with only a few scars. When there were beams of light in the darkness that others couldn't explain, her heart soared, reaffirmed in its faith in the greater force that reached into the madness to leave behind a ray of hope.

Yet, even Jael had to admit it was difficult to see any good in this kind of craziness. The murders were having a domino effect already. How many more had to die? When would it end? Most important, why did it all frighten her so much, and so personally?

Chapter
14

Not having time to keep her vow to have a little talk with Tammy, Jael threw up a quick "Hey, girl" at the receptionist as she passed, before pushing through the glass double doors of the squad room. Sills was at his desk, leaning back dangerously in his swivel chair, his back to her with the phone to his ear. Jael didn't bat an eye. That was Sills, living life on the edge.

Hearing her approach, he turned and held up a "give me a second" finger before Jael was even seated. She tilted her head, rolled her eyes and waited as he continued with his phone conversation.

"Yeah . . . right, sir . . . got it, sir." Sills replaced the phone with a look that was not, by any stretch of the imagination, encouraging. "That was the Captain. What do you want first, the good news or the bad news?"

Jael tossed her purse on the desk. "Too early in the morning for bad. You'd better give me the good news first so I can at least *pretend* to start the day out right." She sat in her seat, gripped the side of her chair and leaned *safely* back.

"For our two victims, the bullets were all the same make. Both dealers went down from an Intertec 9 semiautomatic, including the slugs retrieved from the body found by the railroad tracks."

"And . . . ?" Jael rolled her hand in a circular motion to indicate she expected more to the statement.

"Aaand, if the report I'm getting is confirmed, all were fired from the same gun. Each caliber seems to have a particular groove that came from the barrel of the weapon, which would indicate same gun, same guy."

"Well, that's something. It eliminates the possibility that we're dealing with more than one shooter. Unless . . ."

It was now time for the word game she and Sills often played, tossing thoughts back and forth to review a case situation from all possible angles. It helped to clear the fog and make sure they were on the same wavelength. Sills continued her sentence with, ". . . Unless the same gun is being passed around to make it look as if there's only one killer. But then again . . ."

"Then again, it doesn't seem likely that our drug boys on the street would go that far to cover their deeds, and even if . . ."

"And even if it's not the boys, what would be the purpose?"

Jael nodded in agreement but had no comeback. They both sat in deep concentration, mulling over their thoughts.

"I received a call last night from the president of MAD DADS. He says he's being threatened by someone who thinks he knows what's going on but not telling. I also got a note in a weird way while I was at Brenda's house yesterday."

Jael reached into her purse and tossed Sills the plastic bag
with the bold writing. He caught it with one hand.

"Why didn't you tell me about this earlier?" He frowned,
turning the bag over to inspect exactly what he was holding.

"Bad timing. Too many folks around with big ears."

Sills examined the evidence. "This is bad."

"Tell me about it. I also received a very enlightening call
from Gwen Hayes, a reporter at the *Florida Sentinel*. Seems
she picked up a rumor about one of the MAD DADS members on his own personal revenge crusade. His son's an
addict and he's looking for someone to take up a hit contract. On who, she's not sure."

"Man, oh man, this is getting worse by the second."

"You got that right. Big Jake has given me an ultimatum.
Either keep this madman from offing any more of his
dealers quick, or his boys will consider themselves unofficial
deputies and do the job for us."

Sills smiled and leaned even farther back in his seat.
"Hey, that might work in our favor."

Just another micro-inch, Jael thought, and *I'll be picking my
friend up off the floor.* "So what's *your* bad news?"

"Don't think I can top yours, but that was the Captain on
the phone earlier—bypassed protocol looking for you, but I
took the call." Sills lifted slightly forward in his chair, easing
Jael's tension. "You owe me for saving your butt. He was in
an ugly mood, demanding we bring in some results and quit
with the sloppy police work."

"Sloppy police work?"

"He's calling a press conference at noon, wants you by his
side, wants you to make *his* department look competent and

wants you in his office at least twenty minutes before the conference."

"Ugggh." Jael leaned back and studied the paint-chipped ceiling. "Okay . . . how does this sound? I tell the press we've got a make on the car, so we give that description; we also tell them we have reason to believe we're searching for a single perpetrator, and that we have increased patrols of all known drug areas. I won't mention the rumor, or that I've already told Gwen to run with the threat on Harold Watson, but . . . I throw the ball back into the media's court, suggesting they encourage the community to keep a sharp eye out and report any suspicious activity to our hot line." Jael gave Sills a "whadda ya think?" look.

"Sounds good to me. That's why you're the boss—you're quick on your feet. So, we got a hot line already?"

"No, but you'll have that for me before noon, right?"

"Right."

Two hours later, as Jael stood at the Captain's dark oak door, her nerve ends were doing a tap dance just beneath her skin. A praying woman first and always, she certainly knew when prayer should precede a confrontation. She preceded this one with an extensive line of prayer now. *Let us run with patience the race that is set before us*—Hebrews 12:1. *The Lord is my strength and my shield*—Psalms 28:7. *Be wise in all things.*

"Don't lollygag outside my door! Come in or go away!" came the bark from the other side of the entrance. Nothing less than the typical "welcome" from the Dadesville police captain.

Jael stepped into the Captain's office and immediately realized she was in for more than the average snarling and barking. Today, he wore an ugly, ill-tempered, pit-bull, "waiting for someone to bite" expression. She'd have to throw him a bone or two if she didn't want that someone to be her.

"It's about time you got here. The press conference is in less than thirty minutes."

Comparing her boss to a pit bull wasn't far off. He had a large head covered with thin layers of reddish-blond hair, slightly bulging eyes and thick sagging cheeks. Though he was a big man, he tended to stoop, and even while sitting, he looked like someone had stuffed him into his chair. He was wearing his uniform of dark pants, a loud tie and a dark suit jacket that was a bit too tight.

Straightening her spine, Jael moved toward his desk but didn't take a seat in the scarred mahogany chair before him. "I knew you'd want me to take advantage of every available minute to ensure we had as much information as possible."

Captain Slater looked at her from beneath bushy eyebrows and gruffed, "Okay, so get to it. What do we have?"

"If you've had a chance to review the earlier reports, you—"

"Don't give me that! Spit it out! Where does this case stand?"

" 'Stand' is hardly the right word. As a matter of fact, we're not even wobbling."

"You'd better have something, Reynolds. I'm not going in front of that press mob without some concrete leads."

Jael wanted to remind him he'd asked for the conference, not her. A conference which was a tad premature, she thought. Under normal situations, the Captain would have the Homicide team brief him, then they would toss possible scenarios back and forth before finally calling a press conference.

Instead, she counted to ten as she glanced just beyond his head at the white-oak bookshelf filled with personal photos, underwatered plants, dog-eared paperbacks and an ugly crimson, fur-covered dog with a bobbing head that looked a lot like the Captain.

"We believe we're dealing with one perpetrator. The bullets all came from the same gun, which means we can dispense with the premise that this is a drug war. The dealers are scared out of their minds. They're looking for the guy too."

She didn't mention that she had only twenty-four hours to come up with some concrete answers or they'd have more problems on their hands from Big Jake. She'd report that only if she didn't have a strong handle on things within the next twenty-four hours.

"Well, that's something," the Captain responded slowly. "This appears to give us an inside view and changes the spin the press has, that this is a battle between the dealers." He leaned forward in his chair, placing his palms on the desktop, his head bowed down.

Jael knew she had scored a point in the intimidation battle with him. Her nerves started to settle, and she whispered, "Thank you, Lord." But the battle was far from over. The Captain raised his head and fixed her with a glare.

"What do you have to confirm this?"

"Big Jake's sweat. He's scared, and so are his boys."

"I can't tell the press these are vigilante slayings!"

"And I hope you won't do so." Jael ignored the scowl that quickly etched his face.

"Just be sure you don't bring God and angels and all that stuff into this conference." The Captain twirled his hand around in the air. "We don't want the public thinking we move only on heavenly intervention."

Jael resented the cheap shot alluding to their last press conference, held two years ago after the vandalism of several churches. During a heated interview about her zeal to capture the culprit, she'd answered one reporter's question of whether it was an attack on religion by saying God would not allow this to go unsolved and that He was on their side. The headline the next day read: POLICE DEPARTMENT WAITS FOR GOD TO AVENGE HIS CHURCH. She'd been called on the carpet like never before over that one, though the case was solved almost the next day. She'd proudly framed two copies of the article. One hung on the wall in her den beside Ramon's photo, the other at her desk. For her, God was the victor in that one, through and through.

"I've just met with four homicide detectives to set up a task force," Jael said. "We all agree this has all the elements of a serial killer. Not your norm, of course—no visible tags left behind as his personal brag. With our heads together, we should have a definite plan in place soon."

Captain Slater screwed his lips together and leaned his big head sideways. "Soon . . . as in the next couple of hours, or soon as in the next couple of days?"

Jael took a deep breath and released it sharply. "Captain, you know as well as I do that we have very little to go on right now. It would be premature to speculate without more concrete evidence. We don't want to look like fools with a lot of guessing that might cause the citizens of this community any needless worries. We do want to ensure them their safety takes precedence over anything else and that the city is confident that this case will come to justice swiftly. Now, you called this press conference, and I'll do all I can to make *you* look good. But I can't give what I don't have."

For a moment, Jael was sure she had stepped over the line. The look that crossed the Captain's face was one she hoped not to see again soon.

The Captain leaned back in his seat as foul, angry words swirled through his brain. He cleared his throat. "Well, expand on what you can, and you'd better have some persuasive ways today, Detective. I was told that someone from CNN was already here. Our little town will be scrutinized in its handling of this case. You won't want to have me at your door if this case isn't wrapped up soon. Think of me as the thorn in your side, or better yet, the 'devil in the flesh,' if that works better for you."

Chapter
15

Immediately following the press conference, the exhaustion of the past fourteen hours draped her from head to toe, and she was only half into the day. After all the badgering questions from the press and the glaring looks from Captain Slater as he stood beside her, the muscles in her neck were as taut as if a coarse rope were being pulled around it. The tentacles of a headache teased the nerves just behind her eyes, with the promise of a real whopper soon.

Pushing the glass double doors of the squad room open, Jael halted abruptly in mid-stride. The Rock, or at least a dead ringer for the handsome wrestling hunk, now action hero, was sitting on her desk in living color. He was propped on the edge of it, one long leg swinging back and forth, while in his hand he casually inspected her precious "WORLD'S GREATEST MOM" cup. Whoever he was, he was making himself right at home.

"Uh, excuse me, may I help you?" she inquired, allowing the indignation to saturate her voice.

When the man looked up, Jael could tell it was not the

real Rock but a close look-alike. Her stomach took a leap. The man simply smiled, gorgeously, and placed her cup back on the desk, but didn't move. His reaction fueled her irritation.

Drawing her eyebrows together, Jael stepped up to her desk and pulled out her chair. "Do you mind?"

"Not at all," the stranger said, still smiling, as all six feet and approximately 280 pounds of him rose from her desk. He moved to the side, placing both his huge hands on the client chair. "I'm at your service."

"Excuse me?"

Reaching inside his double-breasted jacket, which Jael noticed seemed to fit him like the clothing was designed for the sole purpose of showing the world how men's clothes *should* fit, he pulled out a black wallet and flipped it open. "Special Agent Eric Grant, Federal Bureau of Investigation." He placed the wallet on the table before her.

The photo on the official card didn't do the man justice. His serious and stern look appeared average in the photo. Jael glanced up at him. No, sir, there was nothing average about this guy, not by a long shot.

"Is there a reason this should somehow make my day?" Jael asked, hoping to establish at least some authority in her voice.

Extending his hand, he said, "Only that I'm here to assist you in bringing in your man."

Well, he'd certainly said the right words to knock the wind out of her sail. Jael took the outstretched hand and gave it a firm, but reluctant shake before sitting down.

"Who authorized your involvement? No one told me about the FBI's interest in this case."

"No involvement yet, just curious observation. You may have a situation on your hands, and our department wants to be ready."

Jael raised a skeptical eyebrow. *Talk about the long arm of the law,* she thought.

"We may have a . . . Well, I would certainly call three murders a 'situation,' but why are you guys curious about these drug dealers?"

"It's not the drug dealers we're looking into, but rather why they're being targeted."

"That makes two of us."

"Who have you spoken to so far?"

Jael instantly resented the man's attitude. The Feds always expected to be in charge, but for now this was still her case. "Am I supposed to report to you or something?"

"No, but I hoped we could work together. If you allow me to review your reports and tag along on this investigation, I believe our department could profile this perpetrator and speed up the process."

Did she see a glimmer of mockery in his eyes? Jael bristled, but she also knew she needed to get to the bottom of these murders and had to be willing to put her professional resentments on the back burner. However, she was not about to hand over everything she had without ensuring she was to have final say.

She was wondering whether it was laughable to think she could possibly have final say *over the FBI* when he continued.

"I understand you had a witness to the third shooting, and even more important, brought in a vagrant from the second shooting at the crack house. I'd like to talk to both of them, if possible." He leaned slightly forward as Jael realized that his voice was soft and full, a Brooklyn quality.

"You can, but I'll be there at each interrogation."

"I'd also like to see the crime photos. At your convenience, of course."

Jael looked down at the folder she'd brought back with her from the press conference. She shoved it across the desk at the agent.

"Enjoy yourself while I get myself a cup of coffee." As she rose, she noticed a smile creep across the agent's face. She hurried away. This was all she needed—a guy with looks her cousin Rhonda would drool over. Jael moved toward the far corner, where a coffeepot sat with age-old coffee burning away at the bottom of the glass container. She'd forgotten her mug, so she reached for a foam cup. Like she was going to drink some of this burned mud anyway. She just needed to get away from *Mr. Fine.* Where the heck was Sills when she needed him? Pouring the black slush into the foam cup, she silently implored, *God, I don't need this kind of confusion right now. Can you send him away?*

He was still at her desk when she returned, deep into the pages of the accumulated reports. He looked up as she pulled out her chair to sit.

"When do you expect a more extensive report? This is good so far, with the accounts, background investigation, coroner's report and numerous interviews, but it's got no leads or theories."

"No problem. How soon do you want them? I've got plenty of theories."

Agent Grant leaned back in his seat. "Okay, let's start over. The resentment is rolling off you like fumes. So please, let me ease your concerns. How about this? Why don't I back off and you simply let me tag along. If I have any ideas about anything, I bounce them off you before I call back to headquarters. If I get in the way, you just say so. You think you could work with that?"

Jael studied Agent Eric Grant before answering. Then did so truthfully.

"You're right about my feeling hostile. I don't particularly care to have someone just stepping up and telling me what I need to have and how soon, especially someone I don't know and have never worked with before. But I also want to capture whoever is doing this. So let's forget how I feel about your sudden appearance and just take advantage of it. Deal?"

"Deal." Grant's smile was unnerving. "You mentioned if I wanted to talk to your witnesses, you'd have to be there. I'd like to talk to this MAD DADS member, Daniel Foster— whom you smartly didn't mention at the press conference— and to the derelict who was at the crime scene at the crack house."

"No I didn't. Members of the press are like hounds and will be on the search for the guy, scaring him away. As for Foster and William Walters, I'll have to make a few calls."

"I can wait."

And he did, sitting there as nice as you please, while she dialed the number for the man who'd seen the car and Foster. As she dialed, she studied Agent Grant's interesting profile.

Actually, the more she thought about it, the more she realized The Rock really had nothing on this guy. Mr. FBI had it going on in the best way.

She got Walters's answering service and left a message. Foster's number she needed from Watson, but his wife said he wasn't home and she didn't know Foster's number.

"Daniel Foster of MAD DADS lives on the other side of town. The vagrant, of course, has no known residence. We'll have to find him on the streets," she said after hanging up.

"If you have the time, my rental's outside."

"We'll take my car."

Together they rose and moved toward the double doors. As Grant reached in front of her to push open the glass door, his left arm accidentally brushed against her. Jael quickly inhaled, then squared her shoulders. *Lord, this is* not *funny.*

Chapter
16

Jael stole frequent peeks at her passenger in his trademark FBI dark shades as he gazed out the window taking in the view. There was no denying it: The man sitting ramrod-straight beside her was gorgeous.

Reluctantly, pulling her eyes away before she was caught, her gaze fell on the hands tightly gripping the steering wheel. *Shoot, my nails look so bad. And so does my hair. I should have made an appointment at Nubian Knots with LaTosha, like Rhonda suggested two weeks ago. My limp hair is waaaayy overdue.* She added this thought as she glanced into the rearview mirror before making a left turn: *And why in the world did I pick this drab outfit instead of . . .*

Heeeyyy, Jael silently shushed herself. Why was she suddenly so concerned about how she looked? *Keep your mind on business, girl.*

Jael cleared her throat. "So, you're here simply to do a profile?"

"As you said earlier, the suspect is possibly a vigilante." Grant answered without turning in her direction, which Jael didn't mind at all, since it gave her the opportunity to absorb *his* striking profile as if she were simply being attentive.

"Regardless of his initial motives," he continued, "vigilantes tend to view their killings as a mission, feeling justified in what they're doing. I hope you know you're dealing with the irrational here."

The statement brought things back into perspective. Jael finally pulled her gaze away and twisted her mouth. Like this was news? Did they need someone from the FBI to tell them this tidbit of priceless information?

The downtown district gradually transformed into residential dwellings with well-kept lawns and high, decorative privacy fences. Overhead the sun flickered fingers of rays through the trees, dropping light glints of yellow and gold on their leaves. As her squad car rolled smoothly down Amberwood Drive heading toward Willow Road, a predominately white section of town with only a handful of blacks, branches waved gently on a soft breeze along both sides of the street. Since it wasn't yet 5 P.M., most of the residents were probably still at work and only a few cars were on the road.

Jael pressed the lever at her elbow and cracked her window. Whatever the brand of cologne this man was wearing, it was making her light-headed. She felt like a woman who'd never been exposed to the allure of an appealing man before. Her mind was wandering, wondering how long it had been since she'd felt attraction for anyone. What had he just said? Something about serial killers being dangerous? How stupid. And was he waiting for an answer? She gave him the first retort that came to mind, something she used often with Ramon when he thought he was one up on her.

"I may be crazy, but I'm not stuck on stupid." She quickly realized this was possibly the wrong answer, and added, "As a homicide detective, I have some knowledge about killers, you know."

The hardy laugh exploding from Grant's throat sounded good, real good. It also gave her a reason to look directly at him again. The first thing she noticed was how the lines had softened around his mouth from the outburst. She was unaware that her own expression had softened as well.

"No one would ever put you in the category of stupid," he said.

Virgil came to mind, and she quickly dismissed any thoughts of him. "Well, just making sure you know I'm no slouch." She gave him her first real smile. He smiled back.

"You can rest assured your talents and abilities have been well noted. Captain Slater didn't have to give me a detailed list of all your service awards to impress me. Nor mention that you're the pride of the force and the possible next lieutenant."

Jael was genuinely surprised. Captain Slater bragging on her? No way, not the bulldog. She was at a loss for words.

Silence filled the car for a moment. Grant was the first to speak.

"Jael. That's a rare name." Without looking, Jael could feel the intensity of his sudden stare. "From the Bible, isn't it?"

Jael was surprised. Usually people mispronounced it, calling her *Jail* instead of *Jay-el.* And for many, it was intentional. Few knew its real meaning or that it came from the scriptures.

"Yes, from the Book of Judges, 4:17–23. My mom said she was so excited to discover this black woman in the Bible named Jael she had to christen one of her children with it. Supposedly, Jael was a direct descendant of Moses' father-in-law and helped the Israelites in battle by nailing their enemy king's head to the ground." Jael looked at her passenger with genuine curiosity. "You acquainted with the word of God?"

"Can't say I'm an avid follower, but I was brought up in the Catholic Church. Took up theology in college for a while, though, before moving off into forensic psychology. I still do a little studying on my own."

Jael respected any spiritual admittance on a man's part, though she had many questions about the doctrine of the Catholic religion. It was refreshing to meet a man who admitted to studying the Word, even though he was not active in any church.

"You don't look like a man who would read the Book on his own, much less study."

"In my field it pays to understand the deeper motives of the human species and what makes their minds tick. I find man's nature has not changed much, if at all, from the days of Noah or Adam. Without getting into a heady debate, this kind of work needs a solid foundation to keep one's head above the mire."

"Tell me about it. I would have thrown in the towel long ago if not for the grace of God. His divine strength has been my strength."

"Well, you're certainly going to need His guidance on this one."

Jael was completely dumbfounded. How likely was she to

meet a guy intellectually endowed, good-looking *and* with a sense of the need for spiritual guidance. She'd better not get her hopes up, though, she thought. His kind were always married off.

"Does your wife study the Word too?" *No I didn't,* she thought in horror.

"In the beginning she did, but by the time we divorced a few years ago she'd 'expanded her mind' to an even higher consciousness than the Bible, like yoga or something to that extent, and there was very little we saw eye-to-eye on after that."

He was still staring at her, but before she could make an intelligent remark, they'd arrived at their destination. She wasn't sure if this was a blessing or not.

Two cars were parked out in front of the MAD DADS member's home. Jael parked behind the second, and as she exited she and Grant stared up at the small frame house. It could certainly have used a new coat of paint, but otherwise boasted of a well-kept surrounding with a manicured lawn and terra-cotta potted plants on each side of the front steps.

Together they walked to the front porch, and before they reached the heavy emerald-green door the sound of muffled arguing could be heard from inside. Jael glanced at Grant, then rang the bell. The arguing instantly stopped.

When the door opened, a ragged-looking Daniel Foster stood before them. Daniel was small in stature, but broad-chested and thick around the waistline. His thinning, jet-black hair sat upon a large head with a jutting jaw, which right now looked as if it hadn't been shaved in a few days. Before Jael could say a word, he attacked with his own verbal demands.

"For once the police are finally on time. Come inside and remove this old fool from my home."

Jael peeked inside as Harold Watson came up to the door behind Foster and yanked it completely open, hitting it against the back wall with a loud thud.

"Yes, do come in, and tell this ignoramus that leaving threats at people's homes can land his butt behind bars!"

Jael gave Grant a rather pensive look, and together they stepped inside the house.

She took the lead. "Mr. Foster, we're here on a completely different matter, but if you did leave the note, this might be a good time to tell us why."

Daniel tossed his hand in Harold's direction. "I've told this fool it wasn't me."

"In that case, we have other questions we need to ask," Jael said. "If you'd like Mr. Watson to leave, we can—"

"No, let the fool stay and learn of my innocence. I haven't done anything I'm ashamed of."

Jael decided to pull a little bit of authority control and get right to the point. "Mr. Foster, did you put a hit out on your son?" Neither Foster nor Watson seemed surprised by the question, only that she knew. "Well?"

"Well what?" Foster said, moving away from the door and rubbing his hands on the side of his pants. Jael and Grant stepped completely into the cozy living room as Harold loudly closed the door behind them. "That was just a farce, a way to get a message into my son's thick skull." He turned back toward them. "Thought that would scare him enough to stay away from my home, give me and my wife a little peace. All that poison out there is killing our young boys. And sometimes it doesn't matter how much you do for them or how hard you try to give them the best of everything, they still fall under the spell of that white stuff. I tell you, that powder, or rocks, or crack or whatever the heck they call that stuff, came straight from hell. It's the devil's own black male exterminator. A young black man doesn't have a chance against that evil."

An image of Ramon leaped into Jael's mind, and she silently pleaded the Blood of Jesus over her son for protection for the umpteenth time.

"Mr. Foster, do you have any knowledge about these recent murders, or who might be involved in any way?" she asked.

"I . . . No." He looked away.

"Mr. Foster, lives are at stake! If you know anything, you have to tell us."

"I believe I talk straight English. I said no."

"Mr. Foster, what about your son?" Grant asked. "If the hit was a farce, as you say, who did you contact to play it out and why are you protecting them?"

Jael turned to Grant, surprised and baffled by the question.

"I'm not protecting anyone but my family, so please leave my son out of this. And if you look for him, you'll find he's no longer around—out of town from what I last heard. Now get out of my house, unless you intend to arrest me."

"Dan, what the heck are you talking about?" Harold stepped forward, his hands held out and his palms up in bewilderment. "What's going on?"

"All of you, out of my house now!"

Harold helplessly looked back and forth between her and Grant. "Well, what about the note he left?"

In reply, Jael pulled a card from her handbag. "Mr. Foster, please call me if you want to talk, about anything, and I promise to give you complete anonymity. And whatever you're afraid of, you'll have the police department's protection."

"Please just leave, all of you." Daniel marched to the front door and held it open.

With a nod, Grant moved toward the door and waited for her. Jael took a deep breath, then placed her card on the cocktail table and followed him.

Harold stood huffing, but had yet to move toward the open door. "I refuse to allow this madman to . . ."

Jael didn't hear the end of his statement as Grant gently took her arm and led her back to the squad car.

"What was that all about?" she asked before his door was even shut.

"I strongly believe you're barking up the wrong tree."

"Wait a minute. How can you come here and say—"

"There are several things here that are similar to what I've been working on in Cleveland. From my research and background knowledge, you're playing a completely different ball game than what you know. With that in mind, Daniel Foster's involvement is purely coincidental."

Jael glanced out the window as she drove the squad car steadily down the quiet street out of Foster's neighborhood and into a less cared for area.

"You've been hinting since I met you that these are not simply vigilante murders. Spill it now, because I'm getting tired of this word game."

"That's fair. As lead detective you should know that you're looking for—"

"There's our man now," Jael abruptly interrupted, pointing out the window and excited that the search for her first witness was just hanging around as if waiting for her.

Leaning against a colorful newspaper stand in front of a small, aged storefront shopping center was Kenneth Peoples, the derelict they'd found at the back of the crack house. His attention seemed totally consumed by a sticky pastry he was stuffing into his mouth.

"We'd better park here before he recognizes the car. He can be very slippery," Jael volunteered as she parked at the corner in front of an old gas station whose pumps had long ago been removed. Before she could turn off the engine, Grant had swiftly doffed his jacket, tossed it on the backseat and jumped from the car. Jael had a moment to admire his sculptured body and quickly asked for forgiveness for the thought that followed. *This is not going to work,* she admitted to herself. She had a serious case on her hands, and Lord, she couldn't afford to be battling with sudden demons of desire at the same time. Then another thought followed: Wasn't this exactly how things worked, the adversary fighting against you from all sides, looking for your vulnerable spots?

As she pulled herself from the squad car, her Rock lookalike was already approaching her witness.

Chapter 17

Jael approached the two men quickly. Her sight landed on Peoples, who was dressed much the same, if not exactly, as he'd been the day of the killing at the crack house, in loose-fitting jeans and a dirty flowered T-shirt. As she closed the distance between them, the sour smell emitting from his unwashed body began to hit her.

Grant had moved up on the bum so fast that Peoples wasn't even aware of his presence until Grant was almost in his face. The derelict looked up startled, but regained his composure by brushing off the crumbs on his stained T-shirt and spreading his lips into a careless grin.

The grin faded just as fast when Grant flashed his badge and got right to the point.

"Eric Grant, FBI. What are your connections to these recent murders?"

Befuddled, Peoples stood up a little straighter. "What?" Grant now had his full attention.

"I don't have time to fool around, Peoples. Who was this other guy you saw at the crack house?"

"I . . . well . . ." Peoples looked back and forth between her and Grant, then around him as if seeking help from some unknown source. "Uh . . . well, uh . . . just some crackhead."

"You've seen him before?"

"Well, not really." The grin was back. "He ain't usually the kind to be seen around places like that." Peoples giggled into his hand, but not before Jael caught a glimpse of stained teeth with food crumbs between them.

"Where'd you get that newsletter sticking out the back of your pocket?" Grant demanded.

"What newsletter? I don't waste money on no newspapers."

Grant reached behind the man and snatched the paper rolled-up from his back pocket. Jael caught the name, *Aryan Report* as Grant unrolled the small newsletter.

"Who gave you this paper?"

"I just found it somewhere, can't remember."

"I think you know how this paper is connected to the recent homicides. It would be to your advantage to tell me what you know."

"Hey, mister, you got the wrong guy. So leave me alone."

"Let me put it this way: One little point in the right direction from you and nobody knows, but if you want to continue with this line of 'I don't know nothing' then we'll have to drop a few hints around that whatever we come up with came from you."

"You can't do that!" If it were possible, his smell seemed to have gotten worse. His face had certainly changed, from a nonchalant expression to one of total distress.

"Who shot TeeTee and Zap Man?"

Jael was shocked. Where did that question come from?
"I ain't talkin' and you can't make me!"

Grant suddenly backed off. He glanced at Jael, then back at Peoples.

"Okay. Just point me to whoever gave you the newsletter or you go downtown for aiding and abetting a murder suspect."

"Hey! You must be crazy! You don't know what you're asking. Are you nuts?" He began backing up.

Grant didn't give up an inch. "No, but you certainly are if you don't start telling me what I want to know."

Jael was about to interrupt when movement to her distant right drew her attention away. Turning her head toward the store entrance, she saw a slim white male with long blond hair exiting the building. His eyes were cast downward, glued to a paper similar in size to the one Grant had just taken from Peoples.

Grant must have threatened Peoples physically in some way, because the derelict suddenly yelped like a wounded puppy, and the sound caused the man at the store entrance to look up in their direction. His eyes locked with Jael's, and she experienced a frozen moment of recognition. Immediately the man broke their gaze as he spun on his heels and took off in a speedy sprint. Jael was in instant pursuit, drawing her weapon and holding it closely in front of her with both hands.

"Halt, police!"

The man ducked to his left at the side of the building and vanished from view. Only a few yards behind, Jael quickly covered the distance to the corner. She threw herself against the rough cement wall, holding her gun before her as she peeked around the building. It was a narrow alley, with little or no light from overhead. She could barely make out the shadow dashing down the distance.

"Stop! This is the police!" Jael shouted into the alley.

Her words had no effect as the man ran the short length of the alleyway, which abruptly came to a dead end at a tall chained fence. Her runner was trapped. Easing herself around the wall in case the man had a weapon on him, Jael dropped to a crouch. "Put both hands in the air."

Realizing he had nowhere to escape, the man slowly turned while raising his hands skyward, giving Jael a better view of his face. Full recognition hit her. He was the man she'd seen that day at the crack house standing amid the crowd of observers. What were the odds of both men having been at the crime scene and now at the same desolate area of town?

Cautiously rising from her crouched position, Jael never dropped the point of her gun from its direct aim at the man's chest.

"Keep both hands high and don't even breathe." She was holding her own breath, aware she could quite possibly be looking into the eyes of a killer.

The man slowly raised his hands higher as terror redesigned his features; she felt waves of it hit her from twenty feet away. She didn't turn when she heard a commotion behind her, and was not surprised to see Grant move past her line of vision and rush up to the man. Jael lowered her weapon only when Grant began to handcuff the man and read him his *Miranda* rights.

"I'm not the guy," he softly mumbled, offering no resistance. His clean-cut look, crisply pressed striped shirt and dark pants gave him the appearance of an average Joe.

"Yeah, yeah, they all say that. So why did you run?" Grant asked.

"I swear, I'm not the one you're looking for."

"You can explain why not down at the station," Jael said as she reholstered her 9mm.

"No, please believe me. If I were the one you were looking for, would I slip you a note telling you there would be more executions?"

"Executions?" Grant said.

"That's what they are."

Jael took a step back. "You're the one who gave me the note at Brenda's house?"

"What are you guys talking about?" Grant asked, pushing the man ahead of him toward the front of the alley.

"Wait a minute." Jael stopped the movement by placing a hand at the center of the guy's chest. She looked into a face marred with acne scars, and watery blue eyes that told her he was telling the truth. "You're trying to help?"

He nodded. "Yes, but I can't get involved."

"Mister, you're involved up to your teeth," Grant snarled.

"Please believe me, if I'm seen talking to you guys, it's over for me."

Jael stepped farther back. "Then how would you suggest we handle this?"

The man thought for a moment, his eyes roaming frantically back and forth between his two captors. He gritted his teeth and with a sigh of resignation said, "Follow me to my house, but don't let anyone see you."

"Wait a minute . . ." Jael began.

"Especially Peoples—he'll say anything for drug money. Let me leave, and let him see you let me go. Then follow me home."

"You must be crazy."

"Listen, my address is in my wallet. I don't live far from here, just a couple of blocks away. I have no car, so it'll be easy to keep up with me." His voice was laced with desperation, and something else. Fear? It seemed there was a lot of that going around. What was everybody so afraid of? Who was this unknown assailant to cause such a reaction in people?

"Just follow me after you're sure Peoples isn't watching. At the end of this corner, pull up into the next alley. My house is the third one with a fence around it. I'll be waiting, and I'll let you in the back door. Then I'll tell you what I know and what I suspect."

Jael looked over at Grant, not sure what to do.

"It's your call," he said.

"Okay, walk casually back up the alley. If one muscle looks like it's attempting to take off, I'm shooting." Jael withdrew her weapon once more for emphasis.

The man nodded. Grant looked at her again and then unhandcuffed the man. Jael held her breath, waiting for him to dash for it.

"Let me see your ID," Grant demanded.

The man reached into his back pants pocket and pulled out his wallet, then handed Grant the Florida driver's license. Grant compared the picture with the man in front of him, then handed the card to Jael. She also compared the photo with the man, then memorized the information. William David Jasper; birth date 7/21/72.

"Come quickly," Jasper pleaded. "I'm not sure how much time we have before someone else is struck down."

Though the statement was alarming, it held an undeniable sense of certainty.

"You can count on it," Jael said, her own voice filled with conviction.

The man moved awkwardly toward the main street, then lifted his shoulders and moved out into the open shopping center, the sun glinting off his blond hair. Jael gave him five seconds, then she and Grant followed.

At the end of the alley, they turned in the opposite direction and headed back to the squad car. She felt stupid letting the man walk away like that but couldn't think of anything else to do. Was she making a grave mistake?

Peoples was nowhere in sight, as she expected, but might be hiding somewhere, watching their every move. She was a ball of nerves and could barely keep from running to her car and burning rubber in pursuit of Mr. Blondie, aka William Jasper. As if reading her mind, Grant did a slight spin on his heels to make it appear as if he were walking backward in order to speak directly to her, while he in fact looked over her shoulder. "He hasn't taken off yet. He may be on the up-and-up."

"It'll be my butt if he's not."

"I held Peoples for as long as I could, but I was worried about you. You were right—the guy can be very slippery."

"I just hope he hung around long enough to see our boy leave on his own."

When she reached the car, she nearly dived in to get a look in the direction William Jasper had taken. He was just turning the corner, but he could take off at any second and lose her. Though she was good, she'd never stepped into a car, sat in her seat, started the engine and pulled off all in the same motion. She did this time, and Grant almost lost a foot in the process.

Chapter 18

So what do you think?" Grant asked as she pulled away from the curb.

"I think I'm taking a foolish risk here, but I need whatever I can get. All my earlier leads are raveling away like loose threads."

"You got a feel about this guy?"

"I'm not sure—only that he's scared. But there seems to be a lot of that going around lately." She kept her eyes focused on the road ahead. "When we get to his house—if he's even there—you start the questioning. That will give me some time to look around and get a better feel of what he's all about."

This was a process she and Sills often used, one that offered a chance to let one of the officers scrutinize a suspect's mannerisms and unobserved habits. Although she'd only known Grant a few hours, right now she felt comfortable enough with him to let him play the role. She could always take over if she needed to.

"What do you think happened to Peoples?" she added.

"It was a lucky break for that guy. I was just about to handcuff him when I heard you shout. I had two choices—waste precious moments handcuffing my man or come see about you."

Jael looked over at him and flushed.

"Not standard procedure by a long shot, but I felt Peoples was much less of a danger than the guy you were pursuing. We can always pick up Peoples later."

"Yeah. We'll find him in one of his favorite holes. He's not going far."

Jael restrained the urge to ram the accelerator to the floor, and drove as slowly as possible to give the impression they were simply cruising around the area. Passing the first corner, she stayed on the trail, traveling to the end of the block. Grant didn't question the action, but followed her gaze down the street as their man strolled along as if he were in no hurry.

Together they watched him stop at a house with a huge oak tree and a green metal awning over the front porch. A brown and black mutt of undeterminable lineage was tied to the tree. The animal rose to its feet, wagging it tail when Jasper reached down and patted him. Then the man moved on to the next house, where he waved at someone sitting on the porch. Jael was too far away to get a good view of the person.

Jasper resumed his stroll in an unhurried walk, and Jael suspected he was emotionally wired, like an escapee on the lam. If he knew they were at the corner watching him, he didn't let on. When he reached a house with a bleached-wood privacy fence, he stopped to check his mailbox, shook his head as if disappointed, then casually walked up the front steps. Jasper fumbled in his pants pocket for a moment, obviously searching for his key. Finding it, he unlocked the door and stepped inside.

Jael did a quick U-turn, headed to the alley they'd been told to enter and drove slowly down the back toward the house.

"So far, so good. He's playing his role like Bruce Willis," she said.

"He must be afraid his house is being watched."

"Or he's pulling our leg."

"For now you can only play it the way he suggests." Grant took in his surroundings to make sure no one was lurking in the bushes or coming out a back door to meet them. The guy could be calling for his own kind of backup right now and his buddies might creep up on the two of them unnoticed. Grant kept his hand on the 9mm Glock at his waist, his senses alert.

When they reached the third house with a fence, Jael drove through the open gate up onto the weedy area a few yards from the back porch. Jasper was standing in the doorway looking anxiously around behind them as she and Grant climbed from the car and moved up his back steps. He waved them in hurriedly, then shut the door and locked it.

"I hope no one was watching you guys hanging around at the corner. I asked you to come straight back to the alley."

"Just making sure you entered the same house you told us to meet you at in back," Jael said, moving past him into the old-fashioned but relatively clean kitchen.

"Let's go to the front so I can keep a watch out in case my old man returns."

They followed him into a cluttered living room where the air was stuffy and stale.

Jael moved away to begin her personal observation of the house. Grant suggested Jasper have a seat on the couch and began questioning him.

"So who's behind these murders?"

"Not the MAD DADS—though unknowingly, they played an important role. I was hoping not to have to go this far, hoping by leaving a note of warning at that Mr. Foster's house, he'd come forward with what he knew. I guess it didn't work."

"I guess not, since you put the warning at Watson's home instead. How are they playing an unknowing role?"

Jasper didn't answer immediately. "Have you ever heard of the Aryan Knights?"

"What about them?"

Jael picked up a hint of excitement in Grant's voice and glanced over at the two men. Grant had taken a seat in an overstuffed chair at the left of the couch and coffee table. Jasper sat on the couch, rubbing his hands across the top of his pants legs.

"There's a branch here in Dadesville."

"Are you a member?"

Jasper reached for a crumbled pack of cigarettes on the top of the coffee table and shook one out. "I went to a few meetings, but it was really too much for me." Digging inside his front pants pocket for a pack of matches, his hand visibly shook as he tried several times to strike a light. "My old man is an active member. I picked up a little about what's going on from his phone conversations."

"And what's going on?"

Still listening, Jael casually moved toward an old scarred wooden desk with a pegboard on the wall directly above it. Attached to the board was a huge rebel flag, newsletters and clippings of the recent murders.

She approached the cluttered desk and picked up a flier lying on the printer tray of a fax machine. Her stomach muscles instantly clinched. It was an old grainy photo of a black male hanging from a tree. Underneath the picture were the words: THEY KNEW HOW TO DO IT IN THE GOOD OLE DAYS.

She dropped the paper as if it had burned her. Heat rushed to her ears and fingers of flame flashed in her eyes as she tossed a cold glare at Jasper. Absorbed as they were in conversation, both men missed the heated look. Controlling herself against her rising anger, Jael moved over to a home-made bookcase standing at the left side of the wall. Silently she prayed as she read the book spines. *The Militias. Adolf Hitler and the Third Reich. The American Nazi Party. Mein Kampf. The Clansman.*

In her many years of duty she'd come across more racism and bigotry than she could stomach, but this was the first time she'd ever been inside the home of someone who advocated pure hate.

She scanned other shelves cluttered with Nazi paraphernalia, a photo of Timothy McVeigh and more revolting messages of violence against Jews, homosexuals and blacks. There were even stacks of clippings from the bombing of the Trade Towers, which made no sense. Wouldn't a terrorist assault be a direct attack on the very symbol of American power? Or was this group simply looking for new ideas? Another flier caught her eye, with the words

"Red Dog" written on it. The name sent a funny chill down her spine.

The atmosphere around her grew heavy with a malignant rot, weighing her down with its vile worship of hate. Disgusted, Jael turned away from the wall and its abominable declarations and moved toward the men. She'd heard everything the two had said about the group's next meeting and jumped in with her own questions, trying to hold back her contempt.

"And where *is* this *meeting* place?" she hissed. Then, pointing to the shaking hand holding the cigarette to his lips, she added, "Those things will kill you."

Jasper glanced at the cigarette. His eyes filled with a deep sadness. "There are worse ways to go," he said, almost to himself.

Jael felt a wave of remorse pour from him. He was caught up in something he obviously did not believe in, but he also knew that if he said too much it could all fall back on him.

"You know where Hanley Road is? Fifteen miles outside of Dadesville?" he asked.

"Yeah."

"If you take Hanley to Wheeler Road, you follow Wheeler about a mile east and watch for a dirt road that veers off to the left. Back about another mile, you'll find an old weathered whitewashed barn. I believe you'll find all your answers there."

"How do I know you're telling the truth about the barn?" Jael demanded, ignoring his remorseful attitude.

Jasper stood up and moved to the bookcase Jael had just left. He pulled out one of the books, flipped open its pages and took out a folded sheet of paper. He handed it to her. It was a hand-drawn map, with the same directions he had just given them. Above it was a large rebel battle flag and the words WHITE POWER.

Grant stood. "Okay, Jael, let's go."

She turned to him. "Let's go?" Then back to Jasper. "Why can't you just tell us what's going on?"

"He's done more than is safe for him to do. Let's go. We've got what we need from here." Grant placed his hand on her elbow and gently directed her toward the kitchen.

"Just wait a minute," Jael said, wrenching her arm free of Grant and turning to glare at him. "He hands us a map that could be anything and you tell me he's done more than he's supposed to do?" Once again she turned to Jasper. "Look, if you need protection, we can provide—"

"Let's go, Jael, trust me," Grant interrupted. "Jasper, here's your driver's license. Stay put and stay out of sight. Don't talk to anyone you don't have to." Then Grant moved toward Jael and, with more force this time, took her arm and led her through the kitchen.

Jael was not ready to relent so easily. "Hold on, we need his license. I still need to run a check—"

"I have it all in here," Grant said, tapping his temple. "And if we don't get away from here, we could be jeopardizing this young man's life."

Jael looked over her shoulder at the man standing there watching them with his hands hanging at his sides. His eyes bore a deep sorrow and regret.

Chapter 19

Since Jael was unable to locate the Captain to clear this latest trip, Grant immediately made another call to his headquarters for further instructions. Once the call was made, he slid behind the wheel as Jael gave the directions to Wheeler Road.

En route, she silently listened as he told an almost unbelievable story.

"Have you ever heard of a book called *The Turner Diaries?*"

"I saw a copy on Jasper's bookshelf, among several other horrifying titles. He has an ugly list of reading material."

"Well, *The Turner Diaries* is the best-seller of ugly material. Today you can easily get a copy on the Net for little or nothing. Unless you have a strong stomach, I'd advise you to let someone give you the condensed version."

"Over the years, I've had to stomach my share of racial pamphlets and other material."

"Unfortunately, that book is the catalyst behind the killings in your town."

Jael looked at Grant, astonished, then glanced out the

window and sighed. "Why do I suddenly have an overpowering feeling of dread?"

"Because you know within yourself you're about to look into the face of pure evil. Hatred at its highest level."

Jael turned back to look at her new partner. "You mean you've believed all along that white supremacy groups are behind the killings?"

"It was only recently that Ben Smith was charged with bombing Jewish synagogues and abortion clinics and that Richard Butler, head of the National Aryan Nations, proclaimed another follower of his as a true American hero for attacks on biracial couples.

"Like I've said, we've been waiting for something to happen in our Southern states for the past three years. Information we picked up on a white supremacist Web site suggested that a pattern of violence could erupt anywhere, but they were too smart to actually announce when and where. Through wiretapping and inside informants, we knew it wouldn't be long before they struck. Black dealers and addicts were at the top of their list.

"I came onto the task force about this time," he continued. "My first case was a low-life vigilante who attempted a shooting in Durham. We were able to squash that one before more than two people died. After September eleven, everything else kind of took a backseat. Unfortunately, these people used this to accelerate their own twisted plans. Because of my profiling expertise, I was sent here to confirm whether these murders where related to such organizations. Once we reach this barn, I'll know a lot more. Turn here?"

"Oh, yeah, yeah." Jael's mind was running a mile a minute.

She was no innocent, and well schooled in hate crime cases, but to actually confront murders being committed in her town by white supremacists was more than she would have ever imagined.

She suddenly remembered the incident involving James Byrd, the black man dragged to death down a Texas road by three young white supremacists. She whispered, "My Lord."

Grant cast her a side glance, nodding his head in agreement. "That's the sad part, because in many ways they're similar to the Taliban. They both believe God is on their side and needs them to purify the land. However, the Taliban are much more extreme, in believing their suicide bombings will be rewarded in heaven.

"In our states, one of the more powerful white supremacist Web sites is called the Christian Identity Group. The hate they spew is sickening. The enormous number of young people following these groups is overwhelming and scary. And they're getting smarter all the time, to the point that many no longer expose themselves as skinheads. They look like your average boy or girl next door. They're encouraged not to work in gangs and bring attention to themselves but to operate as lone hit men of sorts. These individuals are called Lone Wolves, and they're held in high esteem by these groups and considered American heroes."

"Why aren't more people aware of all this?"

"Haven't you heard? The devil's best weapon is to make people think he doesn't exist. He works better that way, and if he can get people to think they're serving the cause of the Almighty, even better."

"How can anyone today believe killing is the will of God?" Jael twisted her lips. "Scratch that—Osama bin

Laden wipes that theory right out." She waved her hand in a gesture of discouragement.

"You're catching on. Madmen will always be behind such actions. As for our guys, they still use the Bible to justify their actions. They believe Jesus cannot return until the earth is cleared of all its vermin. Their list is long."

"Satan is the father of lies." The disgust was apparent in the tone of her voice. "What is this, something like forty years after Dr. Martin Luther King and the civil rights movement and we're still in the dark ages when it comes to racial tolerance? These men in positions of power, like former majority leader Trent Lott, remind us every now and then how real and deep these beliefs go. So many of the cases you hear on the news today seem like isolated incidents. You'd never think it's a well-oiled machine, working in the background."

"That's the way they like it. They're not burning fiery crosses on front lawns anymore, but they're still a very strong secret society. This very minute, they're preparing all over the country for a racial war, which to them is the *real* Holy War. They start teaching their children to hate very early, many before they can even read and write. We have videos of kids barely in their preteens learning how to use guns and practicing military maneuvers at the militia camp sites."

"Why don't you simply break up these sites when you locate them?"

"We do, but these guys are smart, and though they profess to hate government control, they hide behind the Constitution, which allows them to assemble. Don't forget the Waco fiasco."

"That was a religious organization, not a KKK facility."

"The same laws apply. We have to be careful and accurate about what we attempt to prove. These people often use the very laws they despise against us in court, but we're working to correct that. For instance, in Ohio they now provide enhanced sentencing to those convicted of 'ethnic intimidation.' But first, concrete proof has to be established to show the assault was committed for reason of racial bias."

"You know, this sounds like that old saying, 'Not in my neighborhood.' I'm not naïve, but I feel like I've been hit with a Mac truck or something."

"Completely understandable. We all . . . well, most of us anyway, want to believe everyone is good by nature. But that's certainly not the case, never has been, and until people accept the fact that the barrel has a lot of rotten apples in it, they will continue to hide their heads in the sand and hope for the best. Even 9/11 hasn't changed that."

They both fell silent as a few miles ahead, the shape of the old weathered barn began to rise over the horizon. The magnitude of the world they were about to enter pulled her stomach into a tight knot of despair. Jael could not help but think of how ironic life could be. With all the beauty and grace found in living in harmony as God intended, there were still people whose beliefs told them hatred and destruction were the true keys to eternal life.

"Do you think this could be a setup? I mean two black folks headed out to a barn, in the middle of nowhere. Should I call for backup?"

"We'll know in a few minutes."

"Where're your dark shades?" she asked, attempting to lighten the mood. Grim-faced, Grant pulled them from his vest pocket and slipped them over his eyes. The stern pull at the corner of his lips indicated that his easygoing manner of a few hours ago had disappeared with the upcoming chase. His change in demeanor made Jael feel even more uncomfortable than she already did.

Chapter
20

The dirt road was bumpy and uneven, forcing Jael to hold on to the car door handle to keep from bouncing around in her seat. Overhead the sky was a magnificent aquamarine, filled with layers of pregnant white clouds. A typical Florida sky. The landscape around them was serene and unthreatening, the sound of traffic having long ago faded away. Ahead, at the end of the road, the huge whitewashed barn, leaning slightly to the left, seemed out of place and ominous. Another wave of apprehension washed over her. She prayed.

A lone white pickup with a huge rebel flag in the rear window was parked just at the front of the metal double doors. So far, there was no evidence of any hidden group of men waiting in ambush. Grant quickly parked and jumped out, walking straight to the truck. His tall frame moved with authority. Jael followed. At the truck, he placed an open palm on the hood and slowly stepped away from it while reaching under the back of his jacket for a holstered Glock. He nodded at Jael to move to the opposite side of the barn door. This time, she had no trouble following his lead. She had the distinct feeling that Grant had a much better idea of what they were about to face than she did.

With that thought in mind, Jael withdrew her own weapon and stood just on the other side of the door, which was partly ajar. Grant held his gun in the standard precautionary upright pose and stealthily moved forward into the opening. Jael followed close behind.

Once inside, the only light filtering into the vast open area came from the six partially opened windows about twelve feet above the floor on either side. Jael glanced around her as the shafts of light descended on row after row of tables and chairs, boxes and haphazard decor. She took in a deep breath and realized that if hate had a smell, it was here in this cold, moldy, metal and wood building.

From wall to wall, rebel flags hung from poles evenly placed near the ceiling. Against the back wall was a huge Nazi swastika, with framed photos of white men on either side of it. Jael couldn't help but view the Nazi symbol as a warped version of the Cross. Beside it was a blowup of the collapsing Twin Towers, with the words "WHY SURPRISED???" underneath.

Various news clippings of the recent Dadesville killings had been enlarged and lay on a table near the front. Jael's stomach turned as she read some of the vile curse words written across them in heavy black markers. Here again, the name "Red Dog" blazed across the bottom of one of the posters.

At least fifty metal chairs lined the dirt-covered floor. The tables encircling the entire seating area were packed with an arsenal of weapons of death. Under closer inspection Jael identified several varieties of high-point semiautomatics, sawed-off rifles, double-barrel shotguns, grenades, knuckle knives and numerous cases of explosives. The Dadesville Police Department weapons room would have had a hard time competing with this supply.

Tightening the grip on her gun, Jael moved along the left side of the barn, taking in horror after horror. Though steel ceiling fans whirled overhead, Jael felt trickles of sweat slide down the inside of her clothing.

As she slowly made her way down the left side of the building, Jael glanced over at Grant, who had stopped to call in for backup while checking something on one of the tables. It looked like he was picking up one of the hand grenades when her peripheral vision caught a glint of metal milliseconds before her body exploded in shattering pain and she dropped to the ground.

As she hit the dirt floor, pain raced from the base of her head down her neck in fiery waves. For several seconds she fought to catch her breath as her clouded vision gradually cleared. Operating purely on instinct, Jael pulled the trigger on her gun to warn Grant. The roar of the dispelled bullet echoed in her head as she rolled toward the wall and managed to half-sit in time to see Grant's swift response as he raised his weapon in her direction and also fired. Wood splintered inches from her as she turned and caught sight of her attacker.

She expected horns and a tail, but saw only a man dressed in a red shirt and blue jeans. Shielding himself from Grant's view behind a massive beam, the man reached out to the nearest table and grabbed a twelve-gauge semiautomatic shotgun with buckshot that could take a man's face off. Jael heard the slide on the shotgun before he raised it and took aim at Grant.

The explosion of the gun reverberated around the walls, and while he was still ejecting the spent shell, Jael saw the man swing his arm and point the gun in her direction. She pushed herself farther toward the wall, but she couldn't get a clear shot.

Not so for her attacker. He fired twice.

Jael's body slammed against the wall as her mind crashed in on itself from the immediate and excruciating pain. Seconds from impending death, she cried out one word: *JESUS!*

Chapter
21

Without waiting to survey his damage, her assailant did a zigzag dash for the archway, tossing metal chairs behind him as Grant sprinted with feral speed after him. Through a graying haze of agony, Jael heard Grant shout her name. If she could hear him, she was still alive, she thought, and that meant she still had work to do. She felt a warm wetness slide down her arm and a fire of pain centered just at her shoulder. Jael forced her mind to focus—Grant needed her help.

"Grant, stop him," she whispered, thinking she had shouted the words, and looked up just in time to see Grant fly out the entrance and tackle the man. The villain emitted a loud *"whoof"* as the air was knocked out of him and he struck the earth face-first.

Jael pulled herself up from her slumped position, bracing her mind against the pain screaming through her arm with each move. Spitting dirt from her mouth, she pressed herself against the wall, using it as a brace to push herself to her feet. Waves of dizziness threatened to force her back to the ground, but Jael gritted her teeth. A quick scrutiny of her injury verified that the bullet had caused only a deep flesh wound.

"Thank you, Jesus, for your protection and saving me from death. Now bless me with the strength to do my job." Holding her left arm close to her body, Jael pushed herself away from the wall and stumbled toward the barn entrance.

Holding her gun in her right hand, she made it to the open doorway to see the two men struggling on the ground. Jael raised her weapon and aimed it toward them in case she suddenly needed to fire. But Grant was no slouch in hand-to-hand combat and was on top of the guy, walloping him with several tightfisted blows around the head and chest.

Grant swung a final fist, hitting the man with a right hook on the temple. As he rose over the slumped figure on the ground, Grant pulled a small-caliber snubby from his waistband. To Jael, it looked like a European handgun. Her admiration rose several notches.

"Get up!" Grant's bark was cold and strained with control.

Rubbing his head, the man lifted slightly, then dropped his weight on his right elbow. "You motha—"

"Shut your face and get on your feet," Grant said softly, his tone deadly.

The man uttered another oath, but this time he pulled himself to his feet while dropping the gun from his meaty palm. Grant met the other man's gaze evenly, keeping his aim at the man's heart as he rose from the ground.

Their captive's round, white face was livid with rage. Jael noticed the veins popping out on his forehead, his pupils round points of focused hatred. His lips were drawn in a tight expression, nothing remotely human evident in all that animal ferocity.

Now that Grant had control of the situation, Jael allowed herself to fall back against the wall of the barn. Her arm was throbbing as if someone were playing a tune with daggers in her flesh. Her heart was hammering away in a like beat, but otherwise her strength was slowly coming back. Looking over at the men, she thought that they might finally have their murderer. Dressed as he was in loose-fitting jeans, a blazing red V-neck shirt and tattoos on every exposed portion of his thick arms, he was the epitome of a demon from hell. How had he snuck up on streetwise dealers? Or did the dealers simply think a sale was a sale—even to an out-of-place white man? Ballistics would confirm her suspicions—plus the bullet that had grazed her arm.

A surge of righteous victory flushed through her. Of course, others were certainly involved, but for now, one was better than none.

Well, at least for you, Mr. Tattoo, your days of raving madness and murder are over, she thought as she closed her eyes, sucked in her breath and stood up straight. Watching the man literally growl at them as Grant slapped steel handcuffs on him, she knew she'd do everything within her power to make sure this man was buried *under* the jail. She suspected his lawyers would go first for an insanity plea and if that didn't work, then try for a life sentence, since the death penalty was alive and well in the state of Florida.

Grant turned to her, and turned ashen when he noticed the blood on her clothing. He was at her side before she could utter a word.

"Dear Jesus, you've been shot!"

"It's a flesh wound; I'm okay. Hey, we've got our man."

"Well, we've got somebody. Let's get you in the car while I call in."

Grant put his arms around her to assist her, and she smiled at him. She didn't want assistance, but liked the idea of this man's arms around her.

Once she was seated in the passenger side of the car, Grant grabbed the man and shoved him toward the vehicle, the sun's glare glinting off their suspect's nearly bald head. The foul words pouring from his mouth made it difficult for Jael not to reach for her nightstick inside the car and smash him over the head.

"You're digging yourself a deeper hole with every word you say," Grant told him right after reading the *Miranda* rights.

"You niggers have no idea who you're messing with! You're just monkeys in uniform, and this is *way* from over." He laughed a madman's laugh, and Jael felt the evilness of it crawl over her skin. She suddenly didn't want to be confined in the same vehicle with this fiend.

As Grant roughly tossed him into the backseat, the man continued with his vile threats, shoving his head out the car door at Grant with an ugly grin on his face.

"Enjoy yourselves now, coons, because this will be the last time you get to play hotshots. We're everywhere, you know. And when you mess with a Lone Wolf, you mess with the entire Klan!"

Jael tried to ignore him, but his next words brought out the mean side in her.

"All your little nigger girls and boys will soon know that white power is supreme!"

Before she could stop herself, Jael reached over her seat and landed a karate chop at the nape of his neck with her good arm. The man slumped backward and dropped his head on the backseat. Instantly Jael was appalled by her actions. Nothing had ever made her strike out so.

"I was just about to take that pleasure myself," Grant said as he slammed the door shut.

"A little something I picked up from one of Ramon's karate classes," she said sheepishly, with a shrug of her good shoulder as she fell backward against the cushion of the front seat. She was still fuming at the man's words, and at herself for responding to them with such violence.

Grant gave her a look Jael couldn't decipher, but there was nothing "brotherly" about it. Her heart went racing again, and this time over something much better than chasing down a thug. The distant sound of approaching sirens broke the moment.

"After the boys take over here, you and I are going to the hospital to get that wound cleaned up. *Capisce?*"

"Yes sa, boss."

"Okay, glad we've got that straight. And later, how about dinner after we book this villain?"

Jael looked up at Grant as he stood over her in the car's doorway. He looked a bit flushed, but his eyes were bright from the exertion—which only made him look finer, if that were possible.

"My son will be waiting for me after work. I have to get home." Then, as an afterthought, and forgetting all about her wound, she added, "How about you come to my house and I cook us a nice meal."

"It depends on what the doctors say."

Just out of sight over the crest of the field behind the barn, the engine of a lone black vehicle started up and pulled off in the opposite direction, dust following in its wake. The real war had just begun.

Chapter 22

A wounded officer at St. Joseph's Hospital garnished swift and immediate attention. She'd been in and out of the emergency room in less than an hour, allowing her plenty of time to keep things under control back at the station.

By 4:30 P.M. the ecstatic buzz at the station had finally subsided into a reasonably calm hum. However, for hours after Jael and Grant had returned from the hospital to book their suspect for the alleged murders of three people, she couldn't hear a coherent word through all the loud speculating comments.

"It just seems so unreal," Tammy kept saying to anyone within earshot. "I mean, you know they're out there, but white supremacists on a murder spree right here in Dadesville?"

"When they call themselves a 'secret society,' they sure mean it," another added.

The local press was all over the building, and everyone knew it wouldn't be long before media vultures from around the country poured into town to cover the story. For this to have happened in a small town like Dadesville, it was bigger than the Waco fiasco and nearly as shocking as the Oklahoma bombing or the attack on the Twin Towers.

Only Gwen Hayes from the *Florida Sentinel* was given the chance to talk exclusively to Jael and Grant, and even she was provided only limited bits of information. No one was allowed to speak with the alleged murderer, now identified as Whitman James Upton, thirty-two, married with two kids and employed at the Budget Air-Conditioning Company.

Jael knew she needed to be as careful as possible about how they proceeded from here. It seemed Upton wasn't as big a fool as he looked. Though he freely spewed foul words of hatred and white power, he never actually admitted to having any knowledge of the murders. He simply expressed his joy at having some of the scum of the earth removed, a feeling, Jael figured, many other people would probably experience as well, but wouldn't admit to.

Grant spent a little over forty-five minutes in confined quarters, questioning Upton right after booking him. Jael spent the time going over the entire incident with Captain Slater, who eventually went out to the barn himself before giving the press a full accounting.

By now the entire police force was crawling all over the barn, confiscating weapons and collecting any evidence that could be used to seal the case against Upton.

On her way back to the squad room, Jael saw a figure cautiously stepping out of the Captain's office. She was about to call out to him, then realized it was not the Captain but Billups. What was he doing coming out of the Captain's office when the Captain was out at the barn? And why was he rushing away in such a hurry, his head ducked low between his shoulders?

Putting the man out of her mind, she continued on with her own tasks.

After much paperwork and numerous slaps on the back for her bravery—gently, of course, in consideration of her wounded arm—Jael looked up to see Grant standing over her.

"Ready to leave? It's been a long day, and I can't say I remember seeing you eat or drink anything since we met." His smile was warm and caring.

"I was ready four hours ago," Jael answered, closing the open file on her desk and pushing it aside. Shoving back in her chair, she returned Grant's hardy smile before rising. "Let's hit it."

"Why don't we stop and pick something up. I know you have to be too tired to cook after all this. And your bad shoulder may not be up to it."

Jael warmed even more to Grant, witnessing his consideration. During all the excitement, her little dabs of admiration had remained where they belonged—under control. "My shoulder's okay, but I'll admit I'm a little work-weary. My son would love it if I swung by the Golden Arches and picked up some Micky D's, but I feel like I haven't eaten a real meal in days."

"So what do you have a taste for? Chinese?"

"Heck, that goes right through you. I need something that'll stick to the ribs."

"Italian?"

"How about I call this place I know and they'll have it

ready by the time we get there. They make great hot wings and fries. They also have Philly cheese steaks and gyros."

"Sounds good and greasy to me. Let's go."

After picking up three "greasy" bags of hot food, Jael and Grant headed to her house, Grant behind the wheel again. Little of the conversation touched on the arrest and foul character of their captive, as if they were putting off that unpleasantness until they had a full stomach. They were both just thankful Upton was off the streets before there were any more deaths.

"You certainly make a great FBI agent, if I didn't get to say so before. I didn't know they taught you guys how to fly," Jael teased.

"Fly? I was flying?"

"Airborne right through the barn door when Upton tried to take off."

"Oh then, yeah, well, we usually keep those kinds of strategic maneuvers in reserve," Grant said with a laugh, adding, "You didn't do so bad yourself."

"Yeah, like how I stayed on the ground most of the entire capture." Jael felt comfortable with the light banter and with this man she barely knew. "After we've stuffed our faces with food, I'd like it if you'd hang around for a while and tell me why you decided to become a federal agent in the first place."

"Not much to tell; I can give it all to you in a nutshell before we make it to your house."

Jael wasn't sure if this was his polite way of saying he had no plans of hanging around any longer than necessary, but at least she did learn a little more about him, while her stomach growled as the mouthwatering scents rose from the bags on her lap.

"I believe certain things are instilled in us as toddlers," Grant began. "I always loved playing cops and robbers, shoot-'em-up. Even in hide-and-seek, when most kids liked to hide, I had more fun figuring out *where* they were hiding. And in any game where one side battled against the other, there was something about getting the bad guy that always appealed to me."

Jael nodded in agreement. "I know exactly what you mean."

When she added nothing further, Grant continued. "By the time I reached high school I was fascinated by the criminal mind, and when a recruiter from the police academy spoke on Career Day, I was bought and sold. I signed up to join the academy immediately following college. While a handful of my friends went off to get their master's, others into the service, and others just didn't care, I thought I had a jump on them all, because I would be making money in my field in less than a year and have the rest of my life to advance. I eventually went to graduate school to study criminal law. One path led to another, as they say, and here I am." Grant stopped and gave Jael an enthused stare. "What about you?"

"Pretty much the same story for me, just a couple of unforeseen twists."

Grant raised a "come on now" eyebrow, and Jael tilted her head and pursed her lips.

"Okay, maybe one day I'll tell you all about it, but right now, we're two doors from my house, and I'm hungry, starved for a hug from my son, and I want to kick off these shoes."

Grant laughed, and darn it, Jael thought, if it didn't just

tickle her insides. She really needed some food—she was feeling silly.

When Jael slipped her key into the front door and they stepped inside, no one was there to meet her. It didn't take long to put two and two together. She could hear the crowd roaring and the even louder announcer's voice coming down the short hall from the TV.

"Follow me," she told Grant, who'd taken the bags from her outside the car.

As they passed the kitchen divider, Jael pointed for Grant to place the bags on top as she kept on into the den. Both Ramon and Terrell were less than a good foot away from the TV screen, watching the WWF.

"Uh, excuse me, guys, but I'm home."

"Hi, Mom."

"Hi, Ms. Jael." The two boys spoke in unison, neither turning to look her way.

"Okay, boys, let's mind our manners. I have company, and it's polite to show some home training, you know."

Ramon was the first to reluctantly turn around, Terrell following suit milliseconds after him. Blank stares suddenly replaced the noninterested greeting about to pass across their lips. Their mouths gaped open and their eyes became huge round circles. Terrell was the first to speak.

"THE ROCK!"

Ramon spoke in more of a whispered awe: "The Rock."

Jael couldn't help erupting in a loud burst of laughter. "Sorry, guys, not your hero, but certainly mine for today. Please meet FBI Agent Eric Grant."

Ramon jumped to his feet. "Wow, did anyone ever tell you you look just like The Rock on WWF?"

"All the time," Grant admitted, joining in on the fun. "I had a great career before that guy got famous. I'm thinking about either having plastic surgery or becoming a professional wrestler."

"You've got the muscles for it," Terrell said, moving up to Grant and openly checking out the well-defined physique under the agent's suit. "And I believe they pay a whole lot more than the FBI."

"You've piqued my interest," Grant said, smiling and slapping Terrell on the shoulder in a manly gesture. "I think I'd better look into it."

"Okay, okay," Jael interjected. "I know you guys are hungry, and Agent Grant is staying for dinner, so let's start the routine."

"Just call me Grant," he told the boys, and they both gave him broad smiles.

"Okay, Mr. Grant," Ramon said. "Make yourself at home. We'll see about getting dinner out in a sec."

The boys bounced into the kitchen, stealing peeks over their shoulders at Grant. They laid out the food from the various bags, whispering between themselves as they pulled out paper plates, glasses, forks and the necessary condiments for the meal.

"You can wash your hands in the bathroom by the den. Just make yourself at home," Jael offered, then quickly turned her head to keep from staring as Grant eased out of his jacket and headed for the door she'd pointed to.

In the kitchen the boys were busy yakking about their new hero discovery while haphazardly placing the items out on the table.

"Mom, did you see all those muscles?" an excited Ramon asked.

Jael was grateful that her shoulder pain was minimal, thanks to 800 milligrams of ibuprofen, and that her bandages, concealed as they were under her clothing, would not alarm the boys. But she *wasn't* grateful for the question. Not wanting to admit to her own overwhelming admiration of Grant, she sidestepped the truth by saying, "Pay attention to what you're doing with that ice bowl, Ramon," as she washed her hands over the sink. She sent up a quick prayer of forgiveness to justify the wave of longing that attacked her flesh again so unexpectedly. But then, the Lord expected her to appreciate His awesome handiwork, didn't He?

"But did you notice how much he looked like The Rock when you first met him? And why is he here with you anyway?"

Jael sighed: the innocent inquisitiveness of youth. "He's here to help out on the case I'm working on. He's from out of town, so I thought it would be a nice gesture to invite him to have dinner with us."

Ramon tilted his head sideways. "Okaaay."

Jael chose to ignore her son's suspicious nature and took a plate, placing wings, fries and a slice of the Philly cheese steak on it. The boys had already set two-liter bottles of Sprite, Big Red, and Caffeine Free Pepsi on the table with a bowl of ice.

Jael filled her glass with the cold crystal cubes and was about to sit down when Grant reentered the kitchen.

"Here, Mr. Grant, sit by me," Ramon offered.

"Thanks, Ramon." Grant fell right into the swing of

things, as if this was the way he'd eaten all his life. He piled his plate high with fries and wings, adding the other half of the cheese steak to it and pouring Big Red into his glass of ice.

"Mom says you're working on a case with her. It must be pretty special if the FBI is involved. Is it about all those dealers being offed?"

"Ramon, you know we don't discuss stuff like that. Eat your food and behave."

"What's it like being a special agent?" Terrell asked around a mouthful of food.

"Terrell, can we chew our food first?" Jael fussed.

"Oh, yes ma'am."

"What's it like?" Ramon prompted.

"It's nothing like the things you see in the movies," Grant said between huge bites of cheese steak. He wasn't letting the day's excitement curb his appetite. "It's a lot of paperwork, research and long boring interviews."

"Have you ever had to participate in a stakeout or shootout?" Ramon asked, clearly not believing Grant's story.

"I've survived one or two such assignments. But there's a lot of training you have to go through before ever landing an actual case to work on. And you have to have certain skills to fire a weapon, and spend hours learning warlike techniques."

The questions went on for much of the meal, as Jael admired Grant's gentle way with the boys. He never bragged or pretended to be a hero, but didn't minimize what the boys wanted to hear. He served up just enough excitement and logic to keep them interested and on the edge of their seats.

Soon, it was time for Terrell to jump on his bike and head home and for Ramon to take his bath and get ready for bed. Terrell complied with little apparent reluctance, while Ramon put on a real show to stay up a little longer.

"Mom, Mr. Grant says he can play video games. I just want one WWF game with him. Just one, please! I'll never be able to tell my friends I had a real FBI agent in my house who looked like The Rock and I didn't beat him at his own game," Ramon begged.

"Please, Mom, please!" Grant added with a puppy-dog look on his handsome face.

Jael laughed. "Okay, but you'll be sorry, Grant. My son is WWF champ around here."

Ramon rushed to restart a new game on the set, and Jael followed them into the den to watch. Curled up on the couch with a cold drink in her hand, Jael melted with every anxious grin the two displayed. There was certainly a softer side to this man who had just nearly bludgeoned a criminal to death and shattered an entire ring of thugs.

Ramon nearly kept his promise and beat Grant at only two games. As he was passing Jael on his way to his bedroom, he whispered, "He let me win. I can tell when someone is especially good at something and pretending not to be."

Jael nodded. She had thought the very same thing as she watched them play.

Chapter 23

Jael finally kicked off her shoes and curled her feet under her on the couch. Grant moved to the adjacent couch with another full glass of Big Red, making himself comfortable and dispelling her earlier idea that he was ready to get away.

"You've got a nice son there. And Terrell . . . your nephew?" Grant said, taking a sip of his drink.

"No, a young boy I met who needed a little guidance. We sort of unofficially adopted him into the family about a year ago."

"Bighearted woman. I should have guessed," he said before taking a gulp of his drink.

"I don't know about that, just doing my part to keep another black youth off the streets."

"And Ramon's father?"

"We're divorced, three years now."

Grant watched her with a look Jael couldn't decipher. "Three years. And you haven't remarried in all that time? Keeping a boyfriend or two on the sidelines?"

"Too busy for romantic stuff."

Grant raised an eyebrow. "Don't tell me your ex soured you on marriage. It's a great institution, according to the Bible."

"Yeah, I guess for some it's a great institution, but for me it would just get in the way right now."

"So the force has been your lover for all these years?"

Jael squirmed under his intense gaze. "No, God has been all things to me."

Grant continued to watch her, giving nothing away in his expression. He decided not to push. "How long have you been on the force?"

"Next month it will be thirteen years."

"You never told me how you became an officer of the law."

"Like I said, long story."

"Rushing me home?"

"Not before you tell me something about why you came down here in the first place, and how you knew this case was connected somehow to white supremacists."

Grant leaned back against the couch and crossed his left ankle over his knee. He took another sip of the cold red stuff in his glass before answering. "I wasn't sure at first, but close surveillance over the last few months suggested another incident was bound to happen soon. It's usually a Lone Wolf, but he often has powerful forces working behind the scene."

"Upton called himself a Lone Wolf. What does that mean exactly?" Jael took what she hoped was a dainty sip of her own drink and instantly recognized it as a flirty gesture. *Shoot! Watch yourself, girl.*

"In the Klan, they're considered heroes. Almost like men

on a suicide mission. In this case, it was the black drug dealers in Dadesville. An element of society frowned on by just about everyone for poisoning youth and as the cause of most of the negative things happening in our world today."

"So what do we do to stop those behind this? I mean, here I am a member of law enforcement and had no idea our little town was saturated with an organized hate group. In this line of business, you always run into a few rednecks with racist tendencies, but it's usually individual incidents."

"That's why I believe this needs to be publicized more. A lot of people have their heads in the sand about it, and that's why it's growing like wild weeds. We live in dangerous times, and organizations such as these thrive like locusts if they're not completely annihilated."

Watching him, Jael was impressed with his passion. In a flight of fancy, she imagined Grant as an angel hunk from heaven. A man after God's own heart. A man perfect for her and Ramon. A man who would love and cherish her. Fulfill all her needs.

Jael squirmed with that last thought. Right after her divorce she'd fought an almost losing battle with her flesh. It was like love and affection had been suddenly ripped from her life, and the need to be held and to feel special to someone had been overwhelming. Thoughts of picking up a stranger simply for physical pleasure had toyed seriously with her mind. When she'd talked with Brenda back then, while she was still a baby Christian, her girlfriend offered unrealistic advice, like get on her knees and pray it off. She'd wanted to scream.

It seemed so unfair—just because Virgil wanted out, she was left behind with unfulfilled cravings. While he was experimenting with everything from young women to those twice his age, she was forced to rein in her physical need because she wanted to be faithful to God—and because she needed the Lord so desperately for other more important matters at the time.

But the Lord had proven Himself more faithful than she could have ever imagined, giving her the strength she needed to suppress her wanton emotions. In only a few months, the tough part was over. The Word of strength came at her from every direction. While flipping the television channels one evening, the Lord even spoke directly to her through Crefflo Dollar, who said that to chase away evil imaginings, one had to rebuke the devil out loud. She'd immediately stood and verbally demanded control of her own body.

After that, each time ungodly thoughts entered her mind, she'd speak aloud directly to the problem, followed by offering immediate praise. In no time, it was as if a faucet had been shut off and God had completely removed the yearning. Now she realized how she'd taken another of His blessings for granted: When the need left, she'd completely forgotten they had even been there.

But now those old feelings and needs were calling out to her like drugs to a recovering addict. How long had it been? How long since she'd even thought of a man romantically?

"Would you like some more?"

"Huh?" Jael said, caught off guard by the question.

"Your glass is empty. Would you like some more pop?"

"Oh, uh, yeah."

As he rose to take her glass, he let his hand linger on her fingers. His seductive brown eyes held hers for a mind-boggling second. He smiled gently, breaking the moment, allowing her to breathe again.

"Well, as I was saying," he said as he walked to the kitchen. "This is a highly organized group of people, and with the advantages of the computer age, their madness is running rampant. These militia groups are all over the country. Training grounds for racists, claiming that God's their advocate and with names like the World Church of the Creator, or Church of the American Knight, it can be very devious for people unaware. They fill their young with hatred by dehumanizing blacks, Jews, Asians, Latinos—anyone who is nonwhite—to such a degree that these young kids think nothing of taking the life of these people."

"How do they factor God into this hate scenario?"

"They twist actual Bible verse to their own purpose. After 9/11, no one should be surprised that a group of men would kill in the name of their God."

Jael sighed as Grant walked toward her. "But most Christians know the Lord teaches 'Hate the sin but love the sinner.'"

"Most *true* Christians, yeah, but the vast majority of these men and women are *so-called* Christians, twisting Christ's teaching and promoting their own biblical versions. Very few people actually read the Bible, depending on others to translate for them. That's why this stuff has festered for so long, because no one will stand up and say, 'This is not the Word of God.'"

As he handed her a refilled glass of frosty liquid, Jael felt Grant's agitation with each new statement and sensed that he believed strongly in what he was saying. He took his seat again, but this time leaned his elbows on his knees just a few inches away from her.

"They view blacks and other ethnic groups as anti-Christians, idol worshipers with religions like voodoo, Santeria, Buddhism, and thus they feel vindicated in bringing about a Holy War. Their hate for Jews is just as complicated as it has been since the days when Christ walked on earth."

"You know who's really behind this, don't you? I mean if you really know your Bible, you know where it all comes from."

"Yes. The adversary has used man's hatred against his brother for millennia, and ignorant men are his tools of destruction. I believe churches around this country should stop hiding their heads in the sand and finally stand up for what's going to make a real difference. A few ministries have acknowledged the sin of slavery and racism, but it's been so few it's like a ripple in a vast sea. On any given Sunday, whites are in their churches, blacks in theirs and so on and so forth, all praising the same God, but not doing anything to live as brothers and sisters."

Jael thought about what he was saying. Yes, she went to an all-black church, but that certainly didn't mean people of other races were not welcome. And wasn't everyone comfortable in his or her own environment?

"Well, I certainly like my kind of music. It's got more soul, if you get my meaning." She smiled.

He returned the smile. "There's nothing wrong with having individual tastes, but we have to learn to cross the lines of familiarity and make sure we're reaching as many people of other ethnic backgrounds as possible. When churches do outreach, they usually reach out to their own kind."

"Not true." Jael sat up in defense of First Temple Church of God in Christ. Her shoulder gave a little cry of protest. She ignored it. "In our church we financially support many ministries around the country."

"But when was the last time your church invited another church of a different background to a special event?"

Jael waved her hand in front of her. "Okay, we've gotten way off the subject here."

"No, the subject is, 'God's people perish for lack of knowledge.' There are thousands of people out there training for a race war, all in the name of God. Who's taking up their Cross to face this one off?"

Jael thought about that, too, and when she envisioned TeeTee's face and those of the other dead dealers, it hit hard. People around her were dying because someone had decided they were no-good scum of the wrong color. She knew few cared that a dealer was offed. She could see many good and decent people silently saying "Yes, one less criminal on the streets," not knowing where this could all lead.

"As an agent of the Bureau," Grant continued, "my goal is to assist other agencies to infiltrate these organizations—then we can work from the inside. But it's a slow process. All the while, millions of Christians on the outside could do so much more if they'd only decide to leave their comfort zones and really evangelize."

Suddenly, Jael realized how she'd let the zeal of her earlier Christian days slip away. The constancy was still there, but not the passion. She reflected that this was a sad state that many of God's children found themselves in after a while, and possibly why so many churches kept having "revivals." Maybe she needed a personal "soul revival" herself, for more reasons than one.

"How did you get so wrapped up in all this?" she asked.

"It wasn't by personal experience, just a gradual awakening. I went into the agency an innocent. But even there when you're confronted with the prejudice, you think it's only a matter *you* have to deal with.

"A few years ago, I was assigned to the killing of a little black girl in Macon County. As I began my research, case after case kept coming up in the database that were similar. Each new discovery turned my stomach. The Bureau was working to compile a more recent record of incidents, which at first seemed like simple assaults or second-degree murder charges, but were actually racially motivated. One of our infiltrators turned over the Web sites and material that saturate this country. Believe me, skinheads are only a small part of this poison. Often people are confused about the difference between the Klan, Aryan Knights and skinheads. It's simply different generations with varied ideas about how to go about spouting the same hate."

Grant looked down at the empty glass in his hand, attempting to collect himself. "Seems like I'm about to drink you out of house and home. May I have another?" He held up his empty glass. "I guess all of this is making me twice as thirsty. You want some more?"

"No thank you, I'm fine."

When he returned, he completely changed the subject.

"Tell me about you, and don't put me off again about its being a long story." He paused, giving her a sobering look before sitting down again. "I know about the drug charges."

Jael gaped. "How did . . . who told . . . ?"

"No one told me. I told you, I checked your file on the Web before I arrived in Dadesville. You've got a great record and deserve the promotion to lieutenant. The only scar was the time you were called in about drug abuse."

Jael looked off into near space. This was a tender subject with her, something she kept as far back in the crevices of her mind as possible.

"It was a bad scene," she said softly. "I almost lost my job *and* my son."

"Your file indicated the abuse was the result of dependence on Vicodin and Percodan, powerful painkillers."

Jael gazed over at Grant, expecting to see disgust on his face. His look was unaccusing. "Some of us should never dabble with things we have little knowledge about. I've never smoked, alcohol never affected me, and street drugs were the farthest thing from my mind, but after my car accident, which left me with broken ribs in three places, I became addicted to Darvocet. I progressed to Percodan and Vicodin within a few months. Even when I was confronted by my commanding officer, I never admitted to a dependency. Not until the day I was so smashed I passed out."

Like a flood, the past washed over her, with all its buried agonies, but she continued on. "I awoke to Ramon's screams—he was only three at the time. In my pain-riddled stupor I had turned on the stove to boil some eggs for some tuna salad; food in my stomach helped to keep my head clear on the medication. While the eggs were boiling, I lay across the couch and drifted off from all the drugs in my system. If I'd been in my right mind, I would never have left the pot handle facing outward. But the truth is, if I'd been in my right mind I would have seen I had a problem before it went so far. Anyway, Ramon, my innocent baby, with nothing on but his baby pull-ups, reached up to pull at the pot, and the scalding water drenched his little body from head to toe.

"I called 911, and by the time we got him to the hospital, he had second-degree burns over thirty percent of his little body. I was treated at the hospital too, for hysteria. And that's when it all came out about the drugs and how I'd misled my doctor. My husband never let me forget what I'd done. He didn't have to—I tortured myself enough. The department placed me on probation for two years. They didn't have to do that, either: I've had myself on probation ever since."

"Is that when you gave your life to Christ?"

Jael looked at him but didn't say anything at first. "I don't see it as giving God anything. He stepped in and gave *me* everything. I met a lady named Brenda Merrill, the sister of one of our victims, at the hospital. She often came to the children's ward and prayed for the kids, lifting their spirits and reading to them from the children's Bible. She talked to me while Ramon was in intensive care, telling me God would make it all right if I believed. Watching my baby lie there in so much pain, I wanted anything that could make it all right. Up until then I'd pretty much put all the things I'd learned about the Lord on the back burner—too sophisti-cated, you might say, with all my education, and believing I had grown out of that. But right then I prayed to Him to heal my baby. And Brenda began to talk to me about my spirituality and where the addiction was coming from.

"Over the next few months I began to attend her church,

going to the altar for prayer every time they invited anyone up. And then one night . . ." Jael took a deep breath, remembering. "One night something miraculous happened. I felt this power surge through me and I could barely contain myself. I began to shake all over, and something inside seemed about to burst out. I know it was the Holy Spirit. But that was just the beginning. God worked with me so patiently, replacing all the guilt and fear with hope and purpose. And He showed His love in so many wonderful ways. I learned that whatever you do, you can't run away from God. You'll get either His blessings or His wrath, but you'll get something.

"The church prayed continually for Ramon. When he was finally released from the hospital, I took him to church and let the pastor and elders pray for him. A week later the Lord touched my baby like a passage right out of the Bible. I was bathing him in Epsom salts as I'd been told when suddenly all the blackened skin from the burns began to simply fall off. I mean they just fell in the tub of water like a black sea of floating scabs, leaving behind smooth, soft skin. I remember jumping up and shouting, scaring my poor little boy to death. But then we began laughing and praising the Lord, with me getting just as wet as he was. I've lived from that day on thanking the Lord for His mercy. He didn't have to do it, but He did."

"He's an awesome God."

"I wear my uniform now in honor of Him. A soldier in His army, ready to serve any way He calls."

"And is that why you've put men and romance on the back burner, so to speak?"

"Hah, that's a joke. As soon as I gave my life completely to

Christ, the adversary attacked with a vengence. The more I attempted to share my newfound faith with my husband, the more he rebelled. He refused to accept Ramon's healing as anything but advanced medical science, even when the doctors professed they were confused over the quick recovery. My ex seemed to have a blind eye to what was really happening.

"Our disagreements escalated, and his resentment toward me grew out of control. He poured on the blame, constantly reminding me that if not for my drug-crazed state in the first place, the incident would never have happened. He pulled every string he could during the divorce proceedings to take Ramon from me. That would have given him all he needed to prove that without him, I was a useless human being. I was forced to accept my son on a trial basis, to prove I was a good mother. Virgil still hasn't forgiven me for winning custody of our son. My mom and Brenda, my prayer-partner, helped me through it all. But I guess in many ways, my husband made his point."

Jael took a swallow of liquid. Suddenly, her throat seemed very dry. "After divorcing my husband, I didn't think I deserved another chance at love. And when time passed and well . . . "

"I know you know you're a very attractive woman." Grant's voice deepened, transforming into more of a caress. "I'm sure men are constantly approaching you."

Her pulse jumped and gooseflesh crawled up her arms. *Dear Lord, dear Lord, save me from myself.* Aware of where the conversation was headed and her own weakening state, Jael attempted to keep the conversation laced with a strong spiritual overtone.

"God has His time," she murmured.

"And are you patiently waiting or hiding?"

Jael swallowed, her cheeks warmed. "A little of both, I guess. And I will admit, it hasn't been all that easy. I'm human, and sometimes it could just be a casual companion to make the difference."

"When was the last time you were on a date?"

"Date? Dear God. What's that?" She was thankful for the opportunity to lighten the mood.

"Don't tell me you're one of those women who devote themselves so totally to their career and child that life passes them by and one day they look up and ask what happened."

"I'm looking up now, but what I see kind of scares me." *Man, do I have a big mouth,* Jael thought. It was like she was thinking one thing but saying something completely different out loud.

Grant didn't answer right away. "I've only known you a few hours, Jael, but with all that's happened today, it seems like I've known you a lot longer." His eyes seemed to simmer with a hidden message.

"I'm flattered by your compliments, but I believe this time, you're barking up the wrong tree."

The "caution bug" was biting at her conscious, stinging her with remarks like "Who is this man really?" and "It's probably just obvious to him that I might be lonely and vulnerable." He could be thinking of her as just a ship passing through the night. A quick fleshly morsel to digest while on the job in Florida. Another of the women in every port. The thoughts began to spread like webs through her brain, and Jael lifted her chin a tad in defiance. She might be a little rusty when it came to current dating procedures, but she wasn't *that* easy.

Grant leaned back in his seat. His voice dropped to a low rumble. "Really?"

"I think you're picking up on something that's not there."

The look on Grant's face told her he thought it was a lie and that he was insulted.

"Obviously I have. And with that, I think maybe it's time I called it a night—you need your rest and time to care for your wound. I'll be at the station first thing in the morning. We'll deal with whatever this is at another time."

Jael rose from the couch. "I'll walk you to the door."

Chapter 24

Jael kicked back the covers on her bed, feeling way too warm. She'd tossed and turned ever since climbing in bed thirty minutes ago. Sleep eluded her like common sense to a teenager. The conversation with Grant played over and over in her mind. What she should have said and what she had said.

It was okay to be cautious, but she had cut it off at the starting gate. Why? Was she afraid of being let down again, of not being up to par? There was no denying she'd been lonely. A lot, actually. And the loneliness would creep up on her at the oddest times. Like sometimes in church, when a man placed his arms on the back of the pew where his wife was sitting. Jael would glance their way and wish for that kind of comfortable relationship. Or sometimes when she was at Rhonda's and her cousin's husband would come in and pull his wife to him, while Rhonda laughed seductively. And of course the next day, when Rhonda would excitedly give Jael a condensed version of the couple's passionate night, Jael would ache for her own intimate alliance. But whenever those needs or thoughts crossed her mind, she pushed them back, determined to wait until God revealed her time.

But now those emotions were attacking with a vengeance. She'd never been so out of it, thinking more about a man than the case she was on. For the past two years, she'd had her career and Ramon to keep her focused, to fight the demons that threatened to weaken her resolve.

And now she was on the biggest case she'd ever tackled, and here she was sitting up all night thinking about a man instead of getting the rest she needed for tomorrow's demanding day.

Jael yanked the pillow and pulled it over her head. Immediately Grant's image filled her mind.

Oh Lord, what am I to do? I'm so attracted to this man it's scary. And it's not just because he's so good-looking, although that's certainly an added plus, but tonight I got a chance to peek into his mind. He's no slouch when it comes to the things of God. At least not from what I can tell. So what is this I'm feeling? Is it okay? I'm so confused.

Jael crawled out of bed and dropped to her knees; she knew she'd never get any sleep tonight without placing her confusion before the Lord and then leaving it there. But it turned out to be harder than she'd hoped, for once she was back under the covers, thoughts of Grant resumed whirling around in her head, between lines of Bible verse.

Six hours later, Jael's chest was tight with anticipation as she walked into the station expecting to see Grant. He was nowhere around when she entered the squad room, but Sills was in his notorious position, leaning back in his chair.

"Your phone has been ringing off the hook all morning."

"Yeah, Tammy gave me a list of callbacks I don't think I have time for."

Before Jael could take a seat, her phone rang. Giving Sills a twist of her lips, she picked up the receiver. "Detective Reynolds, Homicide."

The voice of a young black man barked through the earpiece. "Hold on. Big Jake wants to talk to you."

A few seconds later Big Jake was on the line. No "hello," no "what's up," just right into his angry complaint.

"What is this shit? Do you mean to tell me my boys have been offed by the Klan? What do you plan to do about it? I ain't taking no—"

"Jake, Jake, calm down. This is out of your hands now. We have a suspect in custody and—"

"Forget that shit! This is war! Man, I can't believe we were the target."

"Jake, listen to me. We're going to handle this by the book. I know you're angry, but there's not much you can do but wait and—"

"The hell there's nothing I can do. *You* just wait. If those crackers think they can walk in on my turf and kill my boys, they don't know who the hell they're messing with. If I have to rip up this whole town, somebody's gonna pay. You got that, Detective? Those mothas will PAY!" The buzz of a dead line screamed in her ear.

Jael hung up slowly and sighed. "That's all I need right now, a riot."

"Big Jake talking retaliation?" Sills asked.

"With a vengeance. I need to get over there and talk to him and his boys before they do something stupid."

She wasn't even halfway out of her seat before the phone rang again.

"Detective Reynolds, Homicide."

"This is Daniel Foster. Oh God, why did I ever think this was going to just all blow over? The world has turned upside down! But I have to tell you how my son is involved in all this."

Jael flexed her fingers in frustration. "Mr. Foster, why didn't you say anything about this yesterday?"

"I didn't believe it myself! But now with all the news coverage about the Klan in Dadesville, and the killings, I have to accept my son's role in it."

"Okay, Mr. Foster, I'm listening."

"Not over the phone. You have to come here."

Jael dropped her forehead into her hand, her arm resting on her elbow, and massaged an imaginary throb. The pain in her shoulder, which had not bothered her until now, began a constant throb. Foster's son's direct involvement with the Klan was a little far-fetched, but the fear and concern in Foster's voice was unmistakable. "Okay. I'll be there within the hour."

Once again, before she could rise from her seat, something stopped her. But this time it was something much more pleasant than the ringing of her phone. Her pulse raced like a champion thoroughbred as Grant walked in and stood before her desk.

Giving Sills a quick acknowledging nod, he turned his full attention to Jael. She could tell that although Sills pretended to be busy at work, his ears perked up several notches.

"I need to talk to you." Grant's voice was stern and commanding, and his look added volumes to those simple words.

Jael swallowed, rising from her seat and nodding her head in the affirmative, bound by his gaze the entire time. Pushing her chair back, eyes still locked with his, she jumped at the shrill ring of the phone. She hesitated in picking it up, but Grant gave her a nod indicating he would wait.

Not looking at what she was doing, she fumbled for the phone and had to tear her gaze from his to recapture the handle before it hit the floor. She lifted the receiver to her ear, looking at Grant's broad chest. "Detective Reynolds, Homicide."

"I think you and your FBI boyfriend might want to cruise by the crack house on 29th Street. There's a little present waiting there for the two of you." The line went dead.

Jael replaced the receiver in its cradle and glanced at Grant in surprise. "I've been getting weird calls all morning, but I have a really bad feeling about this one," she said softly.

Grant waited. Sills looked up.

"A rather unnerving voice just suggested you and I cruise over to 29th Street, where the dealer's body was discovered. 'A little gift' is waiting there for us."

Grant glanced at Sills, then back at Jael, as he rubbed the back of his neck. "I didn't *think* they would lay down on this one. We're too close to the nucleus of their operation. We'd better head over there right away."

Chapter 25

Jael and Grant left together. Sills had offered to come along, but Jael suggested he send along backup and for now keep answering her phone and call Mr. Foster back to see if *he* could interview him about his son.

At the time Sills had given her a funny look, but Jael hoped he didn't read anything into her behavior. She needed to feel out whether or not she'd ruined her chances of getting to know Grant better after her abrupt manner last night.

And even though she knew this was the wrong time to be analyzing how she felt about Grant, she also knew he would be gone soon and that whatever was going on between them needed to be addressed before that. The fact that he lived so far away was something to consider in itself.

Jael, nervous about her behavior last night, noticed that Grant remained silent as he drove. It was obvious he wanted to stick to business and forget what had almost transpired between them.

When he finally spoke, it was in a cold, neutral tone. It

sounded more like he was giving a report than sharing information with her.

"Hate groups have increased by ten percent just over the last two years," he said. "An African-American psychiatrist, Alvin Poussaint, recently reported his findings on extreme racism and believes it should be considered a mental illness and treated as such. I don't know if I agree with him, but at least he's attempting to study the mentality behind the madness."

Jael picked up on the bitter edge that had crept into his voice. In the silence of her mind, she knew full well that Satan was the Prince of Deceit, making men seem wise in their own minds. But as the Bible verse Romans 12:16 said, *Be not wise in your own conceits.*

"Grant, about last night . . ."

"Hold that thought until I fill you in on what you should expect during the trial. I have discovered—"

"Grant, no!" Jael interrupted. "I . . . I apologize for my behavior last night. I was wrong."

Grant turned to stare at her, a sudden sparkle of interest twinkling in his eyes.

"All that talk about romance and dating last night made me a little nervous—very nervous, to be truthful. You hit too close to home. I wasn't ready to admit some of those things, even to myself. And yes, I have been hiding behind my career. And I'm a little frightened that of all people it was you who awakened something in me I thought was long dead."

"What makes it so scary that it's me?"

"Well, look at you. Fine, great muscles, right timbre in your voice, clothes that fit your body as if they were sewn on."

Grant made a throaty chuckling sound. "Thanks for feeding my ego, but what does any of that have to do with your being frightened of me?"

"Well, for heaven's sake, that makes you Mr. Perfect almost. That's scary. Women are probably falling all over you. Tell me you don't have a harem of panting women in every city and a little black book filled with phone numbers."

"I don't have a harem of women or a little black book," he said, laughing and slowly shaking his head. "I will confess to recently breaking up with a nice young lady who quite possibly had marriage on her mind, but we both agreed I wasn't the man for her in the end. The last thing I expected was to be so quickly smitten by another gorgeous sister."

" 'Smitten'?" Jael had to laugh at the term. He was really just a big sweetheart by nature. What could possibly be wrong with another dinner in a more romantic setting than her junky den?

"That's the homeboy in me. But you don't have to be afraid of me, Jael. I understand we've just met. I just want to get to know you better. There can't be any harm in that."

"I feel the same way, and from this moment on, I promise to act like a woman with a little sense and not go running off the deep end."

"Fair enough."

Chapter 26

The day was overcast when they arrived at the crack house and started up the walk to the yellow barrier tape still flapping around the fence and gate.

"Should we wait for backup? That 'little gift' could be anything," Grant asked, but she could tell the question was mostly out of concern for her safety.

"The police tape is still in place, so let's see how much we can feel out before they get here. We're probably only a few minutes ahead of them."

Grant pulled a pocketknife out of his vest jacket, and while he was cutting the warning tape that crisscrossed the entrance, Jael remembered the rush of fear that attacked her the first time she'd placed her foot on this threshold. She experienced another bout of anxiety now.

Once the tape was removed, Grant pulled his weapon from his holster and Jael did likewise. Grant carefully checked for any surprises before slowly pushing the door open. Jael cautiously stepped in and moved past the foyer toward the spot where they had discovered the first dealer. Even with the minimal amount of light falling through the front door, she still recognized the dried bloodstains on the tile. Behind her, Grant moved off to her right to investigate the surrounding rooms. Jael forced herself to check out the one on her left.

"Find anything?" she called out.

"Nothing."

"Think it was a prank call?"

"I wouldn't put anything past these guys. But to send us directly to the first crime scene says volumes. Let's check the backyard."

The scarred wooden door to the back was cracked partially open. The upper hinge had long ago rotted away, making the door stick and lean slightly downward. Jael turned sideways and eased through the tight space, with Grant right behind her.

Her foot stepped in something wet on the floor right by the door. Pulling her foot away, she froze. Grant stared down at her foot, then back at her. They exchanged a wary look.

"Grant, maybe . . ." Whatever she was about to say died in her throat as she turned to stand away from the door, bumping it slightly. There, slumped in a well-worn, over-stuffed chair with cotton hanging out of its arms, was Peoples, propped up like a puppet. His white throat was grotesquely marred by deep rope burns, his mouth hung open in a silent scream and the strong, pungent smell of blood and death floated around him in sour waves. His cold, dead eyes met Jael's in accusation. Jael took an involuntary step backward, her own eyes widened in horror.

Penned on the chest of his dirty stained shirt was a handwritten note.

YOU'VE MADE A BIG MISTAKE, NIGGERS.

Chapter 27

The thunderstorm finally made its promised appearance, with strong, swift rain that drenched the sidewalks like someone had ripped a hole in the sky. The crime team, draped in bright orange rain capes, swarmed the place, along with the coroner, additional police, neighborhood gawkers under umbrellas and, of course, the media.

Jael was back in her element, issuing orders and making sure the crime scene was secured. She was still there long after the body was removed and the forensics team was finishing the painstaking task of sifting through the soggy mess for evidence.

She felt sorry for Peoples. He hadn't told them anything. She wondered if there would be more repercussions as a result of their "big mistake."

Grant had left for the station over an hour ago. Before he'd departed, the two of them had gone over numerous possibilities, even toying with the idea that William Jasper was behind this latest fatality.

The press was out in full force, and this tragedy was

looking bad for the DPD. It seemed their moment of victory was suffering a setback and that the department was at square one again.

Jael heard the rain plummeting against the crack house roof and glanced upward. *Lord, what's going on here?*

She thought about the ruthlessness of these people and how life meant so little to them. She'd been up against a lot while working as an officer of the law, but had never had to deal with organized killers, organized hate.

Dear God, what role do I play in all this? How can you use me to stop these senseless murders?

"Detective Reynolds?"

Jael turned to see Sills approaching from the back of the house, his expression of confusion mirroring her own.

"We've got a bad case on our hands with this one," he said, shaking his head.

"Yeah, you're right there." She rubbed her left hand across her temple. "Grant . . . the FBI agent, was telling me about dangerous militia groups they've uncovered across the country. He was right to suspect they were here. Why did we not know this, Sills?"

"You've got me. It's hard to believe this stench was right under our noses and we never even got a whiff."

"But why Peoples? He couldn't have been a threat to them."

"To get your attention maybe, to say they're not playing games, to keep us on our toes? Who knows what these guys think?" Sills looked over at Jael with concern in his eyes. "You'll solve this one, too, don't worry. It's going to look good when you make lieutenant."

"You think I'm concerned about that now!" she shouted.

"Okay . . . okay, don't bite my head off. Wrong timing on my part."

"I'm sorry. This one has got me puzzled up and down. Every time I think I've figured it out, something new is added."

"Like I said, you'll solve this one, too."

Jael nodded, but with a lot less assurance than Sills seemed to have.

"Grant has taken the note we found on Peoples's shirt back to the lab for prints."

Sills looked at her hard for a moment. "Hope I'm not stepping over the line, but is there anything I should know about the two of you?"

"Sills . . ."

Sills forged ahead, refusing to be put on hold on the matter again. "I've never seen you look at anyone the way you were gawking at our FBI boy back at the station. And he wasn't slack on the emotions either."

Jael's first reaction was to deny his observations. She ran her fingers along the side of her nose, and blew air through her mouth. "Too much on our plate right now to really know one way or the other. Lucky me, huh." She turned and headed into the rain and the night.

Chapter 28

It was eleven-thirty when Jael returned to the office. A small throbbing at the base of her temple was making its presence known while her shoulder beat in awkward time with sharp little jabbing pains. The mound of paperwork on her desk wasn't helping the situation at all. Before forging into the caseload, interoffice memos and the ever-increasing pink telephone slips, she downed three Tylenol tablets with a cup of cold coffee. Within twenty minutes the Tylenol had kicked in and she had sorted the disarray into neatly stacked piles of "Urgent" and "Someday."

The downpour was still at full throttle, and Jael realized she hadn't seen a full day's sun in several days. It was a reminder that a cloud had settled over her perfect little life, bringing with it the electricity of uncertainty and the unknown. When little bursts of brightness attempted to touch her in the form of Grant, darkness quickly reclaimed her each time she had to deal with the madness going on around her.

Her cell phone beeped. She pulled it from her waistband,

glad for the distraction, and clicked it on. Static flickered over the waves as she spoke.

"Detective Reynolds, Homicide."

"Jael? Grant here. I'm heading over to reinterview Upton and thought you might like to come along. The note was a long shot at best—no prints, and common writing paper sold in any drugstore. I didn't expect much more, not with the expertise of these guys, but we have to check out everything. Can you swing it?"

"Should I meet you or are you going to come by here?" she asked.

"How about if I pick you up. I'm only a few minutes away. Meet me at the front steps of the station."

"You got it."

When she hung up, Sills was grinning at her.

"I don't even have to ask who that was. That funny look on your face says it was our FBI boy."

"Sills, give me a break here," Jael responded noncommittally. "I'm still trying to figure out what's going on myself."

"So it may be more than just a professional encounter?" he teased.

Jael knew Sills had her best interests at heart. Over the past few months his matchmaking had increased from casual mention of single men to scheduled meetings. So far, she'd managed to avoid any actual blind dates.

"Yeah, but talk about bad timing," she said with a teasing voice of her own. "I mean, you know me—if it looks like it might distract me from the case . . ."

"Yeah, ain't that the truth, forever the super-police-woman," he kidded. "But you ain't fooling me either, and this guy's no dummy if he's working for the Feds, and to come traipsing into this mess tells me he's got passion. You and I have been partners too long for me to let some out-of-towner prance in here and put claims on you without my making sure it's good for you."

"Well, thanks for the encouragement, if that's what it is."

"Before you go dashing off again, can I get the file on Upton and whatever you have that Mr. FBI has shared with you about this organization? Some of us are expected to do some serious work around here, you know." His words were spoken with a full measure of kindness.

"You're a pal, Sills, you know that? Take whatever you need off my desk; I'll get it from you later. By the way, did you get a chance to speak with Foster?"

Before he could answer, another voice joined theirs.

"Excuse me, but I need to review your file on Upton also," Billups said from just behind her shoulder. Jael hadn't seen Ernest Billups in the past few days. She was always thankful for such small favors.

"Why?"

" 'Why?' Oh yeah, I keep forgetting, you think this is a one-man show and not a team effort. Well, sorry, but we all share information here. Whatever you have, I need to go over it for my own report." He actually sneered. "Every time you go running off half-cocked we're left behind having to clean up after you."

She ignored his sarcasm and made a sound of derision, then added, *"Please."* Her longtime resentment swelled within, but she held on to her temper . . . just barely. At the same time, a thought occurred to her: Billups was white, ignorant and a chauvinist pig—could he have a connection to the Klan? She remembered seeing him leave the Captain's office, too. What had he been doing?

"You'll have to wait your turn, and then you'll get only what I think is necessary for you to have. Until then, I'll call you if you're needed."

Billups opened his mouth to retort, then snapped it shut. As he headed for the double glass doors, she asked for forgiveness from the pleasure she felt at seeing Billups red-faced and at a loss for words.

The county jail was only a few blocks from the Eighth Precinct police station, and both Jael and Grant were quiet during the short drive. Jael had a ton of things she wanted to talk over with him, but didn't want to hit on a really meaningful topic and then have to abort it at a very sensitive point due to police matters.

When they pulled up to the jailhouse, Grant unbuckled his seat belt while giving her one of his stern, no-nonsense looks. "When we finish here, I want at least thirty minutes of your time, uninterrupted."

He didn't wait for her confirmation, but climbed out of the car and walked around it to open her door. He'd displayed a lot of this kind of chivalry from the moment she'd met him. When he opened her door, she smiled. "Thirty minutes—that's all?"

They walked in quiet companionship up to the clerk's desk. She let Grant handle the initial signature clearing, standing back to admire the man while she had the chance.

They entered the inmate visiting room to find Upton in his blazing orange prison uniform staring at them with immense hatred in his eyes.

As soon as they took seats across from the man, Grant got directly to the point.

"Before we start, would you like your lawyer present?"

"I'll tell you if and when I need a lawyer. Shoot with your stupid questions, I'm ready."

"Upton, you're looking the death penalty straight in the eye. There's only one way you can plea-bargain for a life sentence, and I think you know what that is."

A grin spread across Upton's face. "You mean rat on who's working with me, like your little drug addict nigger did when he told us where to find the dealer's hangout in the first place?"

"That's what Foster's son told you?" Jael shouted. She understood why Foster was so upset and fearful.

"I ain't saying nuthin' more. I know the law. You can't come here and try to get me to admit to anything. Remember, you said so yourself, anything I tell you guys can be used against me later in court. That's if this even makes it to court."

"You can count on its making it to court—you have my personal promise on that," Grant informed him with a pleased look of his own. "But I'm not after you. You're not much, just one of the small fries."

"Don't tell me I'm not much!" Upton was livid, his face turning red at the remark. He quickly regained control of himself. "You got no proof I was involved in any of this hoopla, and won't. Kinda ruins your day, huh, Mr. FBI Agent. With all your nigger smarts, you can't prove a thing and you know it."

"Come on, Upton. Why allow them to let you carry the whole rap, let you be the fall guy," Grant said, leaning back in his metal chair. "And you know that's all you are. You'll only be remembered for a few days after we fry you. Then there'll be another Lone Wolf to take your place, getting all the praise and pats on the back, and you'll be all but forgotten."

"I'm not falling for that crap. You think any jury's gonna listen to you and a bunch of fabricated bumblings. I was just protecting my property. Ain't I got a right to do that? How was I supposed to know that the two niggers sneaking around was cops? So see, you ain't so hot. But I will tell you this much, Mr. FBI Agent." Upton leaned forward, and Jael involuntarily backed away. Grant didn't even flinch. "It ain't over till the fat lady sings. And singing 'Dixie,' not that nigger crap y'all love so much." Upton broke into a loud, rambunctious laugh.

Grant still hadn't moved; only a small flex of his jaw indicated he was getting angry. "Once more, Upton, this will be the last chance you get to save your sorry red neck. No plea bargains later."

"Nigger, you don't know what 'later' is. I've got all the time in the world."

Jael was amazed by Upton's bold self-assuredness. Was the note they'd found on Peoples's body a reason for his confidence?

She asked him. "What did the note mean?"

"What note?" he responded with faked innocence. "Somebody using Peoples as their personal mail carrier?"

The man was a trickster with words, admitting knowledge without giving them a thing they could use against him. "You boys fouled up there, Upton. Peoples never told us anything," she taunted.

"Maybe he did, maybe he didn't. But we'll never have to worry about whether he will in the future, now will we?"

"How long have you been a member of the local white supremacist group?" Grant asked.

"I ain't afraid to tell that. We want the world to know we're still in control. I've been an active member for six years," he bragged, leaning back in his chair and folding his arms across his chest.

"What do you mean by 'active'?"

"What else? Attending meetings, paying dues—you know, the regular stuff folks do in any organization."

"Where did the weapons come from?"

"What weapons?" he snickered.

"Don't play games, Upton—we've confiscated all the weaponry from the barn, much of which was military-issue."

Upton thought for a minute, never taking his eyes off Grant. Then the smile returned. "They were donated."

"An arsenal of weapons and explosives were 'donated'? For what purpose?"

When Upton rolled his eyes over them with deliberate disgust, Jael looked away, saying a quick prayer. The empty cold hue of his irises was like looking through the terrifying gates of hell.

"For protection," he spat.

"Protection from whom?"

"For one, from members of this lying government. A government that's prejudiced against whites. We're sick and tired of crying affirmative-action politicians pushing their crap down our throats, when talented white children can't get into major universities because of race quotas. All these black and Hispanic dummies are walking around in our great institutions of learning while decent white students are rejected because of the color of their skin. Reverse discrimination and all that."

Jael could tell Upton was spouting off things he'd been told, but didn't actually know anything about. He'd probably never even seen the inside of a college building.

"God told His people to conquer the land, get rid of the infidels and purify it for His return. That's what we're doing. These so-called innocent people bring the wrath of God upon themselves," Upton scoffed. "But we're the avengers of God! The Bible says 'destruction unto death for those who defy God's law.' That includes homosexuals, Jews, junkies, Chinks and niggers."

Jael prayed silently. *Father, he doesn't know what he's talking about. He's been brainwashed and snared in by Satan himself.*

"Have *you* read the Bible?" Grant asked him calmly.

"Don't have to. It's preached from cover to cover at all our meetings."

"Sorry, buddy, but whoever is teaching you, they're not doing it from the Bible. At least not the Holy Bible."

"You don't know what you're talking about. God is on our side!" Upton suddenly seemed a bit agitated. "You're wasting my time. Guard!" he shouted over his shoulder. "Get me out of here. I'm tired of looking at these nigger monkeys."

Jael noticed Grant's jaw flex again. He was holding back his temper just as much as she was.

They had gotten very little from Upton, and as they left the building in silence, it seemed he still had the upper hand, even behind bars.

Back in the car, as she and Grant headed down Waters Avenue toward the station, Jael wanted to wash the horrible feeling from her person. She needed to be reminded of the good connections people could have with one another.

"How about we try dinner again, and this time let's leave all the craziness behind," she suggested.

"Fair enough, but I have to stop by my hotel to change first. I'll drop you off at the station, then swing back, and we can leave for dinner from there. Unless you want to wait for me in my hotel room while I change?" He raised his eyebrows several times in a Groucho Mark imitation, a teasing grin on his lips.

Jael laughed. "I'll take you up on your first suggestion. I'm way behind on my reports and can use the time to at least get them started before kicking back for the rest of the day."

Back at the station, she made a call home to Ramon.

"Hi, honey, it's going to be another long night. And when I finish this paperwork, I'm going to stop and get something to eat with Grant. Is that okay?"

"No prob, Mom. But hey, what's with you? You digging this guy or something?"

"He seems like a nice man, but I'm not thinking anything serious right now. Just dinner."

"Well, don't feel like you have to rush home on my account. Have fun—you owe it to yourself."

"Well, gee, thanks for the permission."

"No, seriously. I've never seen you go out on a date. It's about time."

"Have I told you lately, you're my own personal angel from heaven?"

"On a regular basis."

"Love ya, honey."

"Love ya back."

Jael hung up and then dialed Rhonda's number.

She could hear the sound of loud music competing with an even louder television program, and then Rhonda shouting into the phone, "HELLO?"

"Hey, Cuz, I know you're busy but I've got to work late again tonight and wonder if you could swing by and check on Ramon and Terrell later on?"

"You know I will," her cousin answered, before shouting to someone to "turn that TV down." Instantly, Rhonda picked up her side of the conversation without missing a beat. "Besides, I like to pop up on those two every now and then and catch them looking at nudie films."

"Quit your mess, girl! You know ain't nothing like that going on in my crib."

"Yeah, I know. You got my poor nephew thinking if he even *looks* at a girl funny he'll burn in hell."

"That's not true, Rhonda, and you know it!"

"Just teasing. You're a great mom with a great son. Don't tell anyone I said this, but I admire the way you're raising that boy. He's going to be one of those special ones smart girls will be after like bees. Still, it never hurts to surprise them every now and then. I'll be there around six or seven. If they're up to something, I'll call after I take their skins off."

"You got it."

Jael hung up and finally began working on the reports. She was still at it thirty minutes later when Grant walked into the room.

"It's still a little early but I'm famished," he said. "Didn't take time out for lunch."

"A little early? It's already five-fifteen. I could eat a horse right now. Any idea what kind of food you'd like?"

"Not especially. Any good Italian restaurants nearby? There's never been an Italian restaurant that didn't have something I loved on the menu."

Sills returned to the squad room, having obviously picked up on the tail end of the conversation.

"How's it going, Grant? Since you arrived in Dadesville, we rarely get to see much of our lead detective." Sills smiled broadly.

Someone coughed loudly, and Jael didn't have to look up to know it was Billups passing by.

"Things can change in a matter of minutes," Billups threw at them on his way out the door.

"Not one of your admirers, I take it," Grant said as he placed his hand at the small of her back and ushered her out the door behind Billups.

"Good observation. I think I bumped him for the post when I was promoted to lead detective. Though he denies it, he's never let me forget the whole thing got under his skin."

Once they were settled in their seats at a window overlooking the bay, Jael realized how long it had been since she'd shared an intimate meal in a romantic setting. Though the interior of the restaurant was still cozy, and still dimly lit by small candles on the table, it had changed a lot since she and Virgil had celebrated their fourth wedding anniversary dinner there.

Glancing around, Jael took in the new decor of checkered tablecloths and a spectacular back wall mural of a bustling

Italian street. An intoxicating aroma of spices and seasoned meats floated in from the kitchen each time one of the waiters entered or exited, while soft violin music played in the background. The place was busy, and the hum of conversation around them was soothing.

"Come here a lot?" Grant asked, watching her intensely between glances at his menu.

"Haven't been here in years. I was here with my ex many years ago. If I remember correctly, the food was excellent."

"You mentioned yesterday that your husband never let you forget what happened to Ramon. Is he the kind of person that holds grudges to a fault?"

"Well, being fair and all, it was a lot more than that. Actually, Virgil is right in saying I brought all of this on myself. You see, I'd heard rumors the day of the accident and was working out my own kind of grudge when it happened." Jael looked down at her menu before continuing. "Someone had told me they'd seen Virgil at Tommy's, a hot nightspot here in Dadesville, with a pretty young woman he'd been seen with before. Said they were all over each other and it didn't look like Virgil cared who saw them together. I jumped into my car and took off in anger, hoping to catch him in the act.

"I never saw the other car coming. While I was at the hospital, he said a lot of things about how our relationship had been deteriorating for a while and that he was feeling trapped. I guess he wasn't cut out for marriage, or maybe simply not with me. Even though his behavior continued to wreck our marriage, I guess I wasn't ready for the last curtain call. I confirmed it by withdrawing; the pills seemed to ease the betrayal and kept me from having to think about it.

Then, of course, over time I needed more and more to deal with the divorce and the whole bit. You know the rest."

Grant reached across the table and placed his hand on hers. "I'm sorry it didn't work out. You deserve to be happy."

There it was again, she thought, those darn butterflies whenever he touched her.

"What about you, Grant? Didn't you ever marry again? Have any kids?"

A veil of inner sadness passed across his face for a fraction of a second, replacing the caring look he'd given her.

"Kids. I would have loved kids. But you make mistakes. Mistakes that follow you for a lifetime. Yes, I was married once, to the Prom Queen, the woman every guy wanted. The woman I thought I wanted. She was 'the perfect woman' all through our engagement. It wasn't until after we were married that I learned she couldn't have children. Or at least that's what I thought for more than four years; it was by accident that I learned she could have them but didn't want any. Not when the birth of a child could leave her body so out of shape." His words carried the bitterness of a deep hurt.

"How did you find out?"

"When the abortion clinic called me."

"Oh, Grant."

"She had forgotten to sign the insurance forms. I was the policyholder, so they called me." His voice cracked. "I was so astonished. I told them they had the wrong name, but after they confirmed their records, there was no doubt it was her. It was her second abortion in three years. When I confronted her, she finally admitted to taking birth control pills all during our marriage and that the two times things went wrong, she'd chosen to have an abortion."

He looked out the window into the dark night. Jael could see his tortured face reflected in the black glass.

"I'm so sorry, Grant."

"No marriage can stand up to those kinds of lies. Even though she promised to get off the pill and make a go at being a mother, it was too late for me. I'd always been a strong pro-life advocate and she knew it, and pretended to believe in the same things I did." Grant let go of a deep sigh. "I felt like such a fool. Preaching against abortion and here my wife was killing off our own kids before they had a chance to see the light of day. It destroyed any hope we might have had for a future."

He turned from the window to look at her. "I did the very same thing I accused you of—I buried myself in work. But unlike you, I did occasionally date, knowing my ex-wife was not the norm. I even got a little serious about a certain lady, as I told you last night."

"I think with me, I never let myself go to places where I might be exposed to my singleness," Jael volunteered, looking out the same window Grant had a moment ago. "I worked, came home and did things with Ramon. There were always a few dads at Ramon's events, but, of course, they were usually married. And if one of the divorced dads hit on me, I let him know right away it was a waste of his time. Virgil was very active in Ramon's life, and many people thought we were still married. I didn't tell them any different, because most of the time it worked to my advantage."

"But didn't you ever miss having someone hold you, whisper in your ear?" he asked in a seductive tone.

Jael turned back to gaze into his eyes for a moment, then looked out the window again. "You have no idea how hard it was at first. But after the Lord healed Ramon, I stopped doing anything outside of church. I stopped partying, stopped seeking companionship and filled my life with Ramon, work and church."

"And now?"

"And now, it seems so strange to be here with you." She gave him her full attention. "But I'll admit I'm loving every minute of it."

"That makes two of us."

They decided to share a Caesar salad, and Jael selected the Shrimp Medici. Just the thought of the plump Gulf Bay shrimp sautéed in garlic, olive oil and basil, on top of a bed of spinach, was enough to make her want to lick her lips in anticipation.

"You read my mind," Grant kidded, and for a moment Jael thought he meant the part about licking her lips. "So I'll have the Veal Marsala."

"Oh, I can change my order," she said, picking up the menu to glance over it again.

Grant politely took it from her and passed both menus to the waiter. "Not on your life. This way you'll have to share more than just the salad."

"Have you always been this type of schemer?" Jael was giddy with the thought of the two of them dipping into each other's plate.

"Always."

After that, the conversation was much lighter and laced with bouts of laughter. For Jael, it was shameless, girlish laughter that she enjoyed to the max. By the end of the meal, she was light-headed with a new kind of freedom, while at the same time getting a pretty good peek into the life of Eric Grant.

She took note of the way his voice softened and filled with emotion when he talked about his parents, siblings and close friends. He'd grown up in Philadelphia and because of the large Italian population, considered himself a bit of an expert on the cuisine.

"I make a mean Veal Piccata. I'd like to let you taste it someday."

"You cook?" She'd thought he was past surprising her and made a mental note to never second-guess him.

"Why not? I love to eat, therefore I cook. When I enjoy something, I dig right in and get all I can from it. I take my pleasure very seriously."

Jael met his eyes, the conversation having moved beyond food. And darn if those ole butterflies weren't back with a vengeance, racing all the way down to her legs. She could not think of a pat answer.

"I'll bet you do." It took all of her will to break the eye contact.

Through the rest of the meal she talked mostly about Ramon, her favorite subject. Grant smiled all the while, knowing she was keeping the conversation from a more intimate nature. Jael saw it as taking things really slow.

"I'm stuffed," Grant said shortly after downing a huge slice of Chocolate Mint Cheesecake. "That stretch of beach out there looks like the perfect place to walk off dinner. You game?"

Jael glanced out the window at the sandy path along the bay beside the restaurant. It was beautiful, and dangerous—dangerous by way of being nearly empty of other beach-combers and the perfect setting for their libidos to run a little wild.

But she was a brave girl, wasn't she? She had control of this situation, didn't she? She moved her legs under the table slightly, testing their sand-worthiness.

"I'll meet you out on the deck after I pay the check," Grant said, not giving her time to answer. So she nodded.

When Jael emerged on the back deck of the restaurant, she had managed to compose herself enough to quiet the thudding of her heart. But one look at Grant as he strolled out the door and the blood-pumping organ God had given her in the center of her chest began its thundering all over again.

When he was beside her, Grant took her arm and escorted her down the wooden stairway to the moonlit beach.

"Tell me what you're looking for in a man, Jael."

The question surprised her, but pleased her as well.

"I don't think I've given it much thought. I mean, yeah, every girl wants certain things: a man who loves her, treats her with respect, brings home the bacon—you know, the whole bit. But after my marriage, I believe God knew what He was talking about when He said not to be unequally yoked."

"You weren't a Christian when you married your husband, right?"

"Let's say I wasn't a devout Christian, but I knew about the Lord and always thought one day I would get serious about it, even though Virgil never had much taste for the things of God. I guess I thought with time everything would fall into place. Now I know that for a marriage to have any success in this day and age, Christ has to be at the forefront."

Grant had stopped to pick up a seashell, and now tossed

it out into the water. His body moved so swiftly and so suddenly that Jael was caught off guard when he swung around and circled her waist with his arms. She froze. Grant responded with a smile and slowly lifted her chin so their eyes met.

"You shouldn't be afraid of love, Jael," he whispered in a husky voice.

"I'm not afraid. It's just . . ."

Jael knew that Grant was about to kiss her. She anticipated the contact before their lips met, inhaling his strong male scent and automatically closing her eyes. As she lifted her arms to wrap around his neck, she silently prayed.

Please, God, is this the one? I certainly wouldn't have a problem with it if he was.

In the car thirty minutes later, Jael was still savoring the taste of Grant's lips. Like the gentleman she was learning to believe he was, he'd ended the kiss with a short peck on her nose, then held her hand as they walked along the beach. The conversation continued to be light, but Jael was feeling like she might soar off into the heavenlies if Grant had not been holding her down by the hand.

"You'd better drop me back off at the station so I can pick up the report," she said now. "I didn't finish it, and I can do that tonight at home."

"Okay, but I'll wait for you. I didn't pay a lot of attention yesterday to where you live. I'll just follow you and then head back to the hotel."

"You're a big ole FBI agent and you didn't take notice where you were going?" Jael teased.

"Had other things on my mind at the time."

Jael basked in the compliment. How long had it been since someone had said such sweet things to her?

When they reached the station, she nearly bounced through the main entrance. She smiled at Tammy, surprised to see her working the late shift today. Tammy didn't return the smile, but gave her a curious raised eyebrow. So what if everyone knew, Jael thought, she had never felt this great in her life. Or at least in a long time. And even Ramon was happy for her. She would call Rhonda later and tell her she'd had a "real live date," a great date. Even with all this madness around her, God had smiled on her with the hope and promise of a better day. Jael felt like her cup was running over.

No one was in the squad room when she stepped inside, and she quickly went to her desk to pick up the file and then head back out. The phone on her desk was ringing, and Jael debated whether to answer it. She ignored it while she gathered the loose sheets of information and stuffed them in a folder, but the phone refused to stop.

Whoever it was could reach her tomorrow; today was too great for another complaint.

She had completely turned away from her desk when the thought crossed her mind that Rhonda could be calling to tell her what the boys had been up to when she'd stopped by to check on them. She'd certainly need her cousin's version of things before she got home. *Oh, shooot.*

Jael answered the phone. "Detective Reynolds, Homicide."

"Is there any sweeter sound than the name 'Momma' uttered by one's only child?"

Jael frowned. She didn't recognize the voice, but the

sound of it instantly sent tiny little fingers of cold tapping along her spine. A knot of apprehension tightened her throat. The next voice she heard made the blood drain from her face.

"Momma?"

Jael sucked in her breath, "Ramon? Ramon honey, what's going on? Who's with you?"

But the voice that answered was not her son's.

"Check your top drawer, *Deeeetective* Reynolds. Then wait for my next call." The line went dead.

Chapter 29

Every vein in Jael's body turned into rivers of ice as she slowly reached for the top drawer of her desk and pulled it open. On top of her normal junk was a white envelope with her name on it. With shaking hands, Jael picked up the envelope and opened it.

Ramon's gold chain with the letters WWJD fell out and dropped onto her desk.

Jael's heart stopped a complete beat. It was the piece of jewelry she'd bought him on his ninth birthday and he never took it off. She could think of only one thing. *Oh God, oh God, oh God.*

Jael sank into her seat. *Dear, sweet Jesus. Don't let this be happening. Oh God, please, not my baby.*

The ring of the phone broke into her fog of denial. Jael snatched the receiver from the cradle and screamed into the mouthpiece.

"WHERE IS MY BABY?"

"Keep your voice down. This little matter is just between the two of us. Now listen and listen good if you want to see your son alive again. You're being watched as we speak, so no funny stuff."

"I want to talk to my son," she hissed through clenched teeth.

"I call the shots now, Detective. And I want you to sit tight until I call again. Tell no one about this or you know what will happen. I'm going to watch how you handle yourself."

"What do you want?"

"Patience, Detective—all in good time. Get some coffee, relax, do what you folks do, but don't go far from your desk. Not a word to anyone. Do you hear me? I'll get back to you. And if you behave, then maybe I'll let your little black boy say something to his mammy."

The click of the phone was like a death toll. Jael fought to hold on to her racing thoughts while her mind refused to accept what was happening to her.

For a solid three minutes, Jael didn't move a muscle and simply stared blindly at the phone. She fought back the urge to hyperventilate. Her mind froze in a state of denial. This couldn't be happening! This evil could not have reached out its ugly, hateful fingers and touched the only thing that meant anything to her in this world. Her God would not let this happen! *Oh, please God, not Ramon, not my baby.*

As her senses began to gradually absorb the sounds around her, the reality of it washed over her in a drowning wave of despair. Inside, she raged with conflicting emotions. She couldn't get a handle on any one feeling. Anger, disbelief, fear all congealed into a whirlwind of agony. At the crest of it all was the conviction that God could not, *would not*, let this happen to her. Not something so devastating, so utterly destroying.

Fixing an image of Ramon in her mind, Jael silently began to pray. *Our Father which art in heaven hallowed be thy name, Thy kingdom come, thy will be done on earth as it is in heaven. . . .* As the words tumbled across her brain, the miracle of flesh and blood and a new soul, all precious elements of who Ramon was, laced itself to her mind.

Jael never took her eyes from the phone, watching it as if it were a living thing, some kind of entity that embodied destruction and terror. When it rang, Jael leaped to grab it, braced for the burn she expected at her touch.

"Yes? Yes?"

"Yes? Girl, when you start answering the phone like you ain't got time to be bothered?"

"Rhonda, I . . . I have to go. I can't talk now. I . . ."

"Well, don't you want to hear about your son?"

"Ramon? What about him?"

"Well, I thought you said the boys were supposed to stay home. Those two have gotten off somewhere and left your back door wide open."

"Oh God!"

"Now don't get all flustered, Cuz. They probably just went off to get something to eat and will be back shortly. I'll swing by again and then I'll put such a scare in those two you won't have to worry about them acting grown for at least a few years. I'll call you again later with an update."

Jael didn't hear the rest of what Rhonda was about to say as she quickly recradled the phone. Thoughts whirled around in her head, never making any clear sense. *Think! Think like a policewoman first, a mother second.*

Okay, so whoever had kidnapped Ramon had left through the back door, she thought. Probably came in that way too!

While she was out, flirting with a man she barely knew, her child had been abducted and taken God only knew where. She could still hear Ramon's voice saying "Momma" that one time. And Terrell was with him! Dear God!

The waiting was killing her. What did they want? Who were they? Was it a they or just a him? But there was no way one man could have wrestled both Ramon and Terrell out of the house. It had to be more than one.

"Ready to go?"

Jael jumped at the sound of the voice and turned around to see Grant standing a few feet behind her. She had forgotten all about his offer to follow her home. But she couldn't say anything. The man had said he was watching, and she had to be careful. Her son was in the hands of a stranger and Jael didn't have any clue why. She only knew that for now she couldn't risk taking chances by telling Grant what was going on.

"Ah . . . I'm sorry, I had much more to gather than I expected. As a matter of fact there's a few things I have to finish up here before I can leave, so I'll be a while."

"I can wait. How long?"

"Oh . . . uh . . . quite a while, I'm sure. Listen, how about I call you later tonight and give you directions. I have some pretty important stuff here that needs my immediate attention."

"Anything I can help you with?" Grant moved closer to her desk. "If it's about the murders, maybe we should—"

The phone rang.

Jael couldn't move. Her eyes widened as she struggled with what to do. It rang a second time. Jael swallowed and reached for it, hoping she looked as casual as she possibly could.

"Detective Reynolds."

"Get rid of him."

Jael could feel Grant staring at her. *Sweet Jesus, help me.* Her villain was watching her *at this very moment.*

"Yes, I'm working on that right now. Can you hold for a second?" She placed her palm over the mouthpiece and looked up at Grant. "I'm really sorry. But this is all going to take a while. I'll call you later. I promise."

Grant gave her an odd look. "Okay. You have the hotel number, right?"

"Yes, yes, I have it."

"I'll be waiting." He gave her another strange look, then turned around and left.

Jael waited a few seconds, took a deep breath and in a whispered voice growled into the phone, "Let me speak to my son, now!"

"You're in no position to make demands. *I'll* be making all the demands. Now listen to me and listen good. You have forty-eight hours to do three things. Do them as you're told and your son will be returned to you unharmed." The voice was Southern, country and familiar, Jael noted.

"What about Terrell?"

"Yeah, his little nappy-headed friend. You can have him, too. But don't even try to screw around with me. I know your every move. Now listen to me carefully. Your first task is to get the phone book that was taken from Upton. I'll give you until tomorrow at this time to have it in your possession. I'll call back then, at this number."

"I can't. . . ."

"You will if you want to see your son alive. Remember, tomorrow." The line went dead. And something inside Jael suddenly died too.

Chapter 30

Jael held Ramon's gold WWJD chain, and could barely hold back the tears choking her. WWJD: *What Would Jesus Do?* What *would* Jesus do in this kind of terrifying situation? What was *she* supposed to do? Just pray? *Oh God, give me strength. Tell me how to handle this. Why is this happening? Why let this evil touch my baby?*

For the last few years she'd been able to pull up a scripture from her subconscious to fit any given situation. Suddenly her mind was a blank and all she could think of was the 23rd Psalm. Yet her soul was crying out, and the Lord did say He heard the cries of the righteous. *Oh please God, hear my cry. Hear me, Lord.*

She tried to think. The caller wanted the phone book the suspect had on him during booking and that was now in the evidence room. How was she to just waltz in there and tell the clerk to hand it over without a legitimate reason? Jael racked her brain to think of a way to confiscate the phone book without actually breaking a law. But there was no other way: She'd have to lie.

In the back of her mind, she knew that what she was planning was illegal. She had every right to take the phone book out of the property room, because she was an officer on the case, but it would have to be returned, and she knew that whoever had her son had no intention of returning the book. A chain of evidence procedure had to always be followed. She could get locked up for this and lose all she had worked so hard for. But she also stood to lose the most precious gift God had ever given her if she didn't do it. Right now Jael could see no other choice for herself. God *had* to understand.

Jael rose from her seat. Her legs felt like lead as she moved past the gurgling water cooler and out of the glass double doors.

The property room was just on the other side of the building. As she passed the receptionist desk, another night clerk, thankfully not Tammy, barely looked up. The lobby was empty of any other officers or drag-ins. The room seemed surreal as Jael passed through the brightly lit area of wooden counters, benches and safety-related wall posters.

As she moved robotically down the hall, someone from one of the outer offices yelled a greeting to her. Jael wasn't sure how she replied, whether by a nod, the wave of a hand or what, as she continued toward her destination. She passed through a small walk-through and opened the door marked PROPERTY ROOM.

A dim light emanated from behind the caged area a few feet from the door. No one was around. But that wasn't unusual. The property clerk in charge would often be found in the back checking labels and re-sorting certain items.

On the counter in front of the cage was a bell. Behind the

counter would be forms to fill out for the removal of any given property. In some cases a subpoena was necessary to retrieve it, but as lead detective she was allowed to remove evidence if she felt it was necessary for her investigation. She would use that privilege tonight to get the phone book in her possession.

Jael stood in the doorway staring at the cage in the heavy silence. It was now or never, because if she thought too much about what she was doing she would buckle under the weight of guilt. And if she didn't handle this right, if any questions arose later, the property clerk would remember her. Jael took another deep breath and attempted a casual air she was afraid she wouldn't be able to pull off.

Stepping up to the window, she slapped the bell with the palm of her hand. A gruff noise spilled from the back of the room and then a distorted shadow crossed the aisle between the lined shelves.

"Just a sec," a deep guttural voice called out.

The shadow began to come into focus, and Jael recognized Officer Manning.

"Detective Reynolds. What can I do for you this late in the evening?" Manning was a huge guy with a head of thick reddish hair and small pinpoint green eyes. His standard gray uniform stretched taut across his chest and midsection. A well-trimmed red beard with flecks of gray covered the lower half of his face.

"Hi, Manning, sorry to take you from whatever you were doing, but I need to check on something so I can finish this darn report before the next millennium."

"Hey, that's the pits. But better you than me. Whadda ya need?"

"The man arrested for the dealers' murders earlier today . . ."

"Man, wasn't that something? I mean what a bastard. Go figure."

"Yeah, I'm boggled too. Probably why I can't remember a simple thing like one of the more important numbers in his phone book."

"Isn't it in the report?"

"Yeah, but Sills filled that in and I'm having a hard time reading his handwriting. I hate to bother you, but could you get the phone book for me?" Jael shrugged her shoulders as if impatient about it all. "I'll have to keep it for a while."

"No problem—we have that scum's personal belongings right up front. Not much, though, just his wallet, watch, phone book and the gun he tried to use to off you guys. Glad to know you all came through that one okay."

"Thanks, Manning."

Manning moved over to the shelf at his left and rummaged through the boxes, pulling one down. He returned to the gated window and looked through the stuff. Jael saw the deep blue worn phone book on the bottom. Her heart began racing.

"Here it is. Just need for you to fill out the form. You know the drill."

Officer Manning pushed a sheet of paper through the slit at the bottom of the window, and Jael hoped he didn't notice the quiver in her hands. Using the pen tied by a white string to one of the rails on the cage, Jael focused on the form, writing in the appropriate information, finally signing her name, badge number and department.

Manning took the form and briefly glanced over it before

passing the phone book in a clear plastic bag through the window. Jael nearly snatched it and took off out the door, but held herself together, refraining from any desperate and betraying acts.

"Thanks again, Manning. Hope to finish up soon and get out of here."

"Lucky you," he called out as he replaced the lid and she began to walk away. "My shift doesn't end until six in the morning."

Once she was on the other side of the property room door, she shut her eyes in shame. She had lied how many times just then? One lie after the other. But this was no time to question her motives. God *had* to know she could think of nothing else. Nothing but her son and getting her hands on the phone book.

She was given a sudden moment of peace as another scripture flashed into her mind—2 Chronicles 18:20–21: *And then the Lord said to the lying spirit, Thou shalt entice him, and thou shalt also prevail: go out, and do even so.* She only hoped she wasn't fooling herself and enticing the Lord's anger by applying scripture for her own purpose.

Clutching the book to her chest, Jael nearly ran back to the main office and only slowed down when she reached the lobby. She casually passed the receptionist again, gave the elderly man a weak and tired smile and pushed open the glass doors. She heard the ringing of the phone before she reached her desk.

Chapter
31

Startled into near speechlessness, she suddenly understood just how carefully she was being watched.

"Now we're at the good stuff. Let's see how well you make this drop and then I'll know if you can play the game called *'Let's Save the Two Little Nigger Boys.'*"

Jael forced herself to listen to the timbre and quality of the voice in the event the time came to recall it later. Whoever was speaking didn't bother to disguise his voice, meaning he had no fear of recognition. She looked around—who was watching her?

"You promised to let me speak to my son."

"Hold your horses, Momma dear. When I have this first item in my possession, then you can talk. So far, you've been a good little girl. So, don't try anything smart now. If anyone even acts like they know what's going on you can say good-bye to Sambo here. Now, listen. Go directly to your car and start driving home. When you get to Jefferson and 42nd, toss the phone book out the window toward the new Laundromat. Keep going, don't look back and you'd better make sure no cops are around waiting. I think you know the drill. Oh, and by the way, make sure the book doesn't get wet. Still a little rain left from the storm, you know."

The click of the phone was terrifying. An icy-cold wave of nauseating fear settled at the pit of her stomach.

Whatever was in the book was important, and Jael knew that someway, somehow, she had to retrieve this information for herself as well. But she'd been ordered to leave and head straight home. The drive was only about fifteen minutes. How could she copy the book and make the drop in so short a time span?

She was being watched closely, but she had to try.

Jael set her purse on the desk, the opening facing her so she could slide the phone book in. The strain of the past hour was giving her a whopper of a headache and as she looked at the gaping mouth of her purse, an idea came to her.

Making a big issue of rubbing her forehead and squeezing her eyes shut, Jael lowered her head onto the desk and dropped her right hand, the one holding the phone book, down between her knees. With her left hand still rubbing at her brow, she used her right hand to slide open the bottom drawer of her desk and pull out a small Instant Shot camera used at crime scenes. With the phone book in her hand facing out, it camouflaged the tiny camera behind it.

With eyes shut, she pretended to heave several times as if she were about to throw up. Jumping abruptly from her chair, Jael dashed for the ladies' room, where she slammed into the nearest stall. With her back against the door, she ripped the cover off the camera, opened the phone book to the front page and quickly began snapping pictures of page after page between forced gags and coughs. Thankfully, only a few pages were filled, with numbers, names and some kind of weird symbols.

She simulated throwing up until she'd shot all the filled-in pages. Slipping both the phone book and camera into her jacket pocket, Jael pushed open the stall door, walked over to the sink and turned on the water. She splashed her face and throat with the cold liquid, then looked up into the mirror. Had anyone seen her? Oh God, was she playing with her son's life? But handing over this obviously important piece of evidence without knowing what it contained was out of the question.

Jael slowly left the ladies' room, holding her stomach in case anyone was watching. And who would that be? Who at the precinct was in cahoots with these terrible people? Was it someone she'd laughed with, or ordered around? For that matter, had the person given her orders? No one was above suspicion. At least no one in white skin. With that in mind she could eliminate who her enemies might not be. *The Lord will make my enemies my footstool. If God be for me, who can be against me!*

As she passed the reception desk, she patted her stomach for the benefit of the elderly gentleman behind it. She finally remembered seeing him a few times before when she'd stayed late to wrap up a case. She was grateful his name tag was visible.

"I guess all this madness is getting to me—stomach did a complete flip-flop."

"Yeah, I saw you taking off like the devil was at your heels. But don't let this case get to you, Detective Reynolds. We need you to take care of these scumbags." The man sounded dead serious, and the look on his face seemed sincere.

"Thanks, Wells." *The devil at her heels? Oh how true that was,* she thought. But the case couldn't get to her any more than it already had. For a moment, a wave of disbelief and doubt aimed toward God swept over her as she moved back into the squad room. How could God have allowed this to happen? Hadn't she done everything she could to show Him she was now a true and dedicated servant? *Why, God, why?*

Instantly, Proverbs 3:5 leaped into her mind. *Trust in the Lord with your whole heart and lean not unto your own understanding.*

Had she crossed that line in trying to figure things out on her own? Would God punish her for a moment of doubt? And what about all the lies she'd told in the last hour? Would God turn His back on her and leave Ramon to perish because of her sins?

Jael shook her head hard and gritted her teeth. The adversary was throwing darts of doubt at her as fast as she tossed them off. She'd have to be on guard like never before. There was no question in her heart that she was in the clutches of a serious spiritual battle. Warfare at the highest level.

At her desk, Jael stared at the phone for a second before picking up her purse and slipping the shoulder strap over her arm. The walk out to the officers' garage was a trek through fog amid an ominous sea of crouching demons, all posing as innocent vehicles in the dimly lit area. The click of her heels echoed throughout the garage, sounding as hollow as the pit of her stomach.

When she reached her Bronco, she slipped in the key, looked around the parking stall before opening the door, tossed in her purse and climbed inside. Adrenaline-fed blood pumped crazily through her veins as Jael turned on the ignition and let the car idle. She lowered all the windows and quickly switched off the radio, which was tuned to her gospel station, in order to hear anything that might be going on around her. Slowly she pulled out of the garage.

Glancing into her rearview mirror, she watched for anyone following and scrutinized every vehicle she passed. Not many cars were in the parking area this time of night, but the few that were she imagined them as demons waiting to pounce. When she hit the end of the ramp, bright street-lights lit up the night beneath a black and cloudless sky.

Positive no one was following her, Jael waited until she'd passed a traffic light and was in the middle of a block laced with buildings tightly pressed side by side before reaching into her pocket and pulling out the phone book. It felt vile in her hand, and she tossed it onto the passenger seat.

She drove for five more blocks, watching every corner, curiously analyzing every passing automobile and late-night pedestrian. Even the bum sleeping in a balled position atop an old cardboard box was a possible suspect in this cloak-and-dagger nightmare. Jael slowed down as she approached another derelict curled just beneath the underpass. He seemed not to notice or hear the sound of her vehicle. Passing, she kept her eyes zeroed in on him for any sudden movement, but he never moved, and seemed deep in his dreams, without a care in the world.

She still couldn't understand why God had allowed this cruel insanity into her life. *What have I done, Lord? Why have you directed your anger toward me? Was it because I was flirting with Grant?* She knew in her heart that the God she served would never be so petty. He was a just and fair God, full of mercy, and she knew that even in this ordeal, all things would work together for the good. Just as quickly, Jael realized she had just fought another bout of doubt.

"Dear Lord!" she said out loud in anguish. "Is this some kind of test? Oh, God, I can barely stand it. Please deliver me from this terrible mental battle. Take away this maddening fear. BRING BACK MY SON!!!"

Jael's insides were crushing in on her. She could barely breathe from the hurt. She wanted to scream at the Lord for letting this happen. She wanted to plead to Him to just make it all go away and take this cup from her. She wanted to curl up in a corner and cry her heart out.

Instead, she began pleading the Blood of Jesus over her son, claiming her right as a child of God and placing her petition of victory at the throne of Jehovah.

"No weapon formed against me shall prosper! I am strong in the Lord and in the power of His might! I will put on the whole armor of God and stand against the wiles of the devil!"

By the time she reached the drop-off point, a peace had settled over her heart, along with the surprise that verses were popping up in her spirit she hadn't known she'd committed to memory.

Jael slowed the Bronco down, reached over for the phone book and tossed it out the passenger window. Her detective instincts continued to kick in as she rolled away, prompting her to observe every moving item around her. She smiled and praised the Lord to spite the worry in her heart.

Chapter
32

Before stepping into the house, Jael proceeded around the side and back of her home, noting any specific changes that might give her a clue as to how the men had entered. Nothing seemed out of place.

As she reached the back door Rhonda said she'd found open, Jael saw that it was now shut. A ragged splinter of wood, just at the curve of the door lock, stuck out like a beacon, increasing Jael's feeling of being violated. As small and slender as the strip of wood was, Jael could see how Rhonda might have missed it, thinking the boys had taken off in haste. But as she touched it lightly with her forefinger, Jael knew someone had used a crowbar to break into her home. That also explained away any doubts that the boys had left the back door unlocked through carelessness while they were still safely inside.

From what little Grant told her, she remembered that these people usually worked as single instruments of destruction, but Jael was positive that more than one person had been at her back door.

Jael pulled her keys from her shoulder bag and unlocked the door. Pushing it inward, she was met with the chaos of the kidnapping. What Rhonda had probably assumed was bad housekeeping on the boys' part, Jael knew was the aftermath of the abduction.

An untouched pepperoni pizza lay open in its box on the kitchen counter. Glasses of Big Red and A&W root beer were spilled across the table, and a single, unused paper plate lay upside down on the floor. And more important than anything else was the fact that one lone counter stool was tilted against the kitchen sink just over the plate on the floor, as if one of the boys had been snatched while preparing to get a slice of pizza.

That was the strike that released the tide Jael had held tightly within her for the last hour. Slumping to the floor on her knees, she crossed her arms before her chest and wailed, rocking back and forth. Her insides felt as if they were being ripped out with a hot iron. For five solid minutes she rocked, pouring her heart out through the tears. Wounded, she reared her head and screamed to the one source she had left.

"Oh God, help me, sweet Jesus, help me! I'm losing my mind with fear. I know your Word tells me not to fear lest that which I fear most come upon me, but dear Jesus save my baby! Save me!"

She sobbed and cried out to God until it felt her heart was as raw as her throat with pain.

When the doorbell rang, Jael chose to ignore it. She brought a hand to her mouth, then dropped it. She pulled herself up, rubbed her hands over her cheeks, hobbled to the kitchen sink and turned on the faucet. Cupping her left hand, she filled it with cold water and splashed it over her face. The doorbell rang again.

Jael reached for the dish towel and wiped her face. *Dear Lord, I can't take the pain. You said you'd never put more on me than I could bear, but oh God, I'm dying inside.*

The doorbell stopped ringing, but whoever it was began a persistent pounding. Jael shut her eyes and sighed. Slowly she moved toward the front door. She had no time for Rhonda, and would be as polite as possible but would get rid of her.

Jael opened the front door a crack. Grant stood outside on the front step.

She spread a grin she didn't feel across her face. "This is a bad time, Grant. I was just about to prepare for bed."

"Aren't you curious how I found your house on my own?"

"You're an FBI agent. I would imagine you could get around in a small town like Dadesville."

"If the boys are already in bed, I thought maybe you and I could go over a few strategy points. I promise not to keep you up too late."

"It's been a long day, Grant. I'm really tired. I'll see you tomorrow, okay?" Her hands began to shake and she clung tightly to the doorframe to still them.

Grant stared at her for a few minutes without speaking. He leaned closer. "You okay?"

"Just tired. Please, I'll see you tomorrow."

Grant finally nodded and stepped back from the door. Jael closed it on him as politely as possible and headed straight for Ramon's room.

There she stood just within the door of her son's room, tears welling up in her eyes. *Lord, please keep my son safe until you deliver him back into my arms.*

Once again, a shadow of doubt that she would ever see

Ramon alive again passed through her mind. Shutting her eyes, she prayed. *I rebuke you, Satan, in the name of Jesus. I will not listen to your lies. For nothing is impossible for God. Faith is the substance of things hoped for, the evidence of things unseen.*

Jael continued exercising her faith as she moved about Ramon's room touching his belongings. When she placed her hand on his pillow, she loudly declared, "BY THE BLOOD OF JESUS, I CLAIM THE SAFE RETURN OF MY ONLY CHILD, RAMON."

She held on to the conviction of that statement in her heart, fighting the urge to fall beneath the weight of fear. Fighting the evil imaginations of her son being cruelly mistreated in the hands of the enemies threatening to defeat her.

Under an anointing she had never experienced before, Jael fell to her knees as if she had been knocked to the floor. Her head slumped onto the WWF blanket on Ramon's bed. She gave herself over to the grief and moaning that claimed her. Yet, within this pain she began to speak as if her mouth were no longer her own. Words poured from her lips, words she had never uttered or heard before. And in her grief she could sense the power and flow of the Holy Spirit over her.

She let Him have His way, grateful for the evidence of the presence of the Comforter. When the fever of the spiritual flow began to subside, Jael praised God for touching her in such an intimate way during her darkest hour. She remained on the floor, too spent to rise and unwilling to break the spell that had wrapped her in its peace.

She felt safe on the floor beside Ramon's bed, felt close to him. Someway, somehow, she believed, she would come through this storm victorious. She arose feeling strengthened and encouraged. For now, the stronghold of defeat had lost its grip, her faith was joyously renewed.

Leaving her son's room, she headed for her own, slipped out of her jacket and tossed it on the chair by the bed. Something heavy inside the pocket struck the arm of the chair. Jael turned and lifted the garment, and the Instant Shot camera slipped out onto the carpet. In her haste to get home, she had forgotten all about it.

Quickly, Jael slipped her jacket back on and headed for the front of the house and out the door. A twenty-four-hour Walgreens, with a one-hour photo department was just a few blocks away. Jael raced to the store, parked the Bronco haphazardly and bolted through the electronic doors.

A teenage girl was waiting in line at the photo counter and the clerk was ringing up her order on the cash register.

Uncharacteristically, Jael stepped up beside the customer, slapping the camera on the counter. "I need this in an hour."

"Just a minute, ma'am, I'll be right with you." The clerk never looked up, obviously used to handling pushy customers.

Jael danced back and forth on the ball of her feet in an effort to control herself while she waited. What lay inside that camera could be very helpful in locating Ramon and Terrell. But waiting an hour would drive her crazy. When the clerk finally finished with the teenager, she politely smiled at Jael as she began filling out Jael's order form.

"Is there any way you can rush this?" Jael asked.

"I'm having a little trouble with the photo printer. If all goes right, I can have it to you . . . let's see . . ." The clerk looked behind her at the huge clock on the wall. ". . . By twelve forty-five."

That was just shy of an hour. Jael gave the young woman her phone number and address and started walking around the store, trying to think of what to do until the pictures were ready.

Then she remembered the extra Bible she kept in the Bronco. Leaving the store, Jael climbed into her car, picked the Bible up from the backseat and turned on the radio.

Tony Evans was preaching on one of the late-night slots. It seemed the message he was delivering in his strong, robust timbre was being spoken purposely for her. As she listened to his commanding voice, Jael smiled. This had happened more times than she could count: There would be a pressing matter she had to contend with, and God would speak to her problem over the Christian airwaves.

"The devil is the father of lies and will take your worst situation, twist it, fill your mind with false images of defeat in an attempt to steal your victory. But the Lord wants you to know that Jesus defeated Satan at the Cross. Take your eyes away from the problem and set them on the Lord. Remember 1 John 4:4: *Greater is He that is in you, than he that is in the world.*"

Jael had caught the tail end of the program, but knew the Lord was speaking encouragement to her. Flipping on the overhead light, she opened her Bible to Isaiah 26:3: *Thou wilt keep him in perfect peace, whose mind is stayed on thee: because he trusteth in thee.*

Those words had always been a source of encouragement for her, lifting her spirits when all else seemed to fail. As she read both them and the passages that followed, she was filled with a surge of hope and expectation. She became so wrapped up in the Word that when she finally glanced at the dashboard clock, over an hour had passed.

Jael closed the Bible, lifted the maroon leather book to her lips and kissed it. "Thank you, Lord. Thank you for renewing my confidence that this matter is in Your hands."

Back inside the drugstore, she rushed to the counter. The clerk smiled again as she handed Jael the photos in a Walgreens package.

"Thank you," Jael murmured as she quickly paid before rummaging through the pictures. Out of a series of twelve possible shots, only eight were distinctly focused. The lined pages were slanted on the prints but clearly revealed names, numbers and those weird symbols.

At first she recognized none of the names, which were actually pen names, like Redneck Fred or Fiery-mouth Thomas. But the name "Red Dog" jumped out at her like a glaring neon sign. It was the same name she'd seen at the barn shed and again at Jasper's house, but it also seemed to ring in her mind from someplace else. Where; where? Jael glanced farther down the list, hoping to jog her memory. Many of the phone numbers were outside Dadesville's area code, and even those seemed to have several digits too many. She would need to have it decoded to garnish any worthy information from it. And just how did she go about getting that done? The FDLE—the Florida Department of Law Enforcement—could take days to get back to her, and she'd have to have others involved during the process.

Jael let out a sigh of frustration. All this photo work may have just been a great waste of time. Still, at least she had the pages, and maybe they would prove valuable later.

Dropping the package of photos back into her purse, Jael

headed out of the store and back home. Once at the house, she threw her purse on the table.

"Show me what to do," she cried to the ceiling.

When she could think of nothing else, she went to the computer. There she spent the next four hours downloading as much information as she could about the Klan, the Aryan Nation, and Nazi sympathizers. She was amazed by the amount of disgusting information readily available to anyone searching the Web.

The more she learned about the organization, the more she realized the sad state of the world around her. The more questions she came up with, the fewer answers there seemed to be. *At what point*, she wondered, *does a man cross the line of dislike and distrust to enraged hate? Is there a certain kind of person whose nature allows him to harm another human being with no remorse? Can you honestly teach a child at a tender age to grow up and be a killer?*

As a woman who'd worked in law enforcement for many years, Jael knew the sad answer to these questions. She knew the kind of world she lived in; it was why she felt such a strong need to protect the innocent. But today, the fight was for herself, and for her beloved son.

Chapter 33

Sometime during the night Jael left the computer, stumbled into Ramon's room and fell asleep across his bed, inhaling the sweet boyish scents of his sheets. An insistent ringing beside her head brought her groggily awake, sore and far from rested. The head-splitting noise continued until the answering machine finally picked up.

Hearing her son's innocent voice during the introduction "This is Ramon"—then her own voice—"And Jael"—yanked a choking cord around her heart. She listened to his hearty completion, squeezing her eyes in sorrow: "We're not home right now. But you know the drill. Have a Jesus-filled day."

The next voice she heard tightened the cord.

"Pick up the next time this phone rings or else."

Jael sprang from the bed as if the mattress were on fire. Even though there was a phone right on the stand beside Ramon's bed, she raced out the door and into her own room, where she'd heard the man's voice speaking from the answering machine. With her hands clutched to her throat she stood before the phone, taking in deep gulps of air, and waited. It couldn't have been more than two minutes, but it seemed like hours before the phone rang again.

Jael took note of the Caller ID number—it was a pay phone—then snatched up the receiver.

"Hello."

"Running a little late to work this morning, aren't we, Detective?"

"Let me talk to my son!"

"Oh, he's waiting anxiously to talk to you, too. A big crybaby, that boy. But when you speak to him, you'd better tell him to keep his teeth off my flesh or he'll come back to you toothless. Now, before you two get too sickening with the Mammy-and-Sambo crap, you'd better listen and listen well. I need the gun that was retrieved at the barn. You've got two hours to get it. I'll call back then on your cell phone. When I know you have the weapon, you can speak to your bad-ass boy. Then I'll tell you what to do next."

"Why didn't you just have me get the gun when I got the phone book?" she screamed.

"Don't get smart-mouthed with me, Ms. Detective. I'm testing you. So follow your orders like a good little nigger and stop thinking you run shit." He slammed the phone in her ear.

Jael immediately hit *69. But the phone rang and rang. She finally gave up after the fifteenth ring. Placing the phone back in its cradle, Jael looked down at the clock beside it. It read 7:53. She was already late.

When Jael arrived at the station, Tammy handed over her messages with a raised eyebrow. Giving Tammy what she hoped was a nonchalant shrug, Jael shuffled through the messages. One was from Big Jake, which was a surprise, and another was from Virgil, which wasn't, reminding her that he was picking up Ramon tomorrow.

For possibly the first time since her divorce, Jael desperately prayed that Ramon *would* get to spend the day with his father.

She debated heading straight for the Captain's office and telling him what was going on. *A smart officer would do that right now,* she told herself; *a smart officer would have done that from the beginning.*

Shoving her messages in the front pocket of her purse, she asked Tammy, "Is the Captain in his office?"

"No, he hasn't come in yet."

"Try his cell phone. I'll wait."

Tammy gave her a strange look, then clicked in the Captain's number on the office switchboard.

"I'm getting his answering machine," she said after the fourth ring. "Do you want me to leave him a message?"

"No, try to reach him at home." Jael turned to leave, then called over her shoulder. "Transfer the call to my desk as soon as you get him."

When she pushed through the double doors, the squad room was in its typical busy state, with officers shuffling back and forth going about their daily duties. Sills was at his desk.

"Not your norm to be running a little late, is it?" he addressed her, whirling a pencil under his nose. "But with all that's happened, I guess you're allowed one 'off the clock' day. So, how're things going on your end?"

Avoiding direct eye contact, Jael pulled out her chair and

busied herself with pushing paper around on her desk. "Haven't gotten much more than what I had last night."

"Seems you had a heavy date last night—could that possibly have something to do with why we're a little late to work this morning?"

"I had no heavy date, and what I do is my business. Why is everyone around here trying to hook me up or marry me off?" The words sounded sharp even to her own ears.

"Hey, don't bite my head off. I just—"

"I'm sorry, Sills, I've got a lot on my mind," Jael said as she scanned the medical examiner's report, still not looking directly at Sills. "I got very little rest last night."

Her partner obviously decided not to comment on that statement. "Well, if you're interested, what I've got so far isn't much either, other than the fact that our suspect is proving to be an arrogant bastard. Got a real smug look on his face this morning and all cocky as hell."

Jael could imagine he was. Whoever he was working with was pulling her strings like she was a puppet. Her nerves were wired to the snapping point. *Oh please, just let me get through this day, Lord,* she thought. Then she'd take her son home, kiss him until he howled and then maybe she'd disappear for a few days with the boys and go fishing or something. She had a lot of vacation time accumulated, and she would share every minute of it with Ramon, after he got back from his dad's. Right now she wouldn't think twice about going along with them. She'd put up with Virgil just to be near her son.

The phone rang.

Jael snatched it up so fast it slipped from her hands and

she had to fumble with it in the air. Sills raised an eyebrow and leaned back in his seat.

"Hello, Detective Reynolds here."

"About time you got to work. Did you get my message?"

Jael could have screamed. It took every ounce of control she had and then some to keep from slamming the phone back in its cradle. "Yes, Virgil, I got the message. Ramon will be ready on time for you to pick him up." *From my lips to God's ear*, she thought.

"I want him to wear his beige suit, the one I bought him last year. He looks sharp in that, like real money."

Jael imagined Ramon in the expensive beige suit and smiled for the first time that day. Yes, her son did look sharp in that outfit. She remembered the first time he'd worn it to church. You couldn't have told him he wasn't the cat's meow.

"I think it's at the cleaners right now. But he can always wear the navy-blue one—he looks great in that one, too."

"I'd prefer the beige one, so see if you can take care of that, okay? I'll swing by somewhere around sixish." Virgil hung up without a good-bye. Typical.

When she replaced the receiver, she could feel Sills staring at her.

"I know this ain't none of my business, but once again, is something going on with you I should know about?"

"No. Why do you say that?"

"For one, it's obvious you're anxious about a certain call. You look kind of rough around the edges this morning too, like you've slept in a dog's bin. Your eyes are all bloodshot and frankly my dear, 'bad hair day' is too gentle a phrase for you."

Jael self-consciously reached up to touch the side of her hair. She had no doubts Sills was telling the truth. She'd taken off right after the frightening call, without looking into a mirror.

Now she thought of heading to the ladies' room and doing what she could to spruce up, but at the same time she was apprehensive about leaving the phone unattended in case her torturer called again.

Yet, if he had spies all around watching her as he'd claimed, he'd know when to call and when not to.

It suddenly struck Jael that Sills was a white guy. Maybe one she rarely thought of as white—more like a human chameleon—but Caucasian, nonetheless. Could she have spent so much time with Sills and still not really know him? Of course, she told herself, that could be true about anyone, but although she couldn't recall him ever acting in a racist way on any of the many cases they'd handled together, how could she be sure that what he put out was genuine?

She remembered that soon after they'd met and she received the first promotion, he seemed happy enough, though not completely *overjoyed* that his new boss was black *and* a woman. Over the years he'd come to adjust as their friendship grew, but had that been a farce all this time? Or was she just getting paranoid about everything?

"Earth to Detective Reynolds, Earth to Detective . . ."

Jael shook the thoughts from her head as she took in Sills, who was waving a hand back and forth in the air to recapture her attention.

"Hey, where were you? You want to talk about it?"

Jael finally gave Sills a full stare. Folding her hands on her desk, she leaned forward and said, "If I remember correctly, you seemed really surprised to learn there was an active white supremacist group in Dadesville, and not simply your average group of racist nuts."

Sills leaned farther back in his seat. "Where is this coming from?"

"I mean, you're a white guy, right? Wouldn't you have just a little more insight or knowledge about what was going on in the white community?"

"Hey, you're confusing these guys with human beings. They mingle with normal people but they know who and who not to approach with that mess. I haven't lived my life with my head in the sand, but honestly, I had no idea we had folks right in our very own town conspiring to *serial murder.* I just don't hang with that sort."

"Never even overheard anything, walked in on a conversation between these kinds of individuals?"

"I've heard a few things, yeah, but not among hard-core racists. I've heard bad racial jokes and slurs. People who say things out of anger. I've even had one or two calls from little old white ladies who swore a black man was following them, but much of that is the nature of the kind of society we live in. Either you believe in the stereotyping or you don't. You forget that as an officer of the law, we're required to take tolerance courses."

"Yeah, but you have to admit, there's been reported racial profiling in police departments all over this country."

"But has that been the case here? Mayor White makes sure Captain Slater doesn't allow that ball game around here. He's tough-nosed about that."

Jael thought about this, and about Sills himself. But someone in the department was the eyes and ears for whoever had her son. Jael glanced at the phone again, and decided to head to the ladies' room now.

"If my phone rings, just let it ring until I return." She pushed back her chair and rose. "I'm going to take your advice and spruce up a bit."

"Hey, you don't have to do it on my account."

Jael offered him a weak smile and headed for the rest room down the hall. Once there, she couldn't believe how rough she actually looked. Dark circles swelled under her eyes from all the crying she'd done last night. And her hair . . . well, she'd seen orangutans with better styles.

As she ran a comb through her thick auburn hair and redid the rubber band, her mind kept wondering what Ramon was doing at that moment. Was he crying his heart out, scared out of his mind and begging for her? These thoughts were the worst kind of torture. She needed the Captain. And since he had yet to return her call, she'd have to try and run him down. That could take time—time she didn't have.

As she reached into her handbag to pull out a tube of lipstick, the door to the ladies' room opened and Tammy stepped in.

"Hey, Detective. We've got a busy day ahead of us, with the media and all. They're having a field day with these killings. I overheard that CNN was stationed outside," she said, taking a quick look at herself in the mirror.

"Yeah," Jael replied without much thought behind it. Then her eyes suddenly widened. Tammy. Why not Tammy?

The girl certainly had access to all the phone calls at the department. She could be the one working for these guys.

As Tammy stepped into one of the stalls, Jael turned completely around from the sink and stared at the closed door. She could see Tammy's high-heeled feet at the bottom of the opening.

"The Captain call back yet?"

"Not yet."

"That's really something about those white supremacists having a murderous group right here in Dadesville, isn't it?" Jael asked loudly.

"Knocked *me* for a loop," Tammy said on the other side of the door. "What do you think's going to happen to this Upton fellow?"

"Well, lucky for us, Florida law has capital punishment. Can't say I'm not rooting for them to fry the guy."

"Well, I don't really agree with capital punishment. It's an awesome decision to say who should die or who should live."

Up until now, that had always been Jael's perspective: Capital punishment was a decision left to God. She didn't support it either, but she was trying to feel Tammy out. "So, you think someone who kills people because of the color of their skin should be allowed to live?"

Jael heard the toilet flush, and then Tammy pushed open the door and came over to the sink. "If he's guilty he should certainly be given life. But death, for killing drug dealers? I just don't know," she said, leaning over the sink to rinse her hands off while at the same time pushing back a strand of frosted blond hair from her forehead.

Jael turned to look at Tammy in the mirror. Tammy fluffed her hair a bit more at the bottom and then pulled a tube of bright pink lipstick from her purse.

"Have you ever heard of this group Upton is supposedly associated with?" Jael asked.

"You'd be surprised the number of organizations that crop up for the sole purpose of sticking their noses in the air at other folks. There's an exclusive country club over in Naples that doesn't publicly say it, but you won't find members of anything other than pure Anglo-Saxon there—well, of course, outside of a few janitors."

It wasn't a direct answer to her question, leading Jael to consider how little she knew of Tammy's life outside of the workplace. She knew she had a daughter and had recently divorced, but other than that she had no idea what the woman did for a social life. Tammy knew a lot more about her life than she knew about Tammy's.

Jael attempted a playful laugh. "Don't tell me you're a member?"

"Have to make more money than I do here to join that club." Tammy gave her hair one more pat. "Well, got to get back to work. Don't want anyone to think I'm slouching on the job." With that, she walked out of the rest room.

Jael turned back to the mirror. Tammy had never said she disagreed with the philosophy of the club. It hit Jael like a sledgehammer to realize how little she knew about the people around her. It was humbling to acknowledge how something of this magnitude could suddenly slap her in the face and she had no idea where most of her coworkers stood. Outside of those who'd joined the Bible study group, she had little interaction with them. And she never asked coworkers about their personal lives outside of the office, thinking it would be nosy. Maybe Billups *had* something when he'd accused her of not being a team player. That didn't sound like a very sharp detective—more like an alien in her own land.

She'd received her share of hostility when she became an officer of the law, and even a bit more when she was advanced to detective. But the things she overheard about herself were words like "pushy," "bossy," or "overachiever," with very few direct racist hits. That didn't mean, however, that those words were not used behind her back.

As Jael left the ladies' room she carefully took in her surroundings, watching her fellow officers stroll back and forth, heading wherever. Some spoke to her in a friendly manner, while those she didn't know personally passed right by.

When Jael stepped through the doors again, thoughts about her coworkers dominated her mind. Then she froze in place. Billups was standing at her desk, holding her phone to his ear.

Chapter
34

"What are you doing?" Jael yelled much too loudly as she rushed up to her desk and snatched the phone from Billups. She covered the mouthpiece with her hand as she glared at him contemptuously.

"Hey, just trying to be helpful," Billups answered with an insulted snort. "What's the matter with you?"

Jael had to catch herself. She was overreacting. Though not commonplace, sometimes fellow officers assisted one another by taking their calls.

"Sorry, I guess I'm a little stressed out with this case."

"Yeah, whatever," Billups said, throwing his hands up with a scowl of his own as he walked away in a huff.

Jael watched him leave the room before bringing the mouthpiece to her lips and speaking into the phone. "This is Detective Reynolds."

"Hey, girl, thought I was going to hear about what happened to the boys last night."

Jael closed her eyes. Rhonda was obviously at work, where she often used the company phone for personal calls. It seemed Jael was getting her own share of personal calls this morning—but not the one she was waiting for.

She flopped wearily into her seat. "Sorry, I got busy and forgot."

"Yeah, well, I hope you told them a thing or two about leaving that house without telling you."

"You were right: They'd gone to the corner store for something to eat. I'm going to make sure they remember to leave a note or something next time." With that, she made a few excuses about being busy, promised to call later and hung up.

Jael looked over at Sills's empty seat. He was probably out working, like she knew she should be doing. It wasn't his responsibility to watch her phone. And of all people to come along and assist, Billups was the last person she'd have expected to find at her desk. He'd always been a thorn in her side, and she wouldn't put it past him to be the one watching her from afar. His very nature seemed to attest that he was more than willing to keep certain people in their places. He had never shown anything but resentment toward her. And he had often used words like "affirmative action" and "quotas" in the negative. Yes, he was a perfect candidate for groups like Upton's. And she still had yet to ask him what he was doing coming out of the Captain's office.

Jael sat up in her seat and began writing herself reminder notes. What did Tammy do when she was away from the station; and what about Billups—what was his social life all about? She also wrote down Sills's and Captain Slater's names. Right now, no one was above suspicion.

But she had a bigger problem on her hands than whether or not certain people were what they seemed. She had to get that gun. She couldn't wait much longer for the Captain's direction.

Rolling back her shoulders, Jael decided not to dwell on it and just do it. She had no other choice.

When she arrived at the property room, an officer other than Manning was behind the cage, filling out forms.

Jael walked up and plunged right in. "Manning off today?"

"Naw," the gruff-looking officer said. "Just on break."

"Well, I'm working on the Upton case and I need to have a look at the gun Upton used during the shooting. I'm sending it over to the FDLE to compare the grooves in the barrel to the one found on the bullets of the deceased." Dear Lord, she was lying like a pro. *Oh please forgive me, Lord, but do I have any other choice?*

"Like who doesn't know you're on the case. But didn't they get a match on that earlier?"

"Yeah, but you know how we always forget to share information with other departments."

The officer—Jones, according to his badge—gave her a curious look, then hunched his shoulders. "Yeah, well, it's your headache, not mine. Wait a sec."

As Jones moved off to collect the gun, again Jael asked for forgiveness, but more important, for her son to be sent back today. Dear Lord, she was going crazy. How much more of this could she take?

"Here you go. Just sign this sheet, Detective, and you're all set."

Jael took the paper he passed through the window, hoping her anxiousness wasn't apparent. She signed the paper and took the gun, still in its plastic bag. Before she was halfway down the hall, her cell phone rang.

"Good girl—you were followed down to the property room, and came out with our nice little package all secured."

Jael quickly glanced around her and stepped as close to the wall as she could get.

"I want to speak to my child now!" she said with as much conviction as possible in a lowered voice.

"And you shall. Just for a moment—to show my good faith and all."

Jael heard a noise like metal chairs scraping across a wooden floor, and then the voice she lived for.

"Momma, Momma?"

"Ramon, my God, oh baby, are you all right?"

"Momma, I wanna come home. When are you going to come get me?"

"Soon, baby, soon, but are you all right? Have they hurt you? Can you—"

The connection was broken, and then the other voice was back. "That's enough. Now, here is your last job; after that you can have your brat back. You've got the gun—now I want you to have Upton released, and to make sure he has the gun on his person when he walks out of there."

"Are you crazy?" Jael hissed into the phone as she pressed herself even closer to the wall. "I have no authority to have a prisoner released!"

"Oh, you can work something out, I'm sure. Aren't you the top coon there? Don't screw with me. Use that so-called brain you've got and have our boy released so we can release your boy."

There it was: the "we" word. Had he slipped before and she'd missed it?

"I can't do it. You've gone too far! I refuse to play any more of your games!" For a moment, hate rose within her, sudden and swift. She spoke her next words through gritted teeth. "You're messing with the wrong woman!" As the anger swelled inside her, Jael could barely hold her temper. "This charade is over. Now release my son or I'll personally see to it that your butt fries."

"So you want to play it like that. Okay, I have someone else who'd like to speak to you."

For at least thirty seconds, Jael heard nothing. She was afraid they'd decided not to come back on the phone when suddenly she heard another voice on the line.

"Ms. Jael. Ms. Jael! Please get us out of here. I'm sorry I didn't do a better job of watching Ramon, but we need to—"

His words were interrupted by the sound of a crude and funny "*pop*" and then nothing. Nothing but empty silence. Icy fingers clasped her heart with a death grip.

"Terrell, Terrell!" She was nearly screaming now. If anyone had been in hearing range they would have certainly come running to her aid.

"Well now, that's one less nigger boy to be trying to get under the skirt of an innocent white girl." The hateful voice was back.

"Oh Jesus, oh Jesus, what have you done? Put him back on! Oh please, put him back on the phone!"

"No can do. Too late for that. If you want to play games, you need to know who's the master game player. Now, I have no qualms about offing this other useless nappy-head jungle monkey. DO YOU UNDERSTAND ME? I want to see Upton walking out of that building in the next two hours. There'd better not be any cops around, because your son will be there watching. When we see Upton, we release your boy." The line went dead.

Jael slumped against the wall. Oh God, she had let anger kill Terrell. How could she have ever believed this evil would come to a quick resolution? How had she allowed the devil to play her so completely? Where was the victory she'd so heartily believed in just a few hours ago? The battle seemed almost impossible for her to endure. "Dear Lord," she pleaded softly, tears clouding her eyes, "forgive me. I know you will not put more on me than I can bear." She spoke the words through obedience, though at this moment they seemed empty and hollow.

Jael had never felt so alone in her life. Never felt as if the world was caving in on her so completely, or that the God she called "Lord" was not supernaturally intervening on her behalf, and bringing this madness to a swift end. And what was even worse, she couldn't tell anyone about it, share her pain and fear.

"Are you all right, Detective?"

Jael jumped, then quickly straightened from her slumped position against the wall to see Officer Stephanie Woo, a Chinese-American street patroller, moving toward her from a back room. She quickly wiped at her eyes and gave the woman, whom she'd given many pep talks, what she hoped was an encouraging smile.

"Yeah, yes, just a little work-weary."

"I can relate. Doing double duty myself, and running late," Woo said, smiling. Moving off, Woo turned back and said, "Oh yeah, Tammy said you were near the property room and to tell you the Captain's back." Then, with a backhand wave she moved toward the exit and out the door.

Jael scanned the hallway for any other observers, then closed her eyes, sucking in a deep breath. The impact of what had just occurred slammed through her soul, and once again she nearly collapsed from the horror of it all. Steadying herself with one hand against the wall, she pushed away from it, completely dead inside.

Chapter
35

Her legs were no longer her own. They propelled her by their own will. Her mind had finally crashed. Her eyes were open, but not really seeing. God had deserted her, and for good reason—she'd allowed her anger to cause Terrell's demise. She'd not followed protocol by involving the Captain. She'd missed her chance to put the matter in the hands of the law. Now she had to do what she had to on her own. Even though a small voice inside her cried that God would not, could not leave her alone, her guilt and pain were too overpowering to allow her to hear it. She felt as if her struggle were hers alone. No guidance, no voice from heaven, nothing but an emptiness and tightness in her chest that hurt so bad it was difficult to breathe. *Where are you, Lord, when I need you so desperately? Why won't you step forward and strike my enemies down?*

In a robotic stroll, Jael headed to the left of the station and to Captain Slater's office. The door was closed. Jael knocked twice.

"Yeah, come in."

Jael shut her eyes, prayed words she would never be able to recall and stepped inside.

"You've been looking for me, Detective? What's up?"

"Captain, I have a proposal I want you to think about. It may seem far-fetched, but if you will hear me out I think you'll see that it's what we need to break this entire case." Jael moved toward the Captain's desk, unaware that another person was in the office leaning against the back wall.

"Far-fetched? Like how far?"

"The prisoner we have in custody is just the tip of the iceberg of something much larger and more sinister. We know he's not talking and will probably never tell us who else is behind his killing spree."

The Captain leaned back in his chair, giving her a quizzical gaze. "Okay, I agree with you so far. But where is this all going?"

"I think if we play our cards right, we can get this guy to lead us to bigger fish."

A movement off to her left caught Jael's eye, and her heart sank as she watched Eric Grant move forward. She hadn't even known he was in the office.

"And how, may I ask, do you propose we do that?" the Captain asked, never taking his eyes from her.

Jael swallowed. "By releasing the suspect and following him."

The Captain sat straight in his chair. He stared at her for a moment and then gave her one of his ugly bulldog frowns. After a moment, he began drumming his fingers on the desk and sucked in a deep breath.

"Okay, Jael, I see this case is really getting to you and becoming too much for you to handle. Maybe it's become a little too personal . . . because of the pending promotion and all. How about I let another of my men take over now? You've done an outstanding job so far, but you look like you could use a little rest. Why—"

"No, wait a minute," Grant interrupted as he stepped closer. "Let's hear her out. She might be on to something."

Jael looked over at him and wished she were dead. She turned back to the Captain.

"Think about it. We could get more birds with this one stone—locate the others, get names and addresses and really clean up the town of this kind of filth. We can't just leave this to a bunch of lawyers ready to make this a federal case and a way to spend more taxpayer dollars. We all know there's more than just this guy involved. It might work."

"It can work," Grant agreed. "Since this is sure to be a federal case, I can have a surveillance team in operation in less than two hours. It could be just what we need to crack this ring and get the big guys at the top."

Jael held her breath. The words "two hours" scared the beeswax out of her. If Grant got involved, he could delay the release.

"If we're going to do it, we have to do it now. Make it look like a screwup on our part, and we're covering our behinds, or whoever he's working with might get suspicious," she quickly added.

"No way am I going to allow this," the Captain said, shaking his head. "It was foolish of you to ask."

"But, Captain—"

"I said NO. This is the dumbest thing I've heard yet. Release a prisoner, Detective? The only suspect we have?"

"I think it might be the only way," Grant offered.

Captain Slater sucked at his teeth, then twisted his lips. "And you think this might work, Grant?"

"It's the best idea I've heard so far." Grant nodded his head at Jael, then back at the Captain, waiting for his answer. Jael waited, trying to keep her body from shaking all over.

"Something like this, as you know, has to be cleared through the State Attorney's Office first. And if it back-fires, I don't want the press trying to hold me responsible for releasing a criminal in this case. They're already waiting around outside like vultures for us to make a slip." The Captain began shaking his head again in the negative. "No . . . I just don't—"

"I'll take full responsibility," Grant quickly interjected, placing both his palms on the Captain's desk. "I'll get the approval from the State Attorney's Office, even if I have to pull some federal coattails. The FBI's not here simply to see that this case is handled by the books, but to completely eradicate this bunch from any further activities."

"I . . . Well, if you're taking it out of my hands," the Captain said, settling back in his seat with his palms held out-ward. He gave both Jael and Grant a look she couldn't decipher. "Then you can do what you feel the FBI thinks necessary."

"How soon can we move this along?" Jael asked, a little too eagerly.

"Why don't the two of you work that out. I'll sit back and see how it plays out. But make damn sure this doesn't fall back in my lap. This department doesn't need any more bad press," the Captain barked. And if the bark had any bite, for once it had little effect on Jael. She was simply glad this part of her plan had worked out so easily.

"Yes, sir. You've got it." Jael glanced over at Grant, gave him a weak smile, then quickly exited the room. She was afraid if she gazed at him any longer, he might see something in her eyes she couldn't afford to let him see.

Thank you, Lord. Please let this be the right thing I'm doing. Please let this all work out.

Jael was passing the rest rooms, just a few doors away from the Captain's office, when suddenly she was pushed through the entrance of the men's room, nearly falling on her face. She heard the loud slam of the door as she fought to keep her balance while swiftly turning to confront her attacker.

Grant was glaring at her, his back against the door to keep out any intruders.

"What the . . . ?" Jael began.

"Okay, talk to me. I want to know right here and now what's going on with you." Grant pointed to the floor for emphasis, his eyes burning with intense anger.

"What are you talking about? Let me out of here." Jael pressed forward, attempting to push Grant aside, but he grabbed her upper arm and held her tightly a few inches away from him. "Let me go," she hissed. "I have no idea what you mean by stopping me like this."

Grant released the tension, but not his hold.

"You know exactly what I mean, Jael. Ever since we returned from dinner last night you've been acting like another person. I don't have to have known you for any great length of time to tell you're scared out of your mind about something. And that little charade you pulled in the Captain's office has a lot to do with it."

"You're wrong. I—"

"Don't play me, Jael. I just went along with your idea because I could hear the desperation in your voice and I wanted to see what this was all about. Now either tell me what's going on with you or I march back in there and tell the Captain it's off."

Jael threw her palms up against his chest as if to hold him back. "Oh please, Grant, no. Let me do this the way—"

"Then talk to me, and talk to me now." Grant placed his hands over her palms with a consoling touch.

Jael's lips began to tremble. She squeezed her eyes shut, fighting back the tide of tears threatening to break forth, and pulled her hands away to clutch them into fists at her side. She struggled to maintain control, but as she realized what he was asking her to put into words, the reality of it all set in.

At first she couldn't speak, couldn't even think of how to say it. Her hand rose to cover her trembling lips; then her entire body began to shake.

"Jael, please . . . talk to me."

The concern in his voice and the gentle touch of his hand on her shoulder was her undoing. As flashes of Ramon in pain, crying out for her when she couldn't help him, raced across her mind, it finally all came crashing down on her. Her head slumped and she couldn't hold back the tears.

"They have my baby! They have Ramon! He was taken last night and unless I release Upton, they'll kill him just like they did Terrell."

"What?" Grant's eyes widened in shocked disbelief.

"I heard it! I heard what couldn't have been anything but a weapon being fired while I was on the phone with Terrell." Jael reached out and grabbed Grant's coat with both hands, her expression naked with pain and desperation. "I know they've ki—done something terrible to him. And if I don't get Upton out of jail today, in two hours, the same thing happens to Ramon."

Grant was silent, digesting all she was telling him. When he pulled Jael into his arms, the burden she'd endured for too long relieved itself in great sobs of despair. Her entire body heaved against him as she let go of the pent-up anguish. The weight she carried for so long gradually began to ebb with the knowledge that finally someone else knew, finally there was someone to share the fear and pain. Grant held her until the shaking began to subside.

As the racking moans turned into pain-riddled sobs, Grant gently pushed Jael back to look into her eyes. "Jael, do you understand what's happening here?"

She tilted her chin, struggling to hold back more tears. "Of course I understand. I have two hours to get Upton out of jail!"

Grant put his finger to her lips and shook his head. "You're allowing your fear to play right into their hands. I've seen too many of these kidnappings not to know that it's rarely that simple." His strong features creased with worry.

"No, don't say it."

"Listen to me, just listen," Grant hushed her. "We're going to follow through with the release, but you have to trust me and let me handle this."

"I can't. I'm being watched. I was going to inform the Captain earlier but things escalated too fast. I—"

"Jael, I want you to walk back to your desk as casually as possible. When I come up to you, begin screaming at me like you hate my guts."

"Wha—"

"Just do it. Say something like you wish I'd leave your case alone, or something to that effect, which will make anyone watching believe you're trying to get rid of me so you can follow through with what they want. After I leave, wait about fifteen or twenty minutes, then head to your squad car—not your Bronco; the press might see you—and drive off. Do you understand?"

"Should I tell the Captain?"

"Just go directly to your desk. Trust me."

She took a deep breath. "All right."

"All right. Play the angry role, then after a while go get in your squad car and drive away. Let me do what I'm trained to do and you do what *you* know how to do."

"What's that?"

"Pray."

Chapter 36

Minutes passed like drug-intoxicated hours. Jael could barely stand the waiting, watching everyone who moved around the office with looks of suspicion, because now everyone *was* a suspect. At the same time, her eyes fell consistently toward the phone on her desk.

At one point, she was so intently studying the phone and thinking how such an inanimate object could be the epitome of so much fear, she didn't hear Grant walk up behind her. When he touched her shoulder, she nearly jumped out of her skin. She didn't have to pretend.

"What is wrong with you? You scared the daylights out of me!"

"Sorry, didn't know you were so jumpy." Grant stepped back holding his hands up in front of him. A broad smile crossed his face. "Just thought we could go celebrate our first arrest together."

"Celebrate? Are you insane? I've told you before, leave me alone. Don't you understand English, or should I write it in some kind of FBI code. LEAVE ME ALONE!"

The change on Grant's face was so abrupt Jael almost rose from her seat to apologize.

"You're coming through loud and clear, Detective," he said, turning his shocked expression into one of anger. "I guess the name they call you around here was well earned." Grant made a gesture of tipping an imaginary hat. "Consider me a thing of the past." With that, he pivoted and left the office.

Watching him leave the squad room, Jael noticed the three duty officers standing in varying parts of the room, transfixed in their spots while pretending not to have overheard her outburst. She offered them each an ugly scowl, which sent them all quickly back to whatever errand they were doing before her shouting match with Grant.

Jael had partly risen from her seat while acting out her part with Grant. Now she slumped back into her chair, drained.

What the heck am I doing? I don't have time for these games when my son's life is in jeopardy. I need to be getting Upton out of jail, not waiting around for precious minutes to pass.

She wondered how Grant expected her to sit patiently for fifteen or twenty minutes while he did whatever it was he was doing. And exactly what *was* he doing? Was he talking to the Captain, putting plans into action to rescue her son?

When Sills walked in, Jael was grateful for the diversion.

"Hey, partner. What you got going?" Jael prayed her voice gave nothing away of her anxiety.

Sills flopped in his seat before answering, then grabbed his trusty pencil and began circling it around his fingers. "A team from the prosecutor's office is in the conference room poring over the Upton file. I hope you don't mind, but when you couldn't be found I had to take what was on your desk and hand it over to them."

"Thanks, Sills, you've covered my butt a lot lately. I won't forget it."

"You'd better not. But if I can be so bold, what the heck is going on with you? I just saw your FBI friend storm out of here. Is he the reason you've been miles away from this case? Normally, you would be all over the prosecutor and defense lawyer. This just ain't like you."

"Yeah, well, I've had other things on my mind, and it hasn't been that FBI agent. I'm just so concerned about whoever else might be involved with Upton and these murders."

"What's this fascination with the phone all of a sudden?"

Sills was a good detective, and Jael realized now that she should have known his keen and observant nature would soon start formulating a reason for her actions. Besides that, he could certainly be the one telling those guys what she was doing.

"Okay, I'm busted. It's my ex-husband and a personal matter that I have unfortunately allowed to interfere with my work."

"He's threatening to seek custody of Ramon again?"

Jael jumped at this line of thinking. "He's gone way past threatening. He's got a lawyer. Can you believe it?"

"Does he have a chance of taking Ramon from you?"

"No one is ever going to take Ramon from me!" The words dropped so cold and harsh from her lips, Sills fell back in his seat.

"And I believe you. Hey, I'm not the villain here, just trying to help."

"Sorry, I don't mean to take my anger out on you, but as the saying goes, don't mess with a lioness's pup. She'll do whatever is necessary to protect her own."

Just then the phone rang. Sills looked at it, up at Jael, then back at the phone again. Jael stared blindly at it, as if she didn't recognize what it was. She took three deep breaths before answering.

"Detective Reynolds, Homicide." Her voice sounded frightened even to her.

"Time's a-wasting. You're down to an hour and fifteen minutes."

The phone went dead, but Jael continued to hold it to her ear. After a few seconds, she said, "You'll want the juvenile department for that complaint, ma'am—this is Homicide."

Slowly she replaced the phone in its cradle. Sills was watching her, his head tilted. Neither of them moved. Then Jael glanced at her watch and began to shift papers on her desk as if she were getting down to work.

"Remember, Jael. I'm a friend."

Jael raised her eyes without lifting her head, casting him a curious stare. Could she be sure of that?

Chapter 37

The parking garage for squad vehicles and employee autos was darker than usual. After getting off the elevator at the ground floor, Jael walked slowly toward the third row and her car. Every footfall seemed intensified as she moved along, her hand on her shoulder holster.

The loud slam of a car door pierced the otherwise dead silence of the garage, and Jael jumped nearly a foot off the ground. Seconds from pulling out her weapon, she heard her name called out in greeting.

"Hey, Detective Reynolds, you know you're the bomb. You're all over the news. You go, girl."

Jael recognized the rookie officer moving toward her as one of the new female African-American recruits she'd taken a liking to and encouraged as often as time allowed. The woman was with a white male officer Jael had never met.

"Hey, just doing my duty," Jael answered, pleased with the casual way her voice sounded.

"All I can say is I'm glad you're getting that kind of trash off the streets. Makes my job a whole lot easier," the woman said, then looked curiously at Jael. "You're off duty already?"

"No, more like on a personal errand, if you know what I mean."

Jael didn't miss the small grin that crossed the male officer's face. She tensed.

"Yeah, I got you. That was another notch for you catching that suspect like you did," the woman said.

"No personal credit for me—it was the entire department."

"Good work, Detective." It was the first words the man had spoken.

Jael moved toward her car, giving him a curious look. "It's far from over. This was certainly not a one-man operation."

The man's grin widened, and Jael's heart began to pump faster. As he moved slowly toward her, Jael stiffened. "Hey, you mean there's more brains behind the operation?"

"That's what we have to look into." Stepping backward toward her car, she slipped her key into the lock, all the while keeping her eyes on the officer. She said her good-byes and got into her car. The man was still standing there watching her. Throwing up her hand in a good-bye wave, Jael pulled out of the garage, a little too fast. In her rearview mirror she could see that the white officer had not followed his fellow officer but stood there gazing after her.

"Keep your eyes on the road and don't look back."

"JESUS!" Jael's heart leaped into her throat, her head just missing the roof of the car as she nearly jumped out of her skin from the sound. The voice was coming from the back of her car.

"Calm down, it's me, Grant."

"Grant? What are you doing hiding in the backseat of my car?"

"More important, what are you doing climbing into your car without checking *out* the backseat. You can't take any chances." Jael heard Grant make a growling sound. "It's tight as I don't know what back here."

Jael could imagine his huge frame wedged between the back and front seat in an attempt to hide from any unknown observers. If not for her current circumstances she might have laughed.

"Where should I be heading?" she asked, keeping her eyes straight ahead as she pulled out of the parking garage. Fortunately, the media was stationed at the front of the police building and not watching the side as she departed.

"Keep a look out for a tail. Make sure you're not being followed; if you're not, head in the direction of my hotel on Brower Boulevard. In the meantime, if you can pull into a gas station or something so I can get out from back here, I'd appreciate it."

Jael drove for about five minutes, keeping an eye out for anyone who might be trailing her. When she was sure she wasn't being followed, she pulled into a Chevron filling station. In the dark isolated area behind the car wash, she said, "Okay, you can come out now."

Grant unfolded his body from the backseat, moving like some kind of huge beast, and exited the back door. He opened Jael's door.

"Move over and let me take the wheel."

Jael was happy to oblige and slid over, then leaned her head back against the rest and closed her eyes.

"Okay, that's better," he said, giving her a quick glance.

"Now we'll head for my hotel while you tell me everything you know so far."

Which wasn't much. After giving him a quick review, she asked, "What are your plans, Grant? I know you mean well, but I can't let you jeopardize my son's life."

"I'd never do that. But these guys are playing ugly. I don't want to scare you any more than you already are, but they may be lying about giving your son back to you alive."

"Don't say that!" She lifted her head, giving him a hateful scowl.

"Jael, you have to be aware of the fact that if Ramon can identity them, they can't take that chance."

That very thought had hovered at the back of her senses since this nightmare began. She'd fought even thinking about it, and now Grant was saying it out loud.

"Father, I give myself completely over to You," she whispered, lowering her head, her hands in tights fists in her lap. "Save my son."

Grant gave her a supportive look. "I'm sure He heard you."

"Believe me, this is certainly the right time for praying without ceasing. Even when I feel no one's listening, I have to remember the adversary wants me to think just that."

"Their venom is the venom of dragons."

Jael frowned and glanced over at Grant. "Pardon me?"

"From the Book of Deuteronomy, 32:33. It's from the ancient eastern Aramaic text of Peshitta. I believe the King James version goes more like, 'Their wine is the poison of dragons, and the cruel venom of asps.' I tend to like the Aramaic translation, which more adequately describes this scum."

Jael shook her head in awed disbelief. "You have amazed me from the moment I met you."

"I'll take that as a compliment. I hope you'll still feel that way after we reach my hotel. I plan to equip you with a tracking device. I also have one I want to attach to your vehicle. Then, I want you to call my cell phone number from your cell phone just before Upton gets in your car. Keep the phone line open so I can trace you and hear your conversation."

With all that had happened in the past two days, Jael wondered if she had remembered to recharge her phone battery. *Oh God, please let it be charged up.*

"With the device and your cell phone, I'll be able to keep in touch with you by an overhead helicopter and know exactly where you're ordered to take Upton."

"Won't these guys be aware of a helicopter hovering in the air?"

"I certainly wouldn't put anything past them. But I know what I'm doing. I need you to follow my instructions to a T. Remember to speak clearly so I'll know how they plan to make the exchange."

"Oh, Grant, it's all . . ."

"I know, but we can't make any mistakes now. Remember, Jael, think like a cop now, not a mom."

Jael wasn't sure if she could.

Chapter
38

Filled with trepidation, and constantly looking over her shoulder for any sign they were being watched, Jael remained silent as Grant pulled the squad car into the hotel parking lot.

Without turning off the ignition, Grant jumped from the car. "Wait here. I won't be a moment."

Those few minutes seemed like hours, as she sat waiting in the idling vehicle.

Sweet Lord, how could something like this ever be allowed to happen? I've lived a good clean life. I gave up painkillers, tried to be a good mother, fought as little as possible with Virgil and I go to church every Sunday. I even go Tuesday night for Bible study and Saturday for prayer meeting. I sing in the choir and read my Bible all the time. I prayed that the Blood of Jesus would always remain over me and my family. I thought I was doing everything right. How could this be happening to me?

Jael waited to hear a voice explain all the whys, but only the hum of the engine answered. Looking around the hotel parking lot, she noticed tourists climbing in and out of vehicles, many in swimsuits and already tanned. For them, life was filled with the promise of a great and blissful holiday.

Overhead the sky was a brilliant powder blue. God had fluffed up the clouds into gigantic misshapen white towers. It was an awesome sight, displaying all the majesty of the heavens. Jael never failed to appreciate such beauty in humbled awe. Just as Psalm 8:3—*When I consider thy heavens*—always filled her with wonder.

"Lord, hear my prayer. Receive my petition for my baby's safe return. I acknowledge I was weak and foolish and had no right to question you, but I now come boldly before your throne. I stand on your promise to never forsake me, and lay my heart on the altar of your mercy. I put aside all whining and false imaginations of the devil, because through Christ's Blood I am more than a conqueror. I will hold that fast to my heart and count on you to see me through."

She knew that right now, more than anything, she needed to keep her spirit saturated with the Word. Leaning forward, Jael pressed the CD button on her dashboard. The music and words of one of her favorite choirs washed over her, delivering the needed inspiration.

> *Never fail to cast your cares on Him,*
> *Because He cares for you*
> *Hold fast to your faith, and*
> *He'll see you through*
> *If you never let go of His hand*
> *He will answer according to His plan*
> *Remember, through every situation*
> *Just hold on, and God will see you through.*

Those words were just what she needed right now, a reminder to HOLD ON. Jael mouthed the words as they filled the car, receiving and absorbing the message.

She jumped at the soft knock on her door. It was Grant. He'd approached unnoticed, and she realized it could have been anyone. In his eyes she saw concern and encouragement. She lowered the volume on the CD with a trembling hand.

"It's going to be all right, Jael. Hold on to your faith and don't let it waver. This is only a dark time you're going through, which may be a test to see how much you truly rely on the Lord."

She thought of her earlier moments of doubt with shame. Of course it was human to have moments of fear, but this was a battle like no other. It was time to stand fast. To speak the words that would give her the victory.

"I can do all things through Christ who strengthens me. I will rely on Him with my whole heart. I have nothing now but my faith. Bless the Lord." She was silent for a minute before continuing to speak. "I haven't put all the pieces together yet, but I feel strongly that Tammy, the receptionist, is involved. She knew about my incoming calls, and another officer let it slip that Tammy knew I was at the property room. Billups is also a prime suspect; he may be Red Dog and the one who put Ramon's chain in my desk."

Grant nodded, then handed her a small mechanical device. "Do you know how to attach this voice-sensitive tracking device to your clothing?"

"I learned at the academy. I still remember."

"Okay, while you do that, I'll attach this other one to the tail of your car."

Jael looked at the small silver instrument that Grant had attached by four small slivers of duct tape. Releasing the top two buttons of her blouse, Jael pressed the contraption to the tender flesh just within her lace bra. She was buttoning the top button back up when Grant returned to the window.

"So far, so good. Now head for the jailhouse and get Upton out. Agents are on their way to pick me up, so I'll be right behind you."

The ringing of her cell phone startled her. Jael glanced at the phone, then back at Grant. He nodded toward it.

"Hello."

"You're down to forty-five minutes. Once Upton is released, wait for my call to tell you where to drop him off."

"Wait a minute! We have to make an exchange. I'll drop him nowhere until my baby is safe in my arms."

"The process for the exchange will be explained after Upton is released. Wait for my call."

"He says he'll explain the procedure for the exchange when I have Upton," Jael said after she'd clicked off.

"Typical." Grant looked around. "Okay, remember everything he tells you. Speak clearly into the mouthpiece. You don't have to worry about the actual release; by the time you get to the jail, I will have taken care of all that. Upton will be released into your custody. I'll be near every step of the way. You'll never be alone for a minute during this ordeal."

For the first time in hours, Jael felt this was true. Where had Grant really come from? she wondered. Had God foreseen all of this and sent her someone she could see and touch to remind her He was there? As she drove away, it gave her a good feeling to think that God loved her so much that He had sent someone to watch over her. She was aware that she could certainly be fantasizing the whole idea that Grant was a guardian angel, but oh, how she needed to believe it, to feel that God was working so personally on her behalf.

"If he is or not, Lord, thank you for allowing him to be around right now," Jael softly whispered inside the car.

When she had driven about five blocks from the hotel, forcing herself to stay within the speed limit, she was so deep in prayer and worship that she never noticed the maroon Buick that pulled out behind her at Jamerson Avenue and 12th Street. Nor that the vehicle followed her, always two car lengths behind her, all the way to the county jail.

Chapter 39

I can do all things through Christ who strengthens me, I can do all things through Christ who strengthens me. I can . . ." Jael allowed the words to flow through her mind and found more courage with each passing phrase. It was a tonic to her soul. A renewed surge of hope lifted her spirit. Her shoulders straightened and her chin tilted with a holy arrogance. She was not in this battle alone. She had to keep remembering that or the adversary would crush her with fear and doubt. It was the toughest battle Jael had ever been in.

When Jael arrived at the Dadesville County Jail, she parked in the space allotted police officers and exited the car. People were milling around outside waiting for their husbands, sons, brothers or whoever to be released or for the next visiting hour.

She entered through the main entrance door and headed for the information booth. No one she was familiar with was at the desk, but the process would be easily handled if Grant had completed his end of the arrangement.

Jael moved up to the caged window. "I'm Detective

Reynolds. I'm here to pick up inmate Whitman James Upton."

"One second, Detective," a white-haired clerk told her as he clicked away at the keys on his computer.

Within the span of a minute or two, the clerk looked up. "Upton is already in the inmate release room. Captain Slater left not too long ago. It shouldn't be more than another ten minutes."

The Captain was here? So he must have decided to assist with her plan. Jael looked at her wristwatch. It was already 4:52. She would be cutting it very close. "Can they rush it a little? This is a very serious case I'm working on here."

The man smiled. "I'll do what I can."

"Thank you."

As Jael moved toward a bench, her cell phone began to ring. She almost dropped it trying to get to it so fast.

"I'm here. I'm waiting for him to be released," she hissed into the mouthpiece.

"Waiting for who to be released?"

"Virgil?" she said, her voice full of exasperation. "Oh, not now, Virgil, you'll have to call me later."

"Don't you dare hang up on me!"

"Virgil, this is a bad time, I—"

"With you it's always a bad time. And you never bothered to return my calls, again. Jael, I don't want any more problems with you. If you keep this up, I'm going to have to force the judge to look into your—"

"Not now, Virgil, please, I don't have the time! I'll call you later." Jael hung up.

She'd forgotten Tammy had told her she'd had several calls

from her ex-husband. She didn't need this additional headache right now. The phone began to ring again.

"Detective, your man is ready."

Jael turned to the door to see Upton standing on the other side of the cage, his grin as wide as the length of the snake that seduced Eve, and just as hypnotic. She completely forgot the ringing phone in her hand.

Chapter 40

Moving through the gate, Jael faltered a bit, not wanting to be near the man. His vile depravity seemed to roll off him in waves. *If ever a person could be described as evil incarnate,* Jael reflected, *it could be said of this man.* And the first words to come from his mouth were like righteous blasphemy.

"God will purify this land of corruption and evil, and I am proud to be his instrument."

Jael pulled out her handcuffs and slammed them on his wrist. "I think you might consider getting a better heavenly connection. You seem to have nothing but a lot of static."

"Yeah, make jokes now, but you'll soon see who's running this show, and it ain't you," he sneered.

"It ain't you, either, and if you open your mouth again you may feel the wrath of God in a very physical way."

"That would be police brutality, something your people are always screaming about, and against the law."

Without thinking about it, Jael used her elbow to give him a quick jab in the side. The man whoofed and doubled over. She gave him a sneer of her own. "If you people want to antagonize me into breaking the law, how about I just go the whole hog. I'd love taking all my anger out on you."

The surprised look Upton gave her was the first moment of satisfaction she'd experienced in a while. For now, at least, he knew she was not playing games. Jael pushed him ahead of her out of the cage and said a hasty good-bye to the clerk.

Upton stumbled before her, grumbling under his breath all the way to her vehicle, but he didn't open his mouth again. When Jael had him secured in the backseat, she waited a few minutes for the next call. It came right on cue, letting her know she was constantly being watched.

"Now, for your next instruction. Drive to Piller Junction and Interstate 301 about twenty miles outside of Dadesville. At the corner of Jackson Street and Washington, you will see a white van with the words 'Budget Air-Conditioning.' Wait across the street for the call as to what you are to do next. Don't do anything foolish. Your son will be in that van, and it can pull off at any time."

Jael was getting sick and tired of all the threats, and finally made one of her own. "Let me make one thing perfectly clear right now: If one strand of hair on my son's head is harmed, whoever you are, I will smell you out and track you down. Make absolutely sure you know what you're doing. Because, believe me, you don't want to make me any angrier than I already am!"

"My, my, getting a little edgy, aren't we?"

"When I get to this corner, will the exchange be made there?"

"It all depends on you. If you've informed anyone, and I mean *anyone*, you can forget any kind of exchange or seeing your dear boy. Do I make myself clear?"

A bitter edge crept into her voice. "Loud and clear."

During this entire encounter, Jael watched Upton grinning his butt off in her rearview mirror.

As Jael started the engine and pulled out, she watched for any vehicle that seemed to be following her. She wasn't more than a mile away from the jailhouse when she noticed a car trailing slowly behind her. To be certain she was actually being followed, Jael made several unnecessary turns, which resulted in a full circle of the jailhouse. The tail never let up.

"I guess that black sedan that's been on my tail since we left the jail is some kind of escort." These words were spoken solely for Grant's benefit. "I guess your people don't trust me."

The man in the backseat grunted.

Jael prayed Grant knew what he was doing. He'd said the hearing device attached to her chest was sensitive and would be able to pick up the conversation on the cell phone. He'd also said to leave the phone line open, but how could she do that when the abductors might attempt to contact her at any moment?

Jael was a mass of wired nerves. *I can do all things through Christ who strengthens me.*

"When you get to Thompson Road turn left." It was the first words Upton had spoken since they left the jail.

"What?"

"You heard me—when we get to Thompson Road turn left. I'll tell you where to go from there."

"But your friend or whoever he is said to keep on Jackson just outside of Dadesville."

"There was a little change in plans prior to my release. Can't have you trying to trick us now, can we? Just do like I tell you and it'll all be fine. The white van will just be in another location."

"But—"

"What difference could it make to you what direction we take to your son? Turn here, yeah. Just do what you're told, Mrs. Smart-ass."

As Jael made the smooth turn at the corner, a late-model, white Ford sedan was idling a few yards away in the middle of the street. Before she was a car's length behind it, two men in ski masks jumped from the vehicle and rushed toward them. With a gun in his hand, the first man ran up to her window.

"Get out of the car. Move!" Jael hit the brakes, threw the gear in park and pushed the door open. While edging out of the vehicle, she pulled the cell phone and concealed it within the palm of her hand, pressing the ON button at the same time. The other man yanked open the back door and Upton jumped out and rushed to the waiting vehicle in front of them.

"Over to the other car. Don't make this any harder than it has to be," the man said, pushing her toward the waiting vehicle. As the other man opened the passenger door for Upton before jumping in the back himself, Jael could only slide in beside him while attemping to avoid the leer she knew was spread across his face.

"Get these damn handcuffs off," Upton said, shoving his cuffed wrists toward the man in the back beside her.

Yanking off his ski mask, a man with a face as ugly as Igor's asked, "Where's the keys to the cuffs?"

"I think I left them in the—" Jael suddenly felt the press of the gun at the base of her skull.

"Don't screw with me, nigger!" Spittle flew from his skeletal, blue-veined lips, his breath a lethal weapon of its own. "Hand them over."

Slowly Jael reached down to her waistband and lifted the keys to the cuff. Without looking into the man's face again, she passed them over, dropping them into his open, meaty palm.

"What I wouldn't have given to see the look on Ms. Detective's face when she saw you guys," Upton said as his partner inserted the key. He was back to his old hateful, grinning ways. Once the cuffs were unlocked, he placed his hand on the back of the driver's seat and leaned farther into the back, his breath only inches from Jael's face.

"Getting a little nervous, are we? Well, I guess you know who's running this operation now."

Jael gritted her teeth. "You better make sure nothing happens to my son."

"I think I'll be giving the orders for a while. Now throw your cell phone out the window."

"What?"

"Okay, once again real slow, so you can understand: THROW YOUR CELL PHONE OUT THE WINDOW."

Jael hit the down lever on her window control and tossed her cell phone out while making a mental note of their location and in what direction they where heading. She didn't recognize any landmarks that might help later, just a lot of open fields.

"Now remove any hearing devices you have strapped to your body."

"What are you talking about?"

"If you won't do it yourself, my buddy here will pull over and personally frisk you. He might even enjoy doing it."

The very thought of the vile man's hands touching her body was beyond repulsive. Jael opened the bodice of her top and angrily pulled the device from inside her bra. The tape ripped a thin layer of skin from her flesh.

"Ohh, really smart. Out the window with it, sister."

Jael did as she was told, her courage and safety net going out the window with her only contact to Grant and rescue. *God, oh God, when does this end? Help me, help my baby. Please!*

Chapter 41

She sat in silence, frightened in her mind and in her body. No one noticed or seemed to care, as the men around her remained as silent as stones. It was obvious this had all been prearranged. She could only be grateful they hadn't thought to handcuff her or tie her up—but she was deeply concerned that they hadn't felt the need to cover her eyes, either.

She had lost all contact with Grant. And if they were taking her captive, there was every likelihood they had no intention of releasing her or her son.

Jael felt completely defeated. Blindly, she had followed their every order in hopes of getting her son back, and all she had actually done was allow them to lead her into a trap. And why wasn't the Lord stopping any of this? How far did He intend to allow this to go? She racked her brains to remember at least one person in the Bible who'd fought battle after battle as she was doing now. Only Job came to mind. Though he'd faced one conflict after the other, not once had he ever questioned the Almighty. But she was no Job. What she wouldn't have given right now to have Brenda talking her through this. Even the strongest of Christians, Jael knew, had to fight a constant battle of faith. There were no super-Christians, even if some of her coworkers thought there were.

Jael looked out the window, her heart heavy with regret and jabs of helplessness. Was this how Jesus felt on the Cross? As if God had left Him out in the cold, just like she was feeling at this moment. She knew she was acting like a wimp, allowing feelings of defeat to beat her down and force negative thoughts to surface again, but she was running out of strength. At every turn it seemed she was beaten. She could only take so much. She couldn't even form the words in her heart to call on Him.

She was near tears, fighting to hide them from her captors, when something caught her eye. At first she wasn't sure she'd seen right, and then there was no mistaking it. It was Deke.

Chapter 42

The wheels screamed in protest just before someone yanked open her door and pulled her roughly out of the car by her collar. Jael tried to break her fall by throwing her hands out in front of her, scraping the skin of her palms raw on the cement in the process. Her wrist took the full impact of the fall, and pain raced up her arm to her bad shoulder.

She was still huddled at the side of the walk trying to get her bearing when three huge black men came out of nowhere and jumped into the vehicle from both sides and began whipping her captors with crowbars and fists. Stumbling away from the sudden violence, Jael had little time to react as she fell again to the concrete street. She could hear screams of agony coming from the car as the attackers—she'd recognized the largest one as Big Jake—lashed out at her abductors. Upton's cries were loudest of all.

For a moment, she remained crouched on her hands and knees, amazed at the swift turn of events, recalling her thoughts seconds before the carjacking. She could barely comprehend the fact that God was using these criminals, these drug dealers, as His instruments of justice. But she also knew the Lord often blessed His people through the hands of the worldly.

Still, she had to stop Jake and his boys—not because she was an officer of the law, but because if she didn't, she might never get her baby back.

Jael leaped to her feet. "Jake, stop, stop! Don't hurt them!"

Big Jake didn't bother to turn in her direction. His fist continued plummeting against the head of his victim. "These mothas offed my boys," he spat, a murdering grimace on his face. "I ain't gonna let them get away with that shit."

Pushing up behind him, Jael grabbed his right arm before the next blow, restraining it with all her might. "Please, Jake, don't kill them. I need—"

"What, and leave this up to you guys?" Jake's eyes smoldered with hatred. "You police ain't gonna do nothing."

"Jake, please." Her next words seemed to strangle in her throat. "They've got my son."

Big Jake pulled back a bloody fist in midair and turned to stare at her.

"What you mean?"

"My baby, my only child—they've kidnapped him and will kill him if I don't bring Upton to them."

Big Jake looked at the man in his grip. His victim's nose and mouth were dripping blood and saliva. The man's eyes were swollen and he was half dazed from the brutal whipping. With a sound of disgust, Jake tossed him back against the leather seat. "So what we do now?"

Jael let go of his arm. "Let them take me wherever it is

they have Ramon. Once I have my son in my arms, you can do whatever you want."

As Jake thought this over, Deke ran up to them.

"Here's your phone, Detective. Picked it up a ways back after you threw it from the car."

Jael accepted the phone from Deke's outstretched hand. The other men who'd come with Big Jake halted their assault, waiting for their leader's instruction. How long had Big Jake and his boys been following her? she wondered. Probably from the moment she'd left the jailhouse, where he was sure to have spies everywhere. But thank God they had.

The Klan members could be heard whining and making lame threats. She gave Jake a pleading look of desperation before pressing the ON button on her cell. It took a second to realize it was already on.

Then Grant was on the line. "Jael, my God, what happened? We lost your signal for nearly eight minutes!"

Jael glanced around her. "I'm at the corner of Spruce and Jefferson. But there's been a major glitch in plans." She turned to look up at Jake. "I believe God has sent some really strong avenging angels my way. You can bet it's been a huge surge in my faith. Big Jake and his boys just carjacked us and beat the crap out of Upton and *his* boys."

Big Jake drew in his brows and made a curious face. She could tell he wasn't sure how to take being called a heavenly angel. Not when he'd had only pure murder in his heart. The bewildered look on his face brought the first hint of a smile in hours to Jael's lips.

Grant barked orders in her ear while Jael reached over to pat Big Jake on the shoulder. She had never been so glad to see someone in her life. When this was all over—and now she had a strong conviction in her heart that it would be a truly victorious end—she would personally sit down with this notorious dealer and get him to tell her just how he and his boys had outsmarted both the FBI and the Klan to attempt such a daring rescue.

But though she was encouraged, she had no false illusion that it would be easy rescuing her son.

She returned her full attention to Grant, who was still yelling over the phone. "We have you back on radar! Get back into the car with Upton, but don't let on you're talking to me on the phone. Got that?"

"But what if . . . ?"

"Listen, we got back the trace on those calls. They came from your very own police station."

Jael's throat locked. His news confirmed her fears. She couldn't say a word as her mind raced.

"Now, listen to me, Jael. These people are the only ones who know where your son is. Don't let them know we're still on your trail. We have to play this like nothing's happened."

"You think they would honestly show us to my son now? After the carjacking?"

"You've got to remember who you're dealing with. They're cowards. Use a little healthy persuasion. I'm sure guns are everywhere around you right now. Get what you feel comfortable with and have the dealers remove all the Klan's weapons—I'm positive they'll love frisking someone else for a change. But above all, make darn sure those rednecks lead you back to their base. If you can get the dealers out of the way after the frisk, do it. We don't want anyone hurt or messing up the original plan. But you've got to move quickly!"

"I understand." Keeping the phone line open, Jael moved

toward Jake and placed a hand on his arm. "Big Jake, I can't thank you enough, but we'll take over from here."

"Listen, if this redneck motha didn't have a brotha, I'd finish this right now. I wanted to use my hands instead of guns for the satisfaction of beating the crap out of them. But for your son's sake, I'll back off." His eyes narrowed in a warning Jael could not misinterpret. "For now."

"God bless you, Big Jake."

Big Jake squirmed. "Yeah, yeah," he mumbled, and quickly turned to move away, nodding at his boys to follow.

"Wait!" Jael called out. "What kind of weapons do you have on you that I could use?"

That got a big grin from the bald-headed dealer. "What kind of weapons do you want?"

"You got a AK47 or Uzi?"

Big Jake raised a skeptical eyebrow. "Hey, pretty heavy stuff for a lady, ain't it, Detective?"

"Right now, I could handle a nuclear warhead. And I need you to remove any guns these guys have on them," she said, pointing with her phone toward the car.

Big Jake put his fingers in his mouth and whistled. One of his boys came running.

"Give the Detective here your Saturday night special."

Without questioning the order, the young dealer handed over the gun. Jael weighed it in the palm of her hand. It would do the job and then some. She stepped back as Jake and his boys roughly checked Upton and the driver for weapons. She wasn't amazed by their expertise as they ran their hands through the glove compartment, under the seats and around the rim of the car. They knew all the major hiding places.

With Upton and his gang, they took extra-special attention, throwing in a lick or two in the process. All together
the search took less than three minutes. She was also handed
one of the Klan's cell phones. She dropped it in the left side
pocket of her jacket.

"Thanks, Big Jake. Now I need you to stay far behind.
Don't give yourself away. We're headed to their campsite,
and there's probably a large number of these fiends just
waiting to hurt someone. I don't want that someone to be
my baby. Remember, any surprise action on your part
without a signal from me might result in that happening. I
don't want to risk my son's life."

"Jael, you've got to move—every minute is precious,"
Grant barked over the cell phone.

Jael nodded once more at Big Jake, then jumped into the
backseat right behind Upton, who was still moaning. The
other Klan members looked at her with a mixture of hatred
and fear.

Jael placed the muzzle of the Special against the driver's
neck. "The ball is back in my court. You have at least ten
very angry black men around waiting for me to let them
loose on you. Every move you make is being watched. But if
one of you so much as looks the wrong way, I won't have any
qualms about taking your face off. And I'll still make it to
where you're holding my son with the other guide. Now
move this car and don't try anything funny."

The driver seemed to get the message right away. He
started the engine and pulled off, leaving a mist of dust
behind them. Upton finally sat up and wiped the blood
from his chin with the back of his sleeve. In the rearview
mirror, Jael could see not only the rapid swelling of his right

eye, but the look of revenge he wanted to convey to her through tightened lips and heated huffs. Jael placed the barrel of the gun at his throat. "Keep your eyes straight ahead. I'm tired of looking at your ugly face."

Upton did as she said, mumbling under his breath. Jael lowered the gun to the base of his head, leaning it against the backrest of his seat.

As a seasoned officer who'd seen plenty of active duty during her time on the streets, she'd shot a suspect in the leg once during a robbery attempt, but had never had to actually kill another human being. Today, however, she was sure she could do it. The only thing keeping her in check was her personal witness of God's intervention on her behalf. No one would ever be able to convince her it was a coincidence that Big Jake and his boys had arrived when they did.

God had proven beyond any more doubts that he was the orchestrator of this entire episode in her life, and never before had she felt so much like a soldier in the Lord's army. Thus, she would continue to believe He was protecting her every step of the way and wouldn't want her to take a life out of anger or revenge. But she felt good having the gun in her hand and having the fear reversed to the other side.

As the car moved along at a more rapid pace than before, Jael took in as much of her surroundings as she could while keeping her eyes trained on the men. With the shrill of a phone, she automatically lifted the one in her hand before realizing it was the cell phone in her pocket. The atmosphere in the vehicle turned to icy tension as everyone seemed to hold their breaths. The driver gave her a warning look in the rearview mirror. Slowly removing the phone from her pocket,

Jael returned the driver's look with one of defiance, as she pressed the YES button and placed the phone to her ear.

"What're you guys doing? Put a rush on it. I have a little something special planned for that screwup, Upton." The caller clicked off without waiting for a reply.

A lump formed in her throat as she instantly recognized the voice. There could be no further doubts, she thought, as she slowly placed the phone on the seat of the car. The voice had been unmistakable. How could she have missed it?

When she noticed a slight movement at her left, she quickly spun her gun in that direction and gave the man one good wallop on the neck. He slumped forward, and that felt good to her.

Suddenly a surge of victorious triumph washed over Jael, and she began to speak out loud in prayer.

"No weapon formed against me shall prosper! The Lord shall make my enemies my footstool! Fret not thyself because of evildoers, for they shall soon be cut down like the grass! The Lord shall deliver me from the hands of the unrighteous!"

With each word that poured from her mouth, Jael jerked her head in a sista's "right on" gesture. Upton and the driver exchanged nervous looks. It was obvious Upton's bravado was for sneak attacks only. He couldn't stomach his own pain. Nor, she thought, would he be able to handle the surprise awaiting him. It seemed just the mere words she spoke filled the men with a fear she could never have imagined. Jael let the anointing pour forth with a holy vengeance.

"I have not seen the righteous forsaken! The Lord is my light and my salvation; whom shall I fear? The Lord is the strength of my life; of whom shall I be afraid!"

Chapter
43

For ten minutes or so they drove through a dense, unpaved area of what seemed to have once been an old cornfield, before veering onto a dirt road surrounded by acres of thick grandfatherly trees. After a deep bend in the road, the car pulled out of the wooded area in front of a huge, dangerous-looking fence with barbed wire across the top. Several men, in military fatigues and carrying rifles over their shoulders, moved in squads behind the fence.

Above them the day was becoming increasingly overcast. Dark ominous clouds crept slowly across the sky in thick patches. Another wave of rain could strike at any moment. The atmosphere made the men marching around behind the fence seem even more frightening. One walked away from the others and swiftly moved toward the gate entrance as it electronically opened. As the car slowly rolled into the tightly secured area, Jael scanned the base for any sign of Ramon. She would not let herself even think about Terrell.

Within the campground were numerous makeshift tents, with both women and men trampling in and out of them, several holding hot camp grills. The place was frenzied with activity as many rushed to break down tents and pack. It seemed they were in the process of clearing out.

Long tables with rows of radio equipment and things Jael couldn't even identify issued static noises, while somewhere in the background a sultry male voice singing some kind of country and western tune poured over the site from a loud-speaker.

Before the vehicle came to a full stop, Jael pressed the nose of her gun between the front seats and into Upton's side.

"If even one man so much as raises an eyebrow of curiosity or gives a sign that something's amiss, I won't think twice about shooting you in the heart, Upton, then your partner for good measure. So don't play me."

Upton nodded, and the driver nodded several times, even though Jael was not speaking to him.

As they pulled farther into the campsite, one of the men, holding a threatening-looking Uzi, glanced over in Jael's direction, and she responded in surprise. It was Officer Manning, the clerk from the property room. She'd not added him to her earlier equation; more of the pieces were now falling in place.

When the car came to a complete stop, Upton leaped out, and for a horrifying second Jael thought he was about to scream an alert. Instead, he hitched his pants up over his hips and spoke calmly to the man at the gate.

"Glad that's over."

"What was the holdup?" Jael heard the man ask him. "You're five minutes behind schedule."

"We got sidetracked. This woman put up a real fight."

The gatekeeper was astonished as he looked first at Upton, then into the vehicle. His face broke out in a wide grin. "I don't believe it. The three of you let one little woman beat the shit out of you like this."

"Hey, she's a trained police officer," Upton huffed with indignation. "The boss said don't kill her, just bring her to him. No one said she couldn't kick our asses."

The man opened Jael's door and grabbed her roughly by the arm, yanking her from the car. She barely had time to secretly stuff the gun inside her skirt under her jacket.

"Okay, Mrs. Police Officer, time to pay the piper."

"Where's my son?"

"Well, well, if we aren't about to have a regular little party here."

The voice came from behind her, and Jael turned, instantly recognizing it as the voice on her cell phone.

Even with the knowledge she'd put together a few minutes earlier, it was still a major jolt to actually see him.

Chapter
44

Jael couldn't help feeling like she'd been slammed in the chest with a two-by-four as Captain Slater sauntered up to her with a grin as big as a slice of watermelon on his face. Her worst suspicions were confirmed. Why hadn't she recognized his voice much earlier? The person on the phone had never seemed to camouflage it, but spoke in a rather natural tone.

Answering her unspoken question, the Captain replied in his standard station dialect. "I see by your expression that you realize I'm a man of many talents, Detective. I've loved doing impersonations since I was a kid. What you heard on the phone was my famous Andy Griffith imitation. Kinda have the ole Mayberry boy down pat now. Never knew how useful his voice would turn out to be someday."

Jael opened her mouth to respond, but could think of nothing to say.

Now she knew why the voice had dredged up memories of years gone by. She'd thought it was someone she'd known personally from her past, and in a way it was. She'd watched *The Andy Griffith Show* on television for years.

When she saw Tammy move up beside the captain, dressed in similar military fatigue, she felt nothing. Everything was making sense now, horrible sense. She only wondered how far the Klan had infiltrated the police force.

"You don't seem surprised. I guess I should have known with a hound dog detective nose like yours, it wouldn't take you long to figure out Tammy was sending the calls through and following your every move." He slipped his arm around Tammy's shoulder, giving her a pat of approval. "She's my girl all right. Proud to have her on my team."

Jael screwed her lips together and with a slight nod of her head said, "As for you, you only threw me for a second . . . RED DOG."

The captain's smirking smile faltered, giving Jael her own minute of satisfaction.

"Actually, I'm the Grand Dragon," the Captain threw back, dropping his arm from around Tammy while puffing his chest out. "And all that time, right under your big nose. You didn't think a little internal affairs probe really cleaned house, did you?"

Jael understood that Slater was referring to the internal affairs investigation into the force three years ago concerning racial discrimination charges. Only one police officer had been terminated from the department, with a few others placed on probation. At the time, Slater had been the driving instrument in the sweep. Apparently his outrage and disgust back then had been as much a masquerade as his later voice change. She, like others, had assumed that the majority of dirty cops had been cleaned out. Obviously they hadn't been. And no wonder, when the corruption started at the top.

"How could you do this? How could you take my baby and use him as a pawn to get your dirty work done?" she asked, aware of the desperation creeping into her voice. She covered it by raising her voice louder. "You could have gotten all those things you demanded from me yourself!"

"This is a war, Detective, and there will always be casualties in war." He grinned a heinous, self-satisfied grin. "But we could never allow even the slightest trace of evidence to lead back to me."

"You won't get away with this."

"Oh no? Well, think about this—everything will lead back to *you*, Reynolds. All the missing items from the property room—the gun, the phone book. And everyone at the station will attest to the fact that you were acting strange. You see, with your interference, I had to keep changing my original plan. When I was bragging to your FBI agent about what a great officer you were, that was to throw him off. Make him believe I was a serious nigger lover." Everyone around her joined the Captain in a hardy laugh at that one. "But he knew without my telling him about the history of your little drug problem. So when they find your body, and your son's, the medical examiner will discover a large amount of it in your system. And I'm sure I don't have to tell you what dirty business *that* will bring up again."

Jael was struck speechless. Slater had supported her when she came up for dismissal, saying she had his complete backing. He'd even fought the reprimand to keep her on his team. Drugs were not the issue then. He was obviously just waiting for the perfect opportunity to use it against her. But it didn't make sense. Why so much support when he could have easily had her terminated?

As Jael stood stunned, a movement drew her attention, and she turned to see Upton attempting to sneak away, a huge smirk on his face. In desperation, Jael pulled the gun from her waistband.

"Everyone hold it right now."

At the sight of the gun, everyone either froze or slowly backed away. But Slater responded with an even wider grin.

"Oh, you're making this so easy for me. Playing right into my hands."

Jael refused to be intimidated. "You've got to be a fool, Slater, if you think no one will put the pieces together and know this was all a setup." Jael knew she'd have to play every card she had. This was no longer just a kidnapping. Somehow, Slater meant to leave her and her son behind to take the rap for the drug murders. "People are looking for me right now."

"You mean your FBI agent? I knew he was sweet on you—that little spat between you two worked in our favor. Still, I don't expect him to give up that easy, so I've got another little trick up my sleeve for him. By the time he locates you, I'll have everything in place."

"You can't fool him. He knows everything!"

"Not everything, my dear. Certainly not that at this very minute, I'm not in my office but out attempting to locate you because of a tip I received: that you've slipped and reverted back to your old ways." His voice took on a phony inflection as he tilted his head with mock sorrow. "I'll be so sad when I have to tell everyone that to hide your addiction from the force—which was far more than simple painkillers as you'd led us to believe—you went to extreme measures. I'll feel regret for covering for you. Sorry I'd given you another chance when so many people's lives were at stake. To cover up, you tried to make it look like the Klan was the culprit. It goes on, and on, but I guess you get the drift."

"That's about the dumbest thing I ever heard. No one will believe that!"

The Captain gave a slight nod of his head in the direction of one of his men. The man stepped up behind Upton and yanked him aside. At the same time, someone behind her knocked the gun from her hand as another man roughly gripped Upton's free arm. It all happened so fast. Surprise and realization dawned on Upton's face as he began to struggle.

"Hey now, wait a minute," he squealed. "I did everything as you asked."

"And you gave your life for the cause," the Captain said with a sickening smile. "As our selfless Lone Wolf, you will be rewarded in heaven." To the men holding Upton he said, "Take him away."

Upton's eyes nearly bucked out his head. "No! You said you'd take care of everything. Keep me from prison!" He struggled uselessly, his voice cracking as tears welled in his eyes. "You can't do this, you lying son-of-a-bitch."

"Tsk, tsk, better watch your tongue. You know how Detective Reynolds hates a foul mouth." The Captain broke out laughing at his own cruel joke.

"Whatever evil plot you are planning will backfire," Jael screamed, rubbing her wrist after the assault by the man behind her. "No one in his right mind will ever believe it."

"Oh yes they will. As you can see"—he waved his hand

in a wide berth to include the many smiling faces around him, as Tammy snuggled even closer to him and gave Jael a coy smirk—"I have lots of witnesses. And your ex will be quick to add his two cents when he learns certain dealers were holding your son as collateral."

She studied him for a long moment, holding herself still, but the fury she felt emanated from her like waves off hot, black tar. "You low-down, no-good—"

Jael didn't see the shadow that suddenly rushed up behind her, seconds before the back of her head exploded into a cistern of pain. The hard dirt ground raced toward her face as blackness claimed her.

Chapter 45

Pinpoints of dancing light fought to penetrate the shroud of fog around her, arousing her out of the depths of unconsciousness. As she slowly began to come awake, Jael's head felt as if it were splitting into a million pieces, while a small voice as familiar as her own soul continued to push its way through the haze. A sound she needed to cling to, a tiny whisper that pressed against the heavy fog, demanding she comprehend. Finally, a single word broke through, bringing her fully awake.

"Momma?"

Lifting her lids was torture.

"Momma, Momma, please. Are you all right?"

The words penetrated the fog and Jael rose, then fell back again. Her head was pounding and something was holding her arms so tightly she felt paralyzed. As she began to focus, zeroing in on the words floating toward her, her world soared with relief. There across from her was the sweetest sight she'd ever seen. Ramon was lying on a military cot a few feet away. His arms were tied in front, he looked extremely frightened, but otherwise he seemed okay.

As she tried to rise toward him, she realized that the feeling of paralysis came as a result of her own hands' and ankles' being tied. Her suit jacket had been removed, along with her shoes. Of course, her stockings were now nothing more than shreds of material along her legs and her blouse was a little rumpled, but otherwise everything seemed intact.

"Baby, baby, you okay?"

The scared look in his eyes and the quiver in his lips tore at her heart.

"I . . . I guess so," he whispered. "I . . . What's happening, Momma? Why are you here tied up like this too?"

"It's okay, sweetheart. Everything's going to be all right."

Ramon continued to stare at her, his worry creasing his sweet face. Jael shifted and gave him a reassuring smile before turning her gaze to take in her surroundings.

They were in some kind of old dilapidated barn, filled with the smells of dried hay, mildew and dung. If windows were anywhere, it was hard to locate them, because the area was dark, with the only glimmers of light coming through the slats in the roof and a few split boards on the walls of the barn. Otherwise, there was nothing in the center area outside of the two cots she and Ramon were on and some misshapen shadows, which were possibly old farming tools and machinery, in the darkened corners.

Where was Grant? Where was Big Jake? And did she dare ask where was God? Why was it each time she could taste victory, the devil seemed to be one step ahead of her? How could God expect her to hold on to her faith when she was blocked at every turn? But all she had right now was her faith. Her only weapon was staying strong in the words of the Lord, even when she was plagued by emotions of confusion and disbelief.

Her eyes returned to her son. "Ramon, did they hurt you?"

"No, but they took Terrell away and never brought him back."

Jael closed her eyes remembering the funny sound over the phone.

"Baby, don't be scared. Momma's going to get you out of this. Just keep saying the Twenty-third Psalm and this will all be over soon."

"But Momma, I thought I'd never see you again!" he cried, ripping Jael apart inside with the sheer dismay in his voice. "It was so bad, so scary, I've done nothing but pray. But God hasn't heard a word I've said."

"No, baby, don't think like that. God would never let us down." But then the thought crossed her mind that she couldn't really be sure *what* God wanted to happen to her and her son. Just because she believed in Him didn't mean that He didn't want this situation to play out, that this wasn't in His great scheme of things and all for a higher purpose. How many martyrs had given their lives for Christ? Maybe God had a plan and she and her son were the sacrifices to perfect it. Terror instantly consumed her.

Just as quickly Jael banished the thought, recognizing it as a ploy of Satan to weaken her and make her give up the battle. *Get thee behind me, Satan!* Until the Lord told her otherwise, she would fight to the end.

"Ramon, can you move your hands at all?"

"I tried—it's no good. Where's Terrell? I'm so scared."

"I know you are, honey, but just pray. God will get us out of this."

"How? I've prayed and prayed ever since those strange men broke into the house. Why did this happen, Momma? How could God let this happen?"

Jael couldn't condemn him for such thoughts, having just fought her own. But she had to believe God was in control. He had proven Himself time and time again, in so many ways. Weren't all those small tests in her life meant to increase her faith and prepare her for this bigger one? And, dear Lord, wasn't this the "biggie"! At each turn it seemed the adversary was one step ahead of them. No matter what she did, she couldn't find the victory. *Deliver me not over unto the will of mine enemies.* Weren't those King David's very words in the 27th Psalm? She certainly knew the outcome there.

"Pray with me now, Ramon. The Lord is listening and ready to dispel His angels on our behalf. I believe this, baby, with all my heart. I know it's scary, but God will not let us be destroyed or defeated by the hands of His enemies. Pray with me, honey. Dear Lord . . ."

"Dear Lord," Ramon repeated in a small whimper. Then he softly recited each word his mother spoke. The shadows in the corners around them seemed to grow darker.

"We ask for your mercy and grace and that you look down upon your servants in their dark hour of need."

Jael spoke while lying stone still, mustering every ounce of control she had as she struggled to breathe under the heavy, suffocating weight of panic.

"Rescue us, Father, from the hands of the enemy; exalt your holy presence by releasing us from the clutches of the adversary."

Beads of sweat began forming on her body, attesting to the inner strain in her struggle to keep from being immobilized with fear. Her pulse raced. She focused on pulling air in and out of her lungs.

"Father, we glorify you and praise you even now in our weakest hour, for we know you are the one true God, the Creator of the universe and the master of all things. Hear us now, oh Lord, shield us with your mercy, protect us with your loving arms, fill our hearts, Father, with courage and—"

"Will you shut the hell up! Just shut your big-lipped, black mouths the hell up!"

Jael heard Ramon cry out as the harsh words were spoken. She looked over to see the Captain step inside the barn doors, his bulldog face a mask of fury. Wasn't it just like the devil to detest words of worship, to interrupt prayer. The thought of this renewed her courage and she screamed at Captain Slater, glad to be able to direct her anger at something she could see.

"God hears the cries of the righteous! Having trouble dealing with the Almighty, Captain?"

"All that whining will do you no good. Your prayers are falling on deaf ears." The Captain stepped closer. It was all she could do not to cringe away. "The true righteous will inherit the earth. We are the chosen of God."

"And the devil knows scripture and how to twist it to his advantage," Jael spit back.

"The Bible says that the pleas of sinners will not be heard, so quit your sniveling crap."

"MY GOD, THE ONE TRUE GOD WILL PREVAIL!" Jael shouted. She refused to allow his arrogant confidence to replace hope with doubt. If she knew anything, she knew in the deepest part of her heart that when one prayed from the depths of his or her soul, crying out to the Lord, He did hear and did respond. This she would stake her life on. And it seemed she was going to have to do just that.

The Captain took another step forward, and Jael saw her son shrink back. "Oh yes, He will prevail," the Captain barked. Then, raising his right hand and pointing his finger at her, he added. "But unfortunately for you, you're on the wrong side. God has no connections with vile sinners such as yourselves."

"How can you even allow the name of the Lord to cross your lips!" Anger bellowed in her voice. "Your truth is twisted and perverted and is a lie from the Father of lies. You are all spawns of the devil, serving him in your ignorance, pride and deluded self-importance."

"Ha! Look who's talking. It seems to me if God were listening to you, then I would be the one in your place and you would be holding *me* hostage. So, I guess whatever voodoo god you serve, it ain't all it's cracked up to be, huh? Not working its magic right now, is it?"

"You are a liar from the pit of hell. You never intended to free my son."

"Oh, here we go with that freedom crap. I can't tell you how sick I was every time I had to look into your black face and hear you spout off about this or that." A grin of pure malice crept onto his face. He folded his hands in front of him and rocked slightly on the heels of his feet. "That's why so many of us have joined law enforcement. We get a legal permit to knock a few niggers upside the head."

In his military garb he looked and behaved like a completely different person. Or was it that she was finally seeing the real man behind the mask? she wondered.

He continued in his confident manner, "I'm sure you thought Lieutenant Peterson falling ill three months before retirement was to your good fortune. You couldn't wait to step in his shoes and strut around the station like the big-wheel nigger you already think you are. Well, that's why my timing is so perfect. I couldn't wait to get you out of my station. And believe me it will be a long time before another like you will ever have such authority again. I'll see to that personally."

"You're wrong there, Captain." She kept her gaze unwavering on his. "We are a mighty people from a proud heritage. It will take more than a few bigots like you to keep us back."

Furious color flooded his face, stealing a bit of his arrogant pose. "Nigger, when we finish with this holy battle, all of you and your kind will be glad just to see another day. I promise this as Grand Dragon of the World Church of the Creator! We are at the crest of a new millennium, a new world order!"

Jael heard the madness in his voice. He had come to believe his own drivel. His eyes shone with the look of insanity of one who has long ago lost his mind. What lived in the darkest basement of his soul, only the Lord knew. And how he had fooled them all for so long, she couldn't imagine.

"If you're so smart, what sense did it make bringing me to your militia campsite? Who would believe my drug-crazed mind would send me to the very heart of your sick operations."

"Oh, but that's the really good part," the Captain said. "You see, you forced me to go to plan B. Originally, we simply took the opportunity that presented itself to remove a few more niggers from the face of the earth, knowing most true American citizens would applaud the removal of a few drug dealers. Upton was more than glad to be our champion. He was promised complete protection. But when you arrested him, well . . . I had to go to plan B. Remove Upton. He would have been too much of a risk. And why not kill two birds with one stone. That's why you were ordered to have Upton released from the county jail. I knew you and your FBI agent would find a way to do it over my head. I had to play as if I didn't like the idea so when things backfired on you guys, well, I could say how I was against it in the first place."

"So why did you visit him at the jailhouse? To say good-bye?"

"No, rather to tell him there was going to be a change in plans—the cars would be switched. He loved that idea and was ready to get out."

"What I still can't understand is why you let Upton leave all the drugs and drug money behind in the first place. Didn't you know that would tip off any smart officer that it wasn't between the dealers?"

"We're working for a higher power. Drugs and drug money are unclean gain. We don't need it, nor will it be used for our cause." Jael realized he didn't understand how twisted this logic was. "How this all plays out is, after you learned Upton was involved in your son's kidnapping, you went over my head with some harebrained scheme to get him out and have him lead you to your son. Once you found out your son was already dead, you killed Upton, and then in despair at the thought of getting caught and defaming your name, you killed yourself. As captain, I'll lead the investigation. Everyone will know about your sad story.

"My sorrow about the whole matter will reach unprecedented levels. I might even take a few days off in mourning." He was loving himself right now. "While our Mr. FBI Agent is trampling around following a decoy transmitter, this camp will be dismantled and relocated."

Jael knew better than to give any hint that Grant was anywhere near the campsite. What was taking them so long, she couldn't figure, but she had to stall for time.

"Why is it I never realized how really stupid you are," Jael taunted. "I guess that ugly face of yours fooled a lot of people. And all this new world order bull has really warped your brains. It won't be you guys running the planet, and you can bet on that!"

He glared at her with unmasked hatred. "Oh, and you think it may be some big-nosed niggers! Don't make me laugh. All of you are just a bunch of no-good, low-life slime. All that brother crap y'all talk about is hyped-up bull. As a matter of fact, it was one of your own nigger 'brothas' that told us where we could find the dealers' hangouts in the first place. For a crappy hundred dollars he told Upton everything, rattling on like a fool, then taking off in fear when the dealers he'd snitched on started dropping dead like flies. As captain of the Dadesville Police Department, I didn't need much more anyway. I had all your reports and all the narcotics target reports to know who was who. I only needed exact times when the scum would be at the locales. But I can always count on you people to sell out your own kind. It's how you all are. And why I'm glad to play such a major part in God's delivery of people like you."

"I pray God have mercy on your soul, Captain. Because if He doesn't, you and your followers will surely bust hell wide open."

"I have no more time to quibble with you. Say good-bye to your son. This will be the last time either of you will see each other alive."

The Captain laughed and backed away, moving toward the huge double wooden doors, the only entrance or exit to the building. Reaching down beside it, he picked up a bright red metal can. Turning to give her a final pleased sneer, he began pouring the golden liquid from the can around the bottom edge of the door. "Oh, and by the way, for some unknown reason, you set the place on fire before putting a gun inside your mouth and blowing your brains out. That's a little security measure on our part. So, stay comfy. One of my men will be back to wrap things up before you burn too badly. For now, it's back to work, trying to locate you and what you've done with the suspect."

The Captain erupted in gleeful laughter filled with triumph and self-satisfaction as he exited the door. Just outside the door, a car's engine was running, and Jael caught a quick glimpse of Tammy's frosted blond hairstyle behind the wheel before the captain slammed the barn door shut.

As the gasoline fumes hit her with a nauseating impact, she heard Ramon begin to pray earnestly. "The Lord is my shepherd, I shall not want . . ."

Having nothing else to cling to, she also realized that

God was at his best when man had nothing in the natural to rely on.

". . . He maketh me to lay down in green pastures, He leadeth me beside the still waters . . ."

Hearing her son praying, Jael used the words as a cloak of protection and strength, as she stretched her neck to look around for something to help them escape. She had to break free, and knew God counted on her to use the wisdom and knowledge He'd instilled in her over the years when she'd handled other dangerous situations.

Though the room was dark, Jael was able to make out the shape of something that looked like an old wheelbarrow against the far wall to her left. Twisting her body in that direction, she pushed herself to the edge of the bed. Her heart thundered as she shifted her weight to the side. *Dear Lord, help me, please!*

Sucking in a deep breath, she swung herself over onto the floor. Her body hit with a loud thud, knocking the air from her lungs.

"Momma!"

She squeezed her eyes shut to still the dizziness, and forced out the words her son needed to hear from her lips. "I'm okay, honey, hush now." But she was far from okay—the impact of the fall had ravaged her body. She steadied herself to get her breath back, but knew there was little time for even that.

The floor was cold beneath her face, and the smells of old hay and the gasoline almost made her choke. Rolling over onto her back, she used her elbows to push herself backward in the direction of the wheelbarrow. Her shoulder screamed in agony with each move. Jael twisted her head backward as far as she could, and from the bottom of the old wheel she could just make out a small gleam reflecting on the barrow's blade. Pushing closer, then squinting her eyes, Jael saw that it was a John Deere plow-blade, used to cut grass.

With every ounce of strength she had, she pushed up to the plow and pressed her tied wrist against the blade's edge. Over the years it had rusted badly, but Jael kept sawing at it until she felt the first strings of the rope give.

"I can't hear you, Ramon," she called out. "Pray louder."

She sawed at the rope as Ramon's weak and tired voice rose to an audible volume. Twice the rusted blade cut into her skin, but Jael never stopped, whispering her own words of prayer.

When the rope finally gave, it was so unexpected she fell back against the blade, ripping the right shoulder of her blouse and probably leaving a gash in her flesh. Quickly spinning her body around, she raised her legs to press the rope around her ankles against the blade. This time the maneuver was much easier, the rope not as tight. Ripping through the treads of the first layer loosened the binding, and instantly she was on her feet, running back to her son.

"Thank you, Jesus," she cried as she pulled him into her arms, smothering him with hugs and kisses. The two cried together for a moment; then Jael untied his hands and grabbed him again.

She untied the rope around his legs and managed to get him to his feet. "Come on, baby, we've got to get out of here."

"I can barely stand," he said, falling back onto the cot.

"I know, sweetheart." She held him close and stroked his hair. "But we have to move quickly."

"But what about Terrell? Where is he?"

Jael prayed her expression gave nothing away. "I'm sure he's okay. Let me get you out of here and then I'll search for him."

She pulled him to his feet, and once he was steady held on to his hand as she raced them toward the double doors. She released Ramon's hand and pulled at the door handle, even though she expected it would be locked. It was. She shook and hammered on it. Ramon joined in, shouting for someone to let them out.

Stepping back, she looked around for something to pry between the door hinges. Then she noticed, to her right, an old sagging door, probably to an inside storage shed. Jael raced to it, yanked it open, then screamed.

There on the floor of the shed, atop what she supposed was a lump of stored hay, was Jasper. He still wore the clothes she'd last seen him in at his house. His arms hung limply at his side, his sunken cheeks were hollowed holes of waxlike skin, and the teal-blue eyes that had spoken so much that day now held only a lifeless, empty gaze.

Jael stared down at Jasper's white face, frozen in death. There were no visible signs of a struggle, no cuts, blood or anything else to label the cause of death—only the tossed-off white sheet beside him that could possibly prove later to have been a weapon of suffocation. Judging by the stage of rigor mortis, he had been dead six to eight hours. He had sacrificed his own safety by telling them what he had, and it had ricocheted back as he had feared, causing his demise.

Jael whispered a silent prayer that God would know this man had fought evil the only way he knew how.

When Ramon raced to her side to see what had caused her to cry out, she roughly shoved him back behind her, not wanting him to witness the awful sight.

Behind her Ramon began praying at the top of his lungs. Jael could hear the strangle of tears mingled in. ". . . YEA, THOUGH I WALK THROUGH THE VALLEY OF THE SHADOW OF DEATH, I SHALL FEAR NO EVIL, FOR THOU ARE WITH ME. . . ."

Backing away and offering her own prayers of salvation, she thought she heard a sound issue from the victim just before she shut the door. She could have sworn the man was dead, but leaned forward to take a second look. Jael immediately leaped backward as the dead body fell to the side.

A dazed and terrified Terrell stared up at her, his eyes filled with fear and the horror of lying for so long in the darkened shed. The Lord only knew how long he'd been there under Jasper's dead corpse.

"Praise the Lord! My God—Terrell!" Jael threw her hands out and grabbed at Terrell's shirt, pushing aside Jasper's cold body with her foot. She pulled him out of the shed and slammed the door before falling to her knees and wrapping her arms around his trembling frame. His clothing was wrinkled and muddied, his face and hair covered with botches of dirt. She also smelled a faint scent of urine around the crotch of his pants. *Poor baby.*

"Oh, Ms. Jael, you're here, you're here. I was so scared."

"I know, honey. I'm sorry you had to go through this, but everything's going to be all right now."

Ramon had thrown his arms around them both, his cries

of relief mingled with his constant words of prayer. *Thank God for my little boy's strength and endurance,* she thought.

"I thought they had hurt you," Ramon cried over her shoulder at his friend. "I thought I would never see you again!"

"I don't know what happened," Terrell said in a shaking voice. "That man hit me in the head so hard, I don't remember much. Then it was dark and I couldn't move. Something heavy and cold was on top of me. I tried to holler over and over, but no one heard me, no one came." Terrell began to sob heavily on Jael's shoulder, and she let him pour out his fear.

"You know it's going to be all right, honey. Everything's going to be . . ." Her words trailed off as her mind began to work. She had to get them out of there. She couldn't wait around for Grant, who might not make it before the Captain ordered one of his men to finish the job he started.

Standing up on her feet with her hand still on Terrell's shoulder, she wasn't even aware she was speaking aloud. "I need to get this door open. Somehow I have to . . ." Turning around in a circle, she quickly reviewed what was available to break the door down. Nothing. *Think, girl, think.* The plow was far too heavy to use, and the storage shed had been empty except for . . . for . . . She suddenly had an idea.

Shoving Terrell aside, she moved quickly to the storage room. "Scrape as much of the dirt around the door into a pile in the center as you can, then try to find a bottle or anything that could be used to fill up," she yelled over her shoulder at the boys as she yanked open the door.

Without looking at his face, she moved toward Jasper and gripped his shoulder with her left hand and ripped at his shirtsleeve with her right. It took several yanks before the sleeve separated from the shirt. Sliding it off his stiff arm, she prayed as she reached inside his front pants pocket. It was there: a book of matches.

"I couldn't find a bottle, but here's an old empty Coke can," Terrell said from behind her as she left the storage room and closed the door with the heel of her foot.

"Okay, it'll have to do." Taking the can, she pressed the metal tab against the small opening in order to make a larger hole. She blew air between her lips in frustration when the cap popped off and into the can instead. The hole would surely be too small for what she planned, but it would have to do. Using the remaining edge of the cap as a kind of tool, she pressed it around the small opening, enlarging it only a tad. It didn't help much, but it was all she could do. Taking the shirtsleeve from under her arm, Jael bent and pressed it down around the pile the boys had made at the center of the door, absorbing as much of the liquid as she could. Then she prayed it would be enough to ignite the cloth. She stuffed as much of the moistened shirt into the opening of the can as would go and pulled out the book of matches.

If she were a cursing woman, she would have used an ungodly word at that moment. When she flipped the cover on the book of matches, there was only a single match left along the cardboard stub.

"God, I need a miracle here." She was unaware she spoke the words with confidence and assurance. A lot had changed in the last hours.

To the boys, she shouted, "Step back!"

In her hands she held the closest thing she had to a

Molotov cocktail. But maybe it might just blow a big enough hole in the door for her and the boys to escape.

Jael closed her eyes briefly and struck the match to the cloth. The material ignited in blazing red and blue flames, scorching her fingers. She threw it at the base of the door. With the remnant of gasoline already there, the impact of the blast was instant—but not enough.

At first Jael couldn't tell if she'd made a hole in the barn door at all, as the fire raced along the bottom and up the sides. Then, as it greedily ate away at the center, a small speck of daylight peeked between the dancing fingers of flame near the bottom. Though she could see through the flames that engulfed its core, the hole was far too small.

And as the tiny fingers of flame continued to lick at the base and sides of the door, blackened smoke was curling out toward them. It wouldn't be long before the entire wall became a blazing inferno.

"Stay back!" she yelled. Her prayers accelerated to frenzied pleas, racing in time with the swift pace of her heart. Even as fear welled up in her for the boys' safety, she held on, counting on the supernatural intervention of her Lord.

If she could somehow get through the small opening, maybe she would have a chance on the outside to find something to pry off the lock or burst the door open. But suddenly thick smoke began to enter from under the barn door, while at the sides, twin pillars of flame danced in twirling circles.

When Terrell screamed, Jael turned to see yellow and orange tongues of twirling flame licking away up the sidewall. A litany of prayers and supplication swept through her head while the chill of realization sawed at her nerves.

Time was running out for them; it was now or never. She hesitated for a fraction of a second, then stepped boldly forward, speaking directly to the fire and her fear.

"And the angel of the Lord was there among them, even in the midst of the fiery furnace. And Nebuchadnezzar blessed the God of Shadrach, Meshach and Abednego!" The words poured forth as if she were in a trance. Ramon and Terrell turned to stare at her in awe, forgetting their fear as they covered their faces to ease the hacking coughs that overwhelmed them.

Forcing the boys to move all the way to the back of the barn, she continued to speak words of faith. Intense heat draped itself over their bodies, declaring the power and promise of death within the fire. And the hole was widening; she could see the dirt ground just outside.

Jael braced herself, prayed and dipped her knees into a crouch. With a sprint equal to that of an Olympic champion, Jael hurled herself through the small opening, taking sharp splinters of burning wood with her. A moment of intense heat engulfed her, while the sharp sting of charred wood ripped at her body.

She hit the outside ground with enough force to knock the air out of her lungs, but was quickly back on her feet and grabbing at the lock. It burned her hands. She spun around, looking for whatever she could find: a hose, a rake, anything. There was nothing. She'd left the boys inside for nothing. The empty expanse of land beyond her seemed endless with despair. Through each cough of her own, she watched as flames spread savagely before her, greedily chewing its way higher along each side door. Again, Jael loudly proclaimed the Word of God. Her boys were coming out of there.

"The righteous will not be defeated!"

Rushing to the right side of the barn, the only thing she could find was a beaten old plastic trash can lying on its side. Grabbing it, she sprinted back to the door and began slamming it with the can. The door rocked with each slam but didn't give; the fire hadn't done enough damage yet. As the fire grew into pillars of flame, she noticed that near the bottom hinge, the flames had spread out, leaving behind black, smoldering wood. She dropped to her knees and began pounding at the weakened area. When she heard Ramon scream, Jael responded with the strongest word resounding in her spirit: "JESUS!"

"JAEL!"

She held her breath, stunned. Had the Lord just called her name in reply? Was she hallucinating out of panic, or were the fumes getting to her? Again she shouted the word as loud as she could: "JESUS!"

The response was a thundering roar as if from heaven itself—only coming from behind her, not above. She turned to see a huge blue Jeep racing toward her, the howl of its engine drowning out all other sounds.

Someone was leaning out the driver side window, frantically waving his arm back and forth. She recognized the man as Grant as he shouted her name again: "JAEL!"

"God be praised! Oh, Grant! Oh, Grant!" She threw both arms in the air, pointing them toward the fiery barn, in reply. "Quick, the boys are still inside!"

Straining his head out even farther, Grant shouted, "Move away from the door, I'm going through! I—"

The rapid spit of gunfire somewhere around the other side of the building drowned out his next words. Frenetic activity suddenly surrounded them as men barked orders and gunfire exploded. And over it all Jael could just make out the sweet, whooping sound of helicopters overhead.

With her adrenaline pumping fast and furious, Jael sprung to her feet and ran for the Jeep, reaching out as it raced toward her. Yanking the passenger door open and jumping in beside Grant, she screamed, "Go, go, go!"

Without further prompting, Grant rammed the accelerator. The tires gave out a long squeal of traction, fighting against dirt, and the Jeep sped through the fiery door of flame. Splinters of burning wood crashed around them, flying helter-skelter.

Just inside, Grant slammed the brakes, as Jael leaped from her seat into the smoke-filled building, the inferno already sending out waves of scorching heat. It was all Jael could do to keep back the cry of terror locked behind her lips.

She screamed their names; then her heart nearly leaped in joy as Ramon and Terrell raced toward her from a far corner, mouthing words she could not read. But they were safe.

"Get in the Jeep," she screamed, trying to shove each boy in.

"Jael, hurry," Grant shouted. "It's only a matter of seconds before this whole building crashes in on itself."

She didn't have to be told twice. Yelling again at Ramon and Terrell to jump inside, Jael helped them up, nearly fainting from the weight of the boys and the overwhelming smoke. She slipped twice trying to push them in before her. Even before the door was shut, she shouted, "Go! Go! We're in!"

"They're here!" Ramon yelled, repeating what he'd been trying to say earlier. "I hear the helicopters!"

Chapter 46

With the wheels screeching, Grant threw the truck in forward and raced ahead through the back wall. It was like a scene from a movie that only stunt doubles would have the nerve to try and pull off. Fresh air hit Jael like a blessed wash of spring rain. She inhaled deeply between coughs, watching the boys do the same.

Leaning out the window, she took a quick look around, taking in the chaotic scene of men shouting and running in all directions. Many were FBI agents in deep blue suits and others had large SWAT letters on their backs. The men were everywhere, like a swarm of bees, on top of buildings and on the ground.

But the one sight she wanted to see most eluded her.

"Where's the Captain?" she screamed. "Do you have the Captain?"

"Not yet," Grant shouted over the deafening noise around them. "My men are—"

"No, no, he's left the campsite." Straining to see around the camp, she asked, "Where's the car they brought me here in?"

"Over by the front gate," Grant said, pointing in the direction of the sedan. ". . . But Jael, we'll get him. You need to—"

"Stop the truck," she commanded. In her haste, she completely missed that Grant understood her sudden need to find the Captain. Before he'd come to a complete stop beside the car, Jael jumped out and pulled the back door of the vehicle open and reached inside. "It's here," she whispered. "Thank you, Father."

She was back in the truck before Grant had finished his statement. "Jael, listen—"

"No, you listen. It's got to be me. I have to be the one to do this. He must have left the campsite before you arrived. Take me back to the station."

"But—"

"Take me back to the station, Grant!"

"Jael, I need to check—"

"Grant, if you don't take me to the station, now, I'll take this truck from you and drive myself."

Grant gave her a look that seemed to say, "Oookaaay." But what he said was "Hop in the back, boys."

"Aw-right!" Ramon said as he climbed over his mother's lap to get out and on to the bed of the truck. Terrell was right behind him.

At the clap of thunder and the sudden heavenly burst of rain, Jael stuck her head out the window and raised both arms high over her head, as Grant rushed past the madness and out the front gate. The cool, drenching wetness was like thousands of heavenly kisses. With eyes closed in wonder, she gave a loud and hearty shout: "THANK YOU, JESUS! PRAISE THE LORD!"

• • •

During the swift ride back to the station, she understood much of the Captain's plan, and she knew that at this moment he would be pretending to try and locate her. If no one had contacted him and informed him the campsite was swarming with FBI agents, which she doubted, he'd assume she was already dead. He'd lead a false investigation out of his office. She couldn't wait.

When they pulled up outside the station, Sills was coming out the door. His facial expression reflected his surprise at seeing them. Leaping from the Jeep, Jael took the steps two at a time. Sills hastily reopened the door for her.

"Jael . . . ?"

"Ask no questions, just follow me."

In her stocking feet, Jael stormed toward the reception desk, her face a mask of rage. At the sight of her, Tammy jumped up, her mouth open as she fumbled to grab the phone.

"Don't even think about it," Jael said between clenched teeth. "Sills, hold her here until I return. Do not let her move, do not let her speak, don't even let her bat an eye."

"Jael, what the—"

"Just do it, Sills!"

As she marched away, heading straight for the Captain's office, she heard Sills say, "Do not move a muscle."

It was gratifying to know she could trust her partner. His actions now confirmed his loyalty to her, and not to some covert organization intent on destroying her.

When she reached the Captain's door, she pushed it open without knocking. His back was to her as he rummaged in a cabinet near his desk. Just to the right of him, she noticed again the bulldog with the bobbing head.

"Whatever you want, you'll have to come back," he said over his shoulder.

"But I want you."

The Captain's head snapped up. With his back stiff as a mannequin's, he slowly swiveled around in his chair. His astonishment showed for only a second, and then with a grin, he leaned back.

"So, somehow you got out of the barn. But whatever you're thinking right now won't work. If you're as smart a cop as you think you are, you know it's still my word against yours. You have no proof of anything. When it all comes out in court, I'll still be the one standing."

With lips barely moving, she hissed, "I doubt that very much, Captain."

The Captain snorted. "You don't know how stupid you are. Whatever you think you have, you have no proof I was involved in any of this."

"Oh yeah? Well, who's the stupid one now?" With a satisfied grin on her face, Jael lifted the cell phone in her hand and pressed REDIAL. Instantly, the cell phone on the Captain's desk began to ring.

"To God be the glory! We've got a trace."

Epilogue

They had been saved! Her desperate prayers had been answered and God had given her the victory. What sweet and precious words: holy victory.

The station was packed with news reporters, lawyers and family members. Virgil was preening over Ramon as if he alone were the hero of the hour, professing what he would have done if he'd gotten his hands on his son's abductors. With hands on her hips, Rhonda walked around demanding someone get a change of clothing for the boys and bring iced liquids to refresh them.

And Terrell's mother, eyes filled with crocodile tears, ranted before the media, spewing words of disgust for the people who had tried to hurt her precious baby.

Sills was keeping everyone away from Jael and Grant, threatening to start his own war if anyone so much as tried to touch her.

Big Jake and his boys had followed her until a mile before the police station and then, with a honk of their horn, had detoured and gone off their separate ways. There would be plenty of time to thank the roughnecks and then get back to harassing them later.

As Sills forced Jael into a private room to escape the bar-
rage of questions tossed at her, she smiled at the thought of
Big Jake's daring rescue, then quickly remembered how close
they had all come to having a major race war. Before Sills
could shut the door behind her, Grant pressed through the
opening and closed the door himself. He'd barely let her out
of his sight since returning to the station.

Still, unable to absorb the magnitude of what had transpired within the past few hours, she involuntarily shud-
dered, and a small whimper slipped past her lips. Grant
quickly stepped forward to encircle her in his arms,
squeezing gently. The concern in his eyes said everything.
For a moment, his lips were only inches from her own. Her
eyes asked, and his answered, just before he pressed his lips
to her forehead. Whatever tension was between them, now
was not the time.

She gently pulled away and smiled up into his face. There
were a thousand and one questions that needed to be
addressed, and only he could answer them.

"I still don't get it!" she said. "You knew all long the Captain was involved and you were here mainly to see what he
was up to?"

"Until I had more proof, I had to make it look as if I
were here merely to watch what was happening to the drug
dealers in town. Thankfully, not many were killed." Grant
still held his arms around her, but seemed glad she was
feeling well enough to want to get down to business and
questions. "After Billups contacted us about Slater—"

"Billups? Our Ernest Billups, the snob?" Jael leaned farther back, completely flabbergasted.

"The one and only. He may have seemed like a bigot to you because of his ideas about racial intolerance, but he was straight across the board each way. He had little in common with Captain Slater, but because of his outspoken feelings about you, the Captain slipped a few times around him, trying to feel him out. When Billups got a whiff of what he suspected, he notified our agency, having serious qualms about how the earlier internal investigation had turned out. That's why you saw him sneak out of the Captain's office—he was hoping for more evidence. Evidence you finally gave us."

"Wow, I would've never believed it. Billups of all people." Jael shook her head in disbelief. "But then again, the Captain had me fooled too. Did you know he was planning to use me as the fall guy for the murders?" she asked, gazing back into his adoring eyes.

"We had our suspicions—that's why I had him watched and followed right after I left his office. As I suspected, he went straight to the Klan's campsite, so when we lost your signal we already knew where they were taking you."

"Why didn't you tell me any of this?"

"You know why, Jael. You were under a lot of strain just trying to get Ramon back. There was no telling what you might have said out of fear."

With a slight nod, she concurred. "I've learned a lot about fear these past few days. But I think it'll take a lot more to frighten me in the future."

"You took more than a normal person could handle this time, and came through it like a champ." Grant touched her forehead gently, then placed another kiss on her brow.

"Yeah, we literally went through fire, didn't we?" She smiled and patted Grant softly on his chest. Man, she was glad just to be able to touch him again, she thought. When all this was over, she'd not act the fool she had before.

She thanked God for the umpteenth time for His mercy, while reluctantly stepping away from Grant, moving to the window and taking in all the rushed activity outside. "God had my back every step of the way. It may seem as if I had things under control, but that's only because I learned to completely trust God and hold fast to my faith. Even when I thought everything kept going haywire, the Lord was one move ahead before it even happened."

"That's what faith is all about. Trusting in the Lord even when we can't see the outcome."

"The Lord has no patience with double-mindedness. I've learned my lesson the hard way. I thank the Lord for His enduring mercy." Turning back toward Grant, who stood watching her with his hands in his pockets, she added, "The adversary plays mean and hard, though; you always have to be on your toes."

"And prayed up and armed with the Word."

"You said a mouthful there, brother!" Jael laughed. "And now we understand why Jasper dropped all those anonymous tips to the press and gave me the note. He couldn't risk going to the police, the very heart of the problem. It seems you guys had everything figured out from the start. What happens now?"

"Well, for one, since there won't be a captain around the station for a while, Lieutenant Reynolds will be in charge of putting things back together."

"Wow, that sounds great: Lieutenant Jael Reynolds." She smiled.

"And since Lieutenant Reynolds was smart enough to get a copy of Jasper's phone book, which can identify certain individuals, before everything went up in smoke . . ." Grant stepped closer, a look of concern on his face. "That was the main purpose of burning down that old barn, you know— to get rid of evidence that might lead back to the Captain."

"So I was an afterthought?"

"No, the Captain had every intention of eliminating you along with any incriminating evidence, but thankfully God had another plan."

"God always has a plan," she said, then added, "Hopefully, you're in the plan He has for me."

Grant reached out, placing his hand on her shoulder. His smile was huge and promising. "Let's speak the positive on that one, shall we? You know, name it and claim it and all that."

"Yeah, let's do just that."

As the two of them headed out the office door, hand in hand, she felt stronger than ever before, having endured so much and understanding that through this trial she was a much stronger Christian. It seemed as if she had gone to hell and back, but during all the moments of wavering doubt, God had been steadfast and faithful. She'd learned an enormous lesson that would carry her through the rest of her life. And whatever plan God had for her life, she had every confidence that He would see it through.

Today is your day for a miracle. Take it by faith!

About the Author

Judy Candis is a native of Detroit and resides in Tampa with her two daughters. She received her BS degree in black studies from Florida A&M University and graduated with the titles Miss Famu and Miss Kappa Alpha Psi. She was a full-time journalist for seven years and currently teaches writing at the University of South Florida. She also helps run the family business, BAR-B-Que King, a legacy in the bay area for fifty-five years. *All Things Hidden* is her first nationally published novel.

Reading Group Guide

Chapter 1
Jael, the main character in this novel, obviously believes in listening to the voice of God. What does the Word say about our ability to hear the voice of God? **1 Corinthians 2:14–15; Ezekiel 44:23**

Chapter 2
It's clear that Jael is not ashamed of her faith nor is she afraid to share it on the job. How does she use her faith in the workplace to glorify God? What challenges do believers face when witnessing in a workplace setting? **Psalm 31:1; Luke 9:26; Romans 1:16**

Chapter 3
Can you relate to Jael's antagonistic coworker? Have you ever had a similar situation at your job? What do you think about the way she's handling him? In the past, how have you handled your personal difficult work situations? What does the Bible say about handling our enemies? **Matthew 5:44; Luke 6:27**

Chapter 4

There is a volatile relationship between Jael and Virgil, her ex-husband. As Christians we're called to live at peace with all men (including family) as much as possible. What steps should Jael, as a Christian, take to improve their interaction, especially for the sake of their child? **Proverbs 20:7**

Chapter 5

Jael explains to her unsaved cousin, Rhonda, that it is God who sustains her so that her physical needs don't get the best of her. Discuss what the Word says about handling temptation. **2 Corinthians 1:2; 1 Thessalonians 5:13; James 1:12; Matthew 26:41**

Chapter 6

In this world Christians are in enemy territory. What precautions can we take when life necessitates that we be in a situation like Jael, where it's clear Satan is busy working overtime on the job? **Matthew 5:14, 13:22; John 1:10, 17:16, 17:18, 18:36; Romans 1:12**

Chapter 7

What is the spiritual benefit of the relationship between Ramon and Terrell? Explain. **Matthew 5:13–14**

Chapter 8

What do you think of Jael's reaction to the death of TeeTee? Is she too focused on finding the killer or should she have been showing more godly compassion? **Matthew 9:36, 20:34**

Chapter 9

Jael tells a "white lie" when trying to get information from Booley. Is lying acceptable in some situations? **Acts 5:4**

Chapter 10
Is TeeTee dead because of choices he made or because of the hand "society" dealt to him? **Philippians 2:12**

Chapter 11
Jael's vendetta is revealed. What do you think about her underlying reason for becoming a police officer? What does the Bible say about revenge? **Psalm 94; Hebrews 10:30**

Chapter 12
Mr. Watson seems prepared to take up arms to defend himself. Do believers have that option? Explain. **Deuteronomy 1:42; 2 Chronicles 20:17**

Chapter 13
As the violence and mystery builds around the murders so do Jael's fears and doubts about how God is moving in the situation. How can she quell her emotions and focus on God, despite what she's experiencing? **2 Timothy 1:7; 1 John 4:18**

Chapter 14
Captain Slater is an intimidating boss, but still he has authority over her. Is she showing him the proper amount of respect? **Proverbs 29:2; Matthew 20:25**

Chapter 15
Jael is clearly attracted to Grant, the FBI agent. At one point she prays for God to not let her make a foolish mistake, but do you think her feelings are harmless at his point?

Chapter 16
Concentrating on the case is becoming increasingly difficult for Jael, and at the end of the chapter she blames the "adver-

sary fighting against you from all sides, looking for vulnerable spots." Is this an attack from Satan? **Job 2:3; 1 Peter 5:8**

Chapter 17
When Jael lets William David Jasper go and agrees to follow him to his house, she's taking a risk. Do you believe the Holy Spirit is guiding her dangerous actions in this case? What is the evidence from the story that backs up your belief? **Psalm 32:8; John 16:13**

Chapter 18
Racism rears its ugly head in a most blatant way and Jael struggles to react rationally to it. What is the root of racism and how should Christians respond to it? **Romans 5:12**

Chapter 19
Grant and Jael have discovered that white supremacy is at the root of the murders. Some are not aware of its evil because of Satan's lies—including that he doesn't exist. Many white supremacist groups operate under the guise that they are fulfilling the will of the almighty God. How does scripture refute this claim? **1 Timothy 4:2; Proverbs 11:9, 6:19; 2 Peter 2:1**

Chapter 20
After Jael is shot, she calls on Jesus. Why does she believe that Jesus will come through for her? **Proverbs 10:21, 17:24; Ecclesiastes 1:13**

Chapter 21
Jael hits the captured man after he makes repeated racial slurs. Would you have done the same? **Proverbs 22:26**

Chapter 22

Jael observes positive interaction between Grant and her son. As a parent, what traits should she be looking for in Grant?

Chapter 23

Has Jael forgiven herself for her past drug addiction? Is this somehow impacting her moving forward with Grant?

Chapter 24

After praying for peace, Jael is still confused. Has her faith weakened? **Matthew 7:22; James 5:15; 1 Peter 4:7**

Chapter 25

Now that Jael has admitted her feelings to Grant and knows it's mutual, is she free to indulge her emotions? Explain. **Colossians 3:5; 1 Corinthians 10:8**

Chapter 26

The horrific discovery of Peoples's dead body is a compelling example of the effects of a sinful world. What can or should the church be doing to stem such violence? Is spreading the gospel enough?

Chapter 27

Like Peoples's death, there are senseless deaths every day. How can we reconcile the fact that God is all-loving even in the face of such violence? **Matthew 28:19**

Chapter 28

Grant and Jael talk about their first marriages and what went wrong. Do you believe remarrying is acceptable in each of their cases? **Luke 16:18; Matthew 19:9**

Chapter 29
Understandably, Jael begins to unravel once Ramon has been kidnapped. What should be her response when there appears to be nothing she can do? 1 Peter 1:7; Matthew 13:21; Romans 2:9; Acts 14:22

Chapter 30
What is the biblical response to our "why me Lord?" Romans 5:3

Chapter 31
Jael believes she is involved in spiritual warfare at this point. Do you agree? Explain. Ephesians 6:12; 2 Corinthians 10:4

Chapter 32
Clearly Jael's facing the biggest test of her life. Do you believe she is truly holding to her faith or is she crumbling? Psalm 62:11, 106:8

Chapter 33
Paranoia and fear are affecting Jael because of Ramon's kidnapping. As human beings can we expect to have power and control over such emotions? 1 Chronicles 25:8; Romans 16:20; Isaiah 40:29

Chapter 34
Should Jael obey the kidnappers' orders or should she simply trust God? What would you do?

Chapter 35
Grant tells Jael to pray. Has she relied on the power of prayer during this ordeal? What can prayer still do? Genesis 20:17; 1 Samuel 1:10, 1:27; Acts 6:4

Chapter 36
Even though she has prayed, Jael is still full of doubt and worry about everything. What Godly counsel would you give her? On what scripture would it be based?

Chapter 37
Can you explain what Grant meant when he quoted Deuteronomy 32:33?

Chapter 38
Jael is beginning to find peace and strength amidst her storm. How is that possible? **Romans 8:6; John 14:27, 16:20**

Chapter 39
Virgil calls at a crucial time. Should Jael have tried to let him know what was going on? As Ramon's father, does he have a right to know? Explain.

Chapter 40
With her cell phone out the window and her wiretaps gone, Jael is completely vulnerable. What biblical character can you compare her to? What should be her prayer now? What scripture should she be standing on?

Chapter 41
Jael compares her despondence to what Jesus may have felt on the Cross. Is this a good analogy? **Luke 11:42**

Chapter 42
Even though victory is in sight, Jael alludes to being capable of killing someone. What is the biblical view on this? **Exodus 20:13; Mark 10:19**

Chapter 43
Deceptions are revealed from various police officers. Should Jael have been more aware of these signs? **Matthew 16:3; 2 Thessalonians 2:9**

Chapter 44
Much to Upton's surprise, he's now a victim of the same sin and hate he perpetuated. Discuss what happens to those who sin against God's people. **1 Samuel 12:23**

Chapter 45
When death appears to be imminent, the Holy Spirit intervenes in a mighty way. Jael and Ramon literally go through fire. What promises of God are demonstrated here? **Genesis 32:11; Psalm 50:15; Proverbs 11:8**

Chapter 46
What spiritual lesson(s) do you believe Jael and Grant could and should have learned through this ordeal?